Once Upon The Black Sky

Part Two

Ghosts

Thomas J.R. Dearn

Once Upon A Time In The Black Country

Part Two

Ghosts

Paberback Edition First Published in the United Kingdom in 2021 Amazon KDP Publishing

eBook Edition First Published in the United Kingdom in
2021 Amazon KDP Publishing

Copyright © Thomas J.R. Dearn
Thomas J.R. Dearn has asserted his rights under 'the Copyright Designs and Patents Act 1988' to be identified as the author of this work.

All rights reserved.
No part of this book may be reproduced or transmitted in any form or by any means, electronic, mechanical, photocopying, recording, or otherwise, without prior written permission of the Author.

Disclaimer
This is a work of fiction. All characters and incidents are products of the author's imagination and any resemblance to actual people or events is coincidental or fictionalised.

Copyright © 2021ThomasJ.R.Dearn
All rights reserved.
ISBN:9798588028783

January 1974

The lonesome figure of a dead man lay face up and partially disintegrated in the rugged rocks of the Andalusian coast. Rats from the skies feasted upon its eyes and the cruel force of the Spanish waves tore at the fabric of its skin. An eye for an eye and a tooth for a tooth. Those that were evil were punished through acts of vengeance, those that were genuine and sought redemption were forgiven…

****

Chapter 1
1906

On the 31st of August 1906, the Black Country saw the peak of a scorching heat wave in which the region had baked for weeks. However, there had been little opportunity for locals to enjoy the sun. The unrelenting heat ensured that working conditions in the many factories, foundries and drop forges were particularly intolerable. The smoke that belched ceaselessly from the tall forbidding chimneys and the hell fires that raged throughout ensured that an endless smog clung to the fabric of every street corner and the region remained black by day and red by night.

On Cradley Road, Cradley Heath, a tram owned by the Dudley, Stourbridge and District Electric Traction Company scuttled along the cobbled paths that ran past the famous Cross Guns Inn which stood adjacent to Samuel Tibbetts the 'High Class' butcher. Further down the hill towards the railway bridge, a row of old cottages lay back from the road and behind them could be found small individual chain shops.

During the nineteenth and well into the twentieth century, Cradley Heath and its surrounding area was world famous for its fine handmade chain that was manufactured from wrought iron. A substantial part of the industry was made up of women who manufactured the smaller chains in little chain shops that often stood at the rear of working-class cottages and terraces throughout the area.

As Susana Mucklow, a widowed mother in her mid-30s worked hard in her chain shop to provide for her four children, a small neglected and skeletal child rummaged through her dustbins in the hope of finding some nourishment. A rat ran over his shoeless foot and the gnawing pain of hunger tore through his tiny, malnourished body. As he desperately searched, two ten-year-old boys watched him cautiously.

"Willie, we should tell aer mother! Hes'a pinchin." Stan Mucklow spoke first, he had light mousy hair and brown eyes.

"Dow be saft Stan. Look at him, poor sod ay ad no food fer weeks!" Willie Mucklow shook his head at his twin brother. They were almost identical and attended the same school in Cradley Heath. He ran into the kitchen before quickly emerging with a piece of stale bread "Gerrit daahn ya wassin!" Willie handed the boy the bread and without delay the small child attacked and devoured it with a ravenous urgency.

"Ar'm a tellin' mother!" Stan turned on his heel and rushed off to the small workshop that was situated at the rear of the family cottage. He knew that he would be scolded for disrupting his mother's work, but Stan had always been a 'do gooder' and he felt an urgent need to inform her of his brother's activities. Willie paid no attention. He stood and watched the child, his eyes filled with pity. Since their father had died in a mining accident three years previously, the Mucklows had led a poor and desolate existence themselves, but their mother worked excruciatingly hard and they rarely went without food. The pathetic and sad soul that stood before him now had suffered a considerably harder existence.

"What's yower name?" Willie extended his right arm to shake the boy's hand. "Ar'm Willie, ar'm 10."

The glimmer of a smile appeared on the boy's face but before he could answer Willie's mother came storming out of the chain shop with a face like thunder whilst being followed by Willie and Stan's older sister Eliza.

"William James Mucklow!" She spat her son's name with a mild irritancy. "Yow know we ay got much to eat! How dare yow give it away to some ragamuffin scrounger!" She picked up a heavy yard brush and beat Willie across the back side before turning her attention to the boy. He did not flinch or cower, he just looked at her with tear filled eyes that had become accustomed to vicious unjustified violence and beatings. She suddenly stopped and could not help but feel pity. He wore a ragged and utterly filthy shirt and a pair of filth-stained shorts. The smell of dirt and urine arose from him pungently and she put down the brush. As she looked closer, she could see that his legs and arms were literally covered with bruises and she wondered how he managed to sustain his feeble weight through the extent of his injuries.

"Eliza, gew and fetch this poor soul some bread, jam and water." Susana Mucklow nodded towards the house and her 12-year-old daughter rushed off obediently.

Susana Mucklow nee Fellows had led a hard life. She had met her husband William at the age of 17 and had quickly fallen pregnant with their first child not long after her 18th birthday. A baby born out of wedlock was not acceptable in the late nineteenth century and she hastily married William Mucklow in the summer of 1888 before their eldest child Tobiaz was born. A few years later their daughter Eliza came along before the twins William and Stanley were born in 1896. Susana's husband had been a hard worker until tragedy struck and he was killed in a mining accident in 1903. Since then, she had worked relentlessly and without complaint to feed and clothe her children as well as make chain in the small building at the rear of the family cottage on Cradley Road.

Eliza returned with the food and the child enjoyed what was possibly one of the greatest feasts of his 9 miserable years of existence. He was of a similar age to Willie and Stan Mucklow but he did not attend the same school as them. Instead, he occasionally attended the 'ragged' school at the top of Ladysmith Road on Mapletree Lane. Ragged schools were charitable organisations set up for the free education of destitute children in 19th century Britain. Such children were often excluded from Sunday school education due to their unkempt appearance and challenging behaviour.

"What's yower name?" Willie enquired again.

The boy paused for a second, still unsure of the intentions of the family before smiling and replying. "Eli, Eli Davis."

Susana gave the child a concerned look and then turned to return to work. "Right, ar bin out here too long. Ar got chain ter meck. Willie, Stan, yow pair gew and play with Eli." She walked purposefully back towards the chain shop and Eliza followed leaving the twins to entertain their new friend.

"Eli, where's ya shoes?" Stan pointed without subtlety to Eli's bare feet.

"Ar bay got none." Eli looked at his bruised feet ashamedly.

"Who did that?" Willie pointed to the many bruises that decorated Eli's legs and arms.

"My ode mon. He does it every night. Sometimes he uses his belt, sometimes he uses his shoes, sometimes he uses his fists." Eli spoke with such a matter-of-fact acceptance that had long grown accustomed to the beatings as a routine part of his daily existence.

"What's he do that for?" Willie Mucklow frowned at the injustice.

"Ar dow know. He just does." Eli shrugged and seemed surprised that there should be a reason for his beatings.

Willie Mucklow thought for a moment. The sun was high in the sky and it shone down with a fierce intensity that was seldom seen in Britain. "Follow us Eli." Willie winked at his newfound friend and the three boys walked swiftly along Cradley Road towards Five Ways and the High street.

They arrived at their destination and lingered outside a neat and reputable cobblers and shoe shop. Willie tapped his brother Stan on the back and whispered something into his ear. The boys laughed mischievously and Willie gestured for Eli to follow him into an alleyway to hide. As soon as the boys were in position, Stan picked up a rock and lobbed it at the shop window with all his might. The window shattered into a thousand pieces and the angry shop keeper emerged onto the cobbles at once, livid and shaking his fist at the boy. Stan stuck out his tongue in a rude act of defiance and turned and ran as fast as he could with the middle-aged shopkeeper hot on his tail and running after him. Willie immediately saw the opportunity and pounced into the shop as the keeper was distracted. Hastily, he picked out a brand-new pair of leather shoes and ran back out of the shop and handed them to his newfound friend.

"Now run, run Eli run!" The two boys made off at full pelt, not stopping for a single second until they came to the stream-like River Stour that passed by the bottom of Cradley Road. They lay down on the floor, basked in the sun and laughed hysterically. Eli Davis put on his new leather shoes and grinned with a pride and happiness that he had never felt before.

That night, an almighty thunderstorm ravaged the night and shook the ground on which the Mucklow's cottage was built. The ground was sodden and the fierce rain pounded hard against the windows and roof of the house. As the family slept uncomfortably amongst the flies of the hot sticky night, the storm brought about a slightly cooling and welcome relief. They did not hear the poor soul that dragged itself along the soaking cobbled stones, leaving traces of his blood that were quickly washed away by the rain. Eli Davis' poor little nine-year-old frame crawled through the mud, the rain and his own fluids as he pulled himself to the front door and tried his very best to beat against it, his feeble attempts inaudible as the thunder and hammering rain continued to ring through the night sky. The young boy lay beaten to a pulp in the doorway and almost died.

The next morning, Willie Mucklow discovered his new friend lying barely alive in the doorway of his home. He immediately alerted his mother and sister who brought the small child inside where they set about seeing to his wounds and assessing the damage. Stan was sent to fetch the doctor and Willie looked on with rage. For a ten-year-old boy, the youngest Mucklow was hot headed and his youthful mind demanded retribution for what had happened to his poor friend.
He sat and watched all day as the doctor came and went alongside a local Police Constable who informed Willie's mother Susana that even though they knew that the child's father was a notorious drunk with a violent temperament, there was nothing they could do unless the child's mother actually spoke out against the man. *What would happen*

next? She thought. She looked at the floor sadly, safe in the knowledge that the child would one day be killed.

Willie narrowed his eyes and thought intently. He waited until he was alone in the room with the barely conscious Eli and seized the opportunity. "Who done this to yer Eli?"

"My ode mon… He was cross cus I ad' them new shoes." A tear appeared in the child's eyes. "He said ar was showing him and the family up by having charity." The nine-year-old lad's lip quivered as he recalled how proud and excited he had felt on the previous day when he and Willie had lay on the grass and his new mate had given him the shoes. Willie Mucklow smiled at his friend and he intuitively knew what he had to do.

Tobiaz Mucklow was waiting to join the Royal Worcestershire regiment of the British Army. He had been assigned to the 4th battalion, a relatively new battalion that had come about in 1900. At this time, the Worcestershire regiment had been ordered to raise two new battalions which became the third and fourth. Tobiaz was 17 years old, tall and slim and was eagerly looking forward to arriving at his regimental home at Norton barracks near Worcester.

On Saturday the 1st of September 1906, Tobiaz Mucklow stood proudly with his friends on Cradley Heath high street smoking cigarettes. Out of the corner of his eye he saw his little brother Willie approach. "What yow want aer kid?" Tobiaz could tell that his brother was angry. "Where's aer Stanley?"

"He's at home. Ar need yer ter do something for me brother." Willie's manner and tone was incredibly mature and serious for a ten-year-old boy and Tobiaz was amused.

"What be that then lad?" Tobiaz coolly dragged on his hand rolled cigarette and exhaled. Willie gestured for his older brother to leave his friends and speak to him in private. Tobiaz smiled again and casually walked over.

"Ar need yow to give a fella a good lampin' for me." Willie spoke in a hushed voice with a deadly serious tone.

"What?" Tobiaz immediately erupted into laughter. "Have some kids bin pickin' on yer aer kid?"

"No." Willie found it hard to hide his frustration. "One of mar mates, his dad keeps beatin' on him and he nearly died!" Willie's face changed and he suddenly looked upset.

"Has he touched you?" Tobiaz Mucklow had a feisty temper and since the death of his father he had taken his role as 'man of the house' very seriously and he was fiercely protective over his mother, sister and younger brothers.

"No… Just mar mate Eli, he's at home now with mother." A sly thought suddenly shot into Willie's mind, a manipulative trait that would become prominent in his character as he got older. "Eli's ode mon said he was gunna gid aer mother a lampin!" Willie lied.

"He did what?" Tobiaz put his own fist into his mouth and bit hard in anger. *He could not leave town to join the army knowing that some drunkard child beater had threatened his mother!* He lent in closer to his little brother and the pair hatched a plan.

John Samuel Davis was a notorious drunk and womaniser. His family lived poor and in total squalor as he drank away his chain maker wages around the various pubs in Cradley Heath. Every night he would beat his son Eli without fail after staggering home drunk and in a state of anger. That Saturday night, John Samuel Davis had 'sunk' more than several ales in The Hand of Providence in Hollybush street, The Heath Tavern on the high street, The Railway off Five ways and The Royal Oak in Lomey town. A few minutes after 'chucking out' time he emerged from the Heath Tavern onto the high street and out into the hot summer night. Barely able to walk he vowed to himself in his drunkard rage that his wife and child would 'suffer' upon his return home for the cheek of the landlord who had dared to 'sling' him out of the establishment. As he staggered back up the high street towards his terraced home a small stone suddenly ricochet off the back his head and a young lad of barely ten years of age shouted abuse at him.

"Oi yow, drunkard fool! Why dow yer pick on somebody your own size?" The young Willie Mucklow sneered at him and the audacity of the youngster speaking to him in such a way angered Davis even more. He immediately rushed towards the boy and almost fell over as the child disappeared down an alleyway.

"Oi you little tow rag!" Davis raged as he staggered around in the darkness of the alley, unaware of who was stalking him from within the shadows. He paused and suddenly felt a little afraid. A rat ran near to his foot and he thought that he heard the sound of human breathing in the stillness of the night. "Come aaht here! Fuckin' now!"

Suddenly, Tobiaz emerged from out of the shadows and eyed Davis with eyes that were livid with the actions of a man who had 'supposedly' threatened his mother. "What yow lookin' for?" He demanded menacingly.

"Some mouthy kid just lobbed a brick at me!" Davis spat the reply with contempt. Before he could utter another word, Tobiaz Mucklow hit him with a hard right-hand punch that sent him straight to the floor. As he struggled to get back up, both Tobiaz and Willie dived in and rained in kick after kick as they summoned all of the strength and energy within them to viciously beat the older man. Davis was far too drunk to defend himself against the youthful attackers and he eventually lost consciousness. Tobiaz put his hand on his little brother's shoulder and informed him that "enough was enough."

Willie paused for a second and looked at his friend's father who lay knocked out on the floor with utter hatred. The man had caused such suffering to young Eli and had made the little boy's life a total misery. He waited for Tobiaz to turn around as if to vacate the vicinity and then he drew a rusty old shaving blade that had belonged to his father and approached Davis. He calmly raised it and then rammed it hard into Davis' throat with as much force as a ten-year-old could generate. Davis' eyes flickered open in horror and blood sprayed violently and forcefully from the remnants of his obliterated Adams apple as he struggled to breathe. Willie Mucklow continued to hold the blade and he forcefully yanked it as deeply as he could from side to side. He pulled the blade out and then proceeded to repeatedly pummel it into his friend's father's throat until eventually the larynx was penetrated and Davis' airways filled up with blood and he lost consciousness for a final time. Tobiaz looked on with sheer shock and horror at his little brother's actions as he stood rooted to the spot, confused and scared about what would happen next! *If the law were to find out then it would be him that would dangle on the end of a rope!*

Willie continued to look on through his mature ten-year-old eyes with amazement and curiosity as Davis choked on his own blood and died. As his throat rattled and rasped its final breath, the young Mucklow continued to watch, safe in the knowledge that his actions here on this hot summer's night may well have saved the life of his young friend Eli.

Chapter 2
1915

On the 28th of June 1914, the Austro-Hungarian heir, Archduke Franz Ferdinand was assassinated in the Bosnia Herzegovian city of Sarajevo. This in turn set off a chain of events that would lead to one of the most destructive and violent conflicts in human history.

At the start of the twentieth century the German Empire was a relatively new major power on the world scene. Great Britain had dominated the centuries that had preceded and had colonized a third of the world. The Germans were a new industrial superpower that wanted to advance its influence and standing in the hierarchy of world politics and after Ferdinand's assassination in 1914 there was an acceleration in military tension between the Austro-Hungarian Empire and Russia. This was an opportunity for Germany to proudly display its military might and back their Austrian allies by declaring war on Russia and France.

The German strategy for war on two fronts was to rapidly concentrate the bulk of its vast army in the west to try and defeat France within 6 weeks before shifting its attention eastwards towards Russia. This became known as the Schlieffen plan. However, in order for the Germans to successfully wage war against France, they first had to gain free passage through Belgium to achieve a swift and comprehensive victory over the French. On the 3rd of August 1914, this free passage was denied and the Germans had no option but to invade Belgium. On the same day, the Belgian government invoked the 1839 Treaty of London, a treaty that obligated Great Britain to declare war on the aggressors and defend their Belgian allies. The following day, August 4th, Britain declared war on Germany and The Great War had all but began.

Tobiaz Mucklow had joined the Royal Worcestershire Regiment 4th battalion in 1906 and by the start of the First World War in 1914 he had risen to the rank of Sargent. At the outbreak of war, the British army embarked on a period of mass recruitment and later conscription. It was around this time that Tobiaz's brothers Stanley and William answered the call at the age of 18 and joined up to the same regiment as their elder brother. After the death of his father 8 years previously, Eli Davis had been taken in by the Mucklows and was unofficially adopted and became all but a 'blood brother' to the Mucklow twins. Like many young boys at this time, Eli lied about his age and proudly enlisted in the Royal Worcestershire regiment 4th battalion alongside his 'brothers.'

As the Mucklow boys trained and prepared at the regimental barracks in Norton near Worcester, the 1st battalion landed in Le Havre France as part of the 24th Brigade in the 8th Division in November 1914. The 2nd battalion had already landed at Boulogne-Sur-Mer in August of that year and they both fought the Germans on the Western front, as did the 3rd battalion that landed at Rouen in August 1914. Meanwhile, the 4th battalion and the Mucklow boys awaited their turn which would not come until March 1915.

Before they were shipped off to war, the Mucklow boys were able to return to their home in Cradley Heath to spend an emotional 48 hours with their mother and sister where they said their final farewells and kissed their mother goodbye. Tobiaz had not been present though as he had returned home a few weeks earlier to say his goodbyes. Before the boys departed for their barracks, they decided to call in for one last beer at The Heath Tavern on High Street Cradley Heath whilst on their way to the railway station. The pub was half full but their khaki green army uniforms attracted little attention as at that time it was relatively commonplace to see soldiers on their way to war.

Willie Mucklow's mind was full of thoughts of his lady friend Helen Hingley. They had been in a courteous relationship for several months now and Willie had seriously considered making her his wife. But this would now have to wait until after the war. To Willie Mucklow this was all very inconvenient. He did not regret signing up to do his bit for King and country, but business had been booming and their small street gang was making them considerably more money from their illegal activities than any factory or mine worker could earn. They had recently moved into the racetracks and were starting to do odd bits of work for the notorious Birmingham gangster Billy Kimber and his young associate Isiah Boswell.

"So then lads." Stan Mucklow looked at his freshly poured pint of ale and wondered when his next opportunity would be to drink another one. "We gunna teach Jerry a lesson then?"

Eli Davis lit a cigarette and leant back on his bar stool. Violence did not scare him, he had grown accustomed to it as a child and, so he believed, there wasn't anything the Kaiser could do to him that his father hadn't already done. He looked at Stan and said nothing.

"Fuckin' army dow pay much!" Willie interrupted the silence unenthusiastically. "We were just getting somewhere when all this kicked off!" He took a gulp of his beer. "Ar better not die! Ar got plans!"

"We ay gewin to France. We woe be fighting Germans Stan." Eli suddenly spoke as he stared aimlessly into the large open fire that dominated the bar.

"Of course we'm fighting the Germans!" Stan looked confused and glared at his brothers. "They'm the enemy ay they?"

"We'm gewin ter Turkey." Eli whispered.

It meant nothing to Stan. He drained his beer and ordered a whisky. "Well, wherever we gew, we will give um' a lampin." His voice quivered with false bravado and both Willie and Eli could tell that their brother was afraid. They had all heard horror stories from the First Battle Marne in September 1914 and rumours were rife of automatic machine guns, advanced new cannons and horrendous gas that were all part of new methods of warfare that had never been seen before.

"Yow ok Stanley?" Willie put a reassuring hand on his brothers back and a small tear escaped from Stanley's eye.

"Ar." He composed himself and then the tear grew more prominent. "Will we see aer mother again Willie?"

Willie looked at his twin and smiled. "Dow be saft Stan. Course we will."

Stan wiped his face and laughed emotionally. "Sorry Willie." He raised a cigarette to his mouth with an unsteady right hand and Willie, cool calm and confidently lit it for him. He inhaled deeply and felt the tobacco smoke in his lungs. "We'll show um' woe we boys?" He blew out smoke and searched his brother's eyes for reassurance.

Willie Mucklow pulled out his pocket watch and checked the time. He paused for a moment and thought of how his mother had embraced them all so intensely as they left the house, even Eli. His mother had suffered a hard life after the death of their father and the last thing Willie wanted was for her to suffer the heart-breaking loss of her sons too. He drained his glass and promised himself that he would not allow his mother to suffer a fate worse than death. He would not allow his mother to lose a child. He checked his watch again and looked solemnly at his brothers. "Right then boys. We got a train ter catch."

The 4th Battalion landed in Gallipoli as part of the 88th Brigade in the 29th Division in March 1915. The allies sought to weaken the Ottoman Empire who were allied with Germany by taking control of the waters that provided a supply route to Russia. The first attack in February 1915 failed so this was then followed up by an amphibious landing to try and capture the Ottoman capital of Constantinople (Istanbul). This was a violent and costly campaign that proved to be unsuccessful for the British Army and in January 1916 The Royal Worcestershire regiment 4th battalion was evacuated to Egypt before it landed in Marseille, France for service on the western front. It was here that the Allied and German forces continued to dig trenches and obliterate each other in an absolute stalemate. Men from either side were simply thrown 'over the top' as 'cannon fodder' to be literally ripped apart by machine gun fire. An almost certain death. This continued for another two years until eventually the German army fell back towards Germany and the allied forces of Britain, France, Russia and eventually the USA were victorious.

Between 1914 and 1918 the total number of deaths was approximately 40 million; a whole generation of men who were butchered and slaughtered for a 'War that would end Wars.' Unfortunately, this would prove to be untrue…

Of the four young sons Susana Mucklow had clung to emotionally, waved goodbye to at the start of The Great War and worried about constantly throughout the hostilities, only 2 returned…

> They shall grow not old, as we that are left grow old.
> Age shall not weary them, nor the years condemn.
> At the going down of the sun and in the morning,
> we will remember them.- Laurence Binyon.

Chapter 3
1948

Arthur Doe looked angrily at the three 'gorgios' (non-gypsies) and then back at his older brother Eladon. He cut his eyes fiercely and drew his finger across his throat aggressively before muttering another gypsy word. "Churi!" The three looked on with some amusement and felt no fear.

Arthur's brother Eladon was the gypsy king. His family had migrated from Ireland many years ago and he had been born on The Black Patch in Smethwick. The Black Patch was a notorious part of Birmingham that from the mid-19th century had been a camping ground for many generations of Gypsy families. Back then the undisputed king of the Gypsies on Black Patch was Esau Smith. Upon his death in 1901 at the age of 92, his widow Henty was elected the new Queen. It had been assumed that the Smith's had gained legal rights to The Black Patch ensuring that the gypsy community were the legal owners of the land. However, upon Queen Henty's death in 1907, her caravan was subsequently burnt as was tradition and ritual amongst gypsy families. Unfortunately for the community, the legal documentation and deeds securing the gypsies ownership of The Black Patch were destroyed and as a result, a 'peaceful eviction' was negotiated and the gypsies left the area in 1909.

It was at this time that the young Eladon Doe and his family left Birmingham and eventually settled in the Worcestershire town of Stourport On Severn where he would establish his own gypsy community just over the Severn Bridge away from the town. The Doe family had risen from strength to strength and during the Second World War Eladon Doe had secured total control over the local underworld. All the pubs, hotels and other businesses paid protection money to the Doe family and anyone who dared not to pay would suffer brutal consequences from Eladon Doe's band of violent and unruly thugs who were often fronted by his sociopathic brother Arthur.

On this day, the 1st of July 1948, a long black 1939 Austin 18 limousine had rolled into the gypsy camp in Stouport and out got three impeccably dressed gangsters. The locals looked on with interest as the arrival of the grand car was unforeseen and without invitation. The three men had then trudged across the muddy campsite and knocked loudly on the side of Eladon Doe's caravan. Leading the trio of visitors was a slightly overweight man of average height who was in his early fifties. He was totally bald, had a neck that appeared to be as thick as a tree trunk and a face that was full, broad and resembled that of a British Bull dog. To the right of him was an associate of similar age. He was a giant of a man and stood at 6 foot five inches tall with wide coarse fists, short curly dark hair that carried a hint of grey and cold penetrating blue eyes that would occasionally display the slightest hint of humour and amusement. The third man was much younger than the other two. He was in his mid-20s and looked like a younger version of the first man. His hairline was high and he had the same wide facial structure as his Bull dog reminiscent boss.

Eladon had emerged from his caravan and his angry looking brother Arthur had quickly walked over to join him. "Calm down Arthur, let's see what these boys want." He put a hand on his brother's shoulder and turned to look at the three 'gorgio' visitors. He had the slightest hint of an Irish accent, though he had never set foot in the country of his ancestors. "Who the feck are you?"

The middle-aged man with the bulldog face smiled politely, took a cigarette from out of his case and introduced himself. "Mar name is Willie Mucklow." He gestured towards the bear of a man next to him and spoke again. "This is mar mate Eli Davis and the lad is mar sister's son Harry Scriven." Mucklow put out his hand to shake that of the gypsy. Doe looked at it for a few seconds and then shook it. He had heard of the Mucklow family from the Black Country… Willie Mucklow was a respected gang boss who controlled the criminal underworld of Halesowen, Cradley Heath, Netherton, Blackheath and parts of Dudley. These were men to be respected.

"What the feck do you want?" Eladon Doe was not afraid of *the flash townies*, they were in his territory and he was not afraid of anyone.

Willie Mucklow lit his cigarette and looked at the floor before fixing his gaze firmly and intently into the gypsy's eyes. He took a step closer and blew smoke provocatively into his face. It had been a long time since a man had possessed the nerve to approach Eladon Doe in such a manner and the gypsy held his cool and hoped that his brother Arthur would practice a similar restraint, at least for now.

"Some of yower lads have been coming raahnd mar pubs in Halesowen and causing trouble… Asking for protection money?" Mucklow posed the word money as a question.

"We do what we fuckin' want!" Arthur Doe lost his cool and took a step closer to the three visitors. Eli Davis watched him closely and prepared to protect his faithful friend Willie. Willie and the Mucklow's had saved his life when he was just a child and they had taken him in and given him a family. Davis felt thankful for this every day and he had developed an overwhelming urge to protect his family from anything and anyone. He had not been able to protect Stan and Tobiaz when they were 'blown to kingdom come' in France in 1917, but since his return to England after the First World War, he had been a constant at Willie's side and the pair had forged a close bond. They looked out for each other and had rose to become two of the most feared and respected men in the Midlands.

Eladon Doe put an arm on his brother's shoulder and gave him a stern look. "Let's not be too hasty brother."

Willie Mucklow took another drag of his cigarette and looked at the Gypsies again. "If yow lot keep bothering my businesses, then I think it is only fair that I start to branch out my activities over this way." He blew smoke into the air and looked around the camp site as Eladon Doe pondered his next move. The gypsy camp stood on banks of the River Severn on the outskirts of Stourport towards the town of Bewdley. Doe thought for a few seconds before coming to the conclusion that fighting the Mucklow family probably wasn't worth the hassle. He was satisfied with his lot and he had no desire to expand his organisation. Some of his men were young with wild oats to sow and they had been venturing further afield into what was Willie Mucklow's territory, but Eladon Doe had no knowledge of this and he certainly had no wish for a war of any description.

"Mr Mucklow, I will have a word with my lads… I was not aware that any of them were venturing into your territory." The gypsy spoke the truth. "I will make sure that it does not happen again. But, if you or your boys ever start making moves around here on my turf, then I will be down on yers' like a ton of feckin' bricks!" The gypsy stared deep into Mucklow's eyes and spoke with sincere and aggressive intent. Willie Mucklow was by no means scared. He blew smoke out, smiled and put out his right hand again. Eladon Doe spat into his own palm and shook Mucklow's hand firmly. The three Black Country men nodded their respects to the Doe brothers and returned to their Austin limousine whilst Arthur Doe sloped off to find some of his best men. He was not prepared to be humiliated by these *'townie gorgios'* and he was *not as weak as his brother!* He would have these three men regretting ever setting foot on a gypsy camp before the sun was down.

Harry Scriven drove the large Austin away from the campsite as Eli Davis and his uncle Willie sat in the back smoking cigarettes. During the Second World War Scriven had served as a technician in the RAF in Cornwall and before that he had worked as a motor mechanic at Henn's garage in Cradley Heath. He knew that he had been brought along by his uncle today as a test of his character and fighting abilities. Scriven's uncle Willie was a notorious criminal and he had made more money in these last few months working for his uncle than he had made in years working as a mechanic. Harry Scriven had proven himself to be a good boxer and more than capable in a fight and he knew that this meeting today had been his opportunity to prove himself as a worthwhile member of his uncle Willie's crew. The meeting at the campsite had gone smoother than anticipated and Scriven had been disappointed that the opportunity had not arisen for him to prove his fighting prowess and demonstrate that he was just as capable as his cousin and Willie's son Billy Mucklow. He watched the road in front of him and wondered why Billy had not been present today and then he realised that this was probably all part of the test. The last thing he needed was Billy or 'The Captain' as Willie and Eli had christened him on account of his impressive army rank during the Second World War taking over and leaving little opportunity for him to impress 'Uncle Willie.'

Scriven nudged the accelerator pedal and figured that he would soon be crossing over the bridge at Stourport to travel back towards the Black Country.

"Harry!" Willie Mucklow called from the back seat and leant forwards to speak to his nephew. "Ar fancy a drink. What der yow pair think?"

Eli Davis and Harry Scriven both nodded their heads enthusiastically and Willie directed them to a country pub in a small village called Dunley. Harry Scriven pulled up outside The Dog Inn and the three men got out and ventured inside. It was a small pub with low ceilings and oak floorboards which was popular with local farmers and gypsies alike.

The door slowly creaked open and the local drinkers all turned and stared suspiciously at the three dapper men who looked noticeably out of place amongst the farm labourers and gypsies. Mucklow, Davis and Scriven drew further attention when they ordered their drinks at the bar and revealed their thick Black Country accents. They were deep in the Worcestershire countryside and Harry Scriven thought that everyone around him sounded like an inbred 'yokel' as he sipped his beer.

"Do yer think the bastards will behave themselves now Willie?" Eli Davis took a long gulp of his ale and looked at his friend.

"Ar dow know Eli. But I ay gunna mess abahht. Anymore problems and ar'm gunna toss them fuckin' caravans in the river!"

Scriven said nothing, safe in the knowledge that his uncle was not joking. He so desperately needed to prove himself to the family and ensure that he was there on his own merits and not because his mother was Willie's sister.

As the three men from the Black Country sat and supped their beer, a large group of local thugs from the gypsy camp sat and watched on the orders of Arthur Doe. They watched and waited until the men had drained the dregs of their ale and then they ventured out onto the car park to wait.

Davis and Mucklow sat nestled and comfortable in the back of the large Austin as Harry Scriven started the engine and put the car into gear. He drove slowly to the edge of the car park when suddenly a group of rough looking young men surrounded the car and attempted to stop them from driving off. Scriven's first reaction was to simply carry on driving through them but then he suddenly stopped upon realisation that this could be his opportunity to prove himself to Uncle Willie and Eli Davis.

Eli sighed and went to get out of the car but Willie tapped him on the shoulder and gestured for him to stop. This was the chance they had both been waiting for. Would Harry be a worthwhile addition to the 'business end' of the family?

Scriven wound down the window and spoke to the men. "What yer doing?" He frowned and waited for a reply. "Get ahht the fuckin' oss road!"

The ringleader gave Scriven a threatening stare and remained defiantly in front of the Austin as his younger associates watched on. "You boys are a long way from home!" The leader had a thick country/gypsy accent and he spoke with a cocky arrogance that Scriven found irritating. He shrugged his shoulders and waited for further comment. "I think you is best giving us your wallets… You is not local and that is the toll that you will pay for passing through these parts."

Eli Davis and Willie Mucklow heard the whole thing and instantly erupted into fits of laughter. Harry Scriven felt a rush of adrenaline as he realised that his time had come and that all eyes were upon him to see if he could sort the problem. He got out of the car and strolled casually over to the gypsy. "Ar'm sorry mate, yow'm gunna have to say that again, ar day quite hear yer."

The Gypsy sniggered and Scriven grimaced at the thick smell of his body odour and rotting teeth. "I said!" the Gypsy raised his voice aggressively "You is gunna have to hand over your wallets before we let you come past here! Isn't that right boys?" The gypsy raised his voice again and the other men replied in unison. "Yeah that's right."

Scriven half smiled and averted his gaze to one side before suddenly smashing the gypsy in the eye with a right hook that almost knocked him over. Scriven pummelled another hard punch into his gut and the gypsy fell forwards, winded and in pain. Before his friends could move to help him, Scriven pulled the man by his dirty, thick ginger hair to the open doorway of the car and they watched on in horror as Scriven slammed the door hard shut one, two, three times, trapping the man's head in the doorway each time and spraying fresh blood onto the floor and across the front wing of the limousine. The men instantly froze and wandered if their friend would escape with his life. Scriven's face looked demonic as blood covered his wide forehead and dripped down his cheeks onto his white shirt. He turned to face them with a grotesque anger that was accentuated by the scarlet droplets that decorated his full and snarling features. "Who else fuckin' wants some?" He growled, teeth clenched and foam flying from his mouth. The men took a step backwards and sheepishly said nothing. Scriven pulled the semi-conscious gypsy to his knees and spat aggressively into his face.

"How many fuckin' sheep did you have to fuck before you could talk like that you filthy, inbred bastard?" The gypsy said nothing as he struggled to retain consciousness. Scriven grabbed him by his collars and threw him away from the car with force so that he collapsed in a heap on the floor. He took one last look at the dispersing gypsy 'yokels' and got back into the car and drove off. Mucklow and Davis said nothing. Each one of them within the car knew full well that Harry Scriven had proven himself, but not a word would ever be spoken of it ever again. Davis and

Mucklow were not the type to give compliments, if you were fortunate enough to be in their presence, then no further words were necessary.

Chapter 4

It was early July 1948 and Harry Scriven sat in the driver's seat and watched his alluring female companion. She had the kind of heavily made-up blue eyes that Scriven found totally irresistible. Lily Cole was just 22 years old but had a confident sophistication that appealed to her older lover Harry who was 27. She was relatively short with light blonde hair that was styled in the typical 1940s fashion, complete with curls and victory rolls. She always wore slightly too much make up with long eye lashes and bright scarlet lipstick. Her figure was slight and she would have preferred to have had fuller breasts but her pretty face more than made up for this.

"Harry, me Mom and Dad am out, do yer wanna come back to the house for a little while?" She sat in the passenger seat of Scriven's 1931 Morris Isis. It was a luxurious old saloon with an overhead cam 17.7hp engine that had quintessentially 1920s styling. The Second World War had only finished three years previously and new cars were scarce. Harry Scriven was one of very few men that Lily Cole knew who actually owned his own car and even if it was old and smelt of oil and petrol, it certainly gave her bragging rights amongst her female friends.

"Ar cor bab, it's Sunday afternoon and you know Uncle Willie likes all the chaps to be in the pub before we gew back to his fer tay." Scriven felt slightly disappointed. He could get a beer anytime, but the opportunity to be alone in the house with his young lady friend was a rare occurrence that he was reluctant to waste. Lily sighed and crossed her legs provocatively, raising her knee length skirt further up her thighs to reveal her black stocking tops. Harry Scriven took a deep breath and bit into his lower lip. "Fuck it bab, Uncle Willie can wait!"

An hour later, Scriven sat upright in Lily Cole's bed and smoked a cigarette as Lily nestled in besides him. A Glen Miller record span on the turntable and Scriven enjoyed life as he sucked in the tobacco smoke, savoured it and then blew it back out. They had been out for a drive that morning and Scriven was very much aware that his presence was required at The Haden Cross pub where his uncle Willie and Eli Davis would be drinking beer and discussing their 'business' plans for the week ahead.

Lily Cole lived with her parents in a relatively affluent 3-bedroom semi-detached house at the bottom end of Barrs Road in Haden Hill. Her father, Norman Cole, owned his own scrap yard and had 'done well' financially.

"Ar'm gunna have to gew soon Lil." Scriven exhaled smoke whilst feeling fulfilled. He was particularly fond of her and he was even entertaining thoughts that one day she would become his wife, but for now he had had his fun and now he was ready for the pub.

"What happened Harry?" Lily suddenly noticed the cuts and bruises on Scriven's knuckles and she instantly sat up in bed. "Who did Willie Mucklow pay you to beat up this time?" She gave a look of disgust and disappointment before shuffling away from his side.

"It ay like that bab." Scriven protested even though he knew what she was saying was true.

"Mar Dad would gew mad if he knew ar was mixing with the Mucklows!" She looked away from him and folded her arms in sulk.

"Well, yer dow seem to mind when yum out and abaaht in me car? Or when we're in the picture house?" Scriven raised his voice slightly and turned to face her. "Yow gew on abaaht my suits and how ar dress so smart." She gave a hint of a nod but she did not look at him. "Have yow seen mar Uncle Willie's house?" Lily nodded and turned to look him in the eye. Willie Mucklow lived in an exceptionally large detached art deco house on Halesowen Road which had been built in the early 1930s. "Well, my ode mon lives in a terraced house up Talbot street… He's worked hard all his life meckin' chain. He aye gorra car or nothing but he's happy ar guess." Scriven was proud of and loved his father but he had bigger aspirations. "What do yer want Lil? A big house in Halesowen, loads of nice clothes and a car? Or a terraced house down

Cradley Heath? Tell me when yow med your mind up." Scriven swiftly got of the bed and began to button his shirt up with a sense of annoyance.

"Wait Harry." She followed him, placed her chin on his back and wrapped her arms around his waist. "I'm just scared Harry. Willie Mucklow is demanding protection money from my father, but I know mar Dad. He's stubborn and he is refusing to pay." A tear emerged in her eye and her make-up began to bleed down her right cheek. "Promise me you won't hurt my father Harry."

Scriven stared out of the window and felt torn. His job was to help make sure people paid his uncle Willie. He hoped in that minute that he would never be asked to pay Norman Cole a visit. "Dow worry bab. I ay gunna lay a finger on yower ode mon." He turned and pulled her slim face into his and kissed her on the head, hoping that he would never have to break his promise to her.

"Where the fuck yow bin?" Eli Davis was in the main bar area of the Haden Cross when Harry Scriven entered the pub through the back door. Davis was buying beer and Scriven was relieved to see his cousin Bill emerge through the front door even later than he was. "The pair on yer!" Davis half smiled and told the barman to get a drink in for the two cousins. Everything went on Willie Mucklow's tab and he always insisted on paying for everything, knowing that he would get most of it back in the form of protection money! "Ar'll tell Willie yow'm here at last! See yer in a bit." Davis nodded towards the small snug that stood behind the main bar which Willie Mucklow treated as his own personal office and went back in with his and Willie's beer.

"I heard all about yow in the week!" Bill Mucklow took a long drink of his beer and winked at his cousin. Bill Mucklow was a big man in his mid to late 20s who looked remarkably similar to his father Willie Mucklow and his cousin Harry Scriven. They had grown up more like brothers than cousins and the pair shared a close bond. Bill was a distinguished war hero and during World War 2 had risen to the rank of

Captain, partially on account of his somewhat privileged upbringing and him having attended grammar school in Halesowen.

"What yow on abaaht?" Scriven lit a cigarette and gratefully accepted his beer from the barman.

"My ode mon told me abaaht yow sortin' ahht them gypsies. Ar told him yow had it in yer. Remember, ar seen yer in the boxing ring!" Bill Mucklow gave him a pat on the back and Scriven could not help but feel a little patronised. He was slightly older than Bill but his cousin always had a way of unintentionally making him feel inferior. Bill certainly never meant to come across like that but it had always been his way.

"Ar well, it had to be done I suppose."

Bill Mucklow smiled again and took out his cigarette case. "Suppose we better gew through to the ode mon. Ar swear if some fucker calls me The Captain again ar will fuckin' lamp em!"

Harry Scriven half smiled but Bill could tell by his eyes that something was bothering his cousin. "What's up aer kid?"

"Nothing mate, it dow matter." Scriven blew smoke across the bar and took a sip of his beer.

"Fuckin' spit it ahht kidda, yow can tell me cor yer?" Bill Mucklow persisted.

Scriven sighed and looked Bill in the eye. "Yer know that wench ar bin a courting?"

Bill nodded enthusiastically. "Ar mate. Nice bit of stuff. About time yow settled down like me and aer Mary." Bill Mucklow had married his wife Mary soon after returning home from War and the couple were expecting their first child.

Scriven extinguished his cigarette in a white ashtray. It was a rectangular shaped barroom with a large Victorian fireplace that stood at the end of the room adjacent to the bar. "Well, she is Norman Cole's daughter and she is worried cus yower ode mon is on his back!"

"Oh…" Bill Mucklow extended the spoken syllable and instantly understood his cousin's dilemma. "Ar'll have a word with the ode mon, see what he says… But yow better be serious about this wench Harry. If aer Dad meck's allowances for Norman Cole yow better fuckin' marry her or summet!" Bill half laughed but Scriven knew that he was not joking. They picked up their drinks and went through to the side bar.

The brilliant sunlight pierced the solitary window on the left-hand side of Willie Mucklow's personal drinking spot within The Haden Cross. It exuded a rich brightness into the small room and Willie Mucklow was relaxed and lay back in his seat. His suit jacket was draped over the back of his chair and he had loosened his top button and tie in the heat of the summer's day. Harry Scriven was hoping his heroics with the gypsies would cut him some 'slack' for being late. He had earned himself a new respect within the gang and he felt more confident that he was now there on his own merit as opposed to because he was the boss's nephew. Bill was late too and Scriven had never seen Willie 'loose it' with his precious son so he figured they would be ok.

"Took yer time day yer?" Willie Mucklow took a long drink of his ale and enjoyed the soothing feel of the beer quenching his thirst on this hot July day.

Scriven said nothing but Bill laughed as he confidently took a seat opposite his father and Eli Davis. "Stop yer moanin' ode mon." He could do no wrong in his father's eyes. Bill Mucklow was as tough and as good in a fight as anyone (with the possible exception of Eli Davis) and three years previously he had fought bravely and ferociously against the Germans in Europe as both Eli Davis and Willie Mucklow had done 30 years earlier. Harry Scriven always felt a little 'out of' this exclusive club for war heroes. He had done his bit in the RAF but he had never been directly involved in military conflict as had the other 3 men who were gathered around the table.

Willie Mucklow laughed and raised his eyebrows in mock annoyance. "Right then lads." He sat upright, took another drink of his beer and then his eyes turned deadly serious. "A couple of things ar want sortin' this week." He looked at Scriven with a newfound respect.

"Harry, yow ay servicing the motors no more… Ar want yer to gew over to The Black Oss at Illey with Eli. Word is the gaffer ay gunna pay us protection money no more cus bloody Isiah Boswell's lot have took over the place." Willie turned to face Eli Davis. "Sort em aaht and teach them flash Brummies a lesson." Willie paused for a minute to recall memories of the past. "Years agew we used to call em The Peaky Blinders, but fuck em. They come onto mar patch and ar'll shove them Peaky things up their fuckin' arse holes!"

Isiah Boswell was an established and respected gang boss from nearby Birmingham. He had risen to prominence within the feared 'Brummie boys' gang and had taken over from the former leader and founding member Billy Kimber who had died in 1945. Boswell was of similar age to Willie Mucklow and the pair usually tolerated each other, but Willie had been hearing about how Boswell had been 'pushing his luck' and beginning to expand into pubs and factories that were outside of his territory. Harry Scriven nodded coolly, hiding his inner pride at finally being accepted into the 'inner circle' of The Mucklow gang.

Willie Mucklow looked at the cloudless blue sky outside of the window and paused again for a few seconds as he tried to remember what else it was he wanted to say. "Oh yes." He regained his focus and his attention came back to the men that sat around the table as he took another drink of his beer. "Ar want that bastard Norman Cole sortin' ahht this week too…" A sudden flash of worry came over Scriven at the mention of his lady friend's father. He could not believe the timing and the sheer bad luck of the fact that she had only mentioned it to him less than an hour previously. *Bloody typical!* He thought to himself. He fixed his gaze on his Uncle, gave away nothing in his eyes and missed the knowing look his cousin Bill had given him from across the table. "That bastard has been teckin' the piss for far too bloody long." Willie banged his glass down hard on the table. "Ar dow know who he thinks he is! He has ter pay just like everybody else!" Willie looked at Eli with a look of annoyance. "Eli, meck him pay. Do whatever yow have ter do." Davis nodded and smiled. He had known nothing but violence since birth and he was good at it.

Bill Mucklow sat casually at the table and smoked an expensive cigarette. "Can I have a word Fairtha?" He looked at his father and gestured to the far corner of the room with his head. Willie looked at his son with a look of bemusement and slowly got up and went into the corner to talk with Billy. Harry Scriven sat uncomfortably in his chair knowing that the conversation would be about him. He opened up his silver-plated cigarette case and pulled out a woodbine. He did not show his nerves as he lit it and sat back in his chair casually. *What would Bill say? What would Willie think? Would he have to marry Lily?* Scriven had grown incredibly fond of Lily Cole and had very much enjoyed his time spent in her company. But he knew that in asking his Uncle to go easy on Lily's father he was taking things to a whole new level. He would probably have to get engaged and he still wasn't completely sure if this was what he wanted. A thousand thoughts and questions rushed through his mind but still he chose to remain silent as he sat and smoked his cigarette with a confident swagger.

Bill Mucklow and his father stood whispering in the corner of the room for what seemed to Harry Scriven like an eternity until finally the pair approached the table. "Well then. Looks like aer Harry has got himself a wench." Willie Mucklow playfully rustled what was left of Scriven's hair as he sat down. "Ar suppose we can negotiate some special 'family terms' fer Norman Cole aer kid… He will have ter pay for the weddin' though Harry… Yow better sort aaht a fuckin' engagement ring!"

Chapter 5

The Saturday morning singing of the birds awakened Harry Scriven from his post pub Friday night slumber. It had been getting on for a week since Willie Mucklow had instructed him to go with Eli Davis to The Black Horse at Illey and reclaim the pub from The Brummie Boys gang. Davis had heard on the grapevine that one of Boswell's top men and two of his associates drank in The Black Horse on Saturday nights and after discussions with Willie it was agreed that Davis and Scriven would go down there and sort things out. As Scriven awoke, his mind was filled with thoughts of the night ahead.

The pub protection racket was remarkably simple. Local pubs and clubs paid Willie Mucklow to protect their businesses, which basically meant that he would ensure that there was no fighting inside the pubs and he would deal with any individual trouble makers. More importantly it meant that he would use his bought influence with the local Police to ensure that the pubs could have 'lock ins' and go on serving alcohol 'after hours.' Of course, if any business refused to pay, the Police would enforce licensing laws to the full extent and customers and staff would suddenly begin to encounter violent episodes inside the pub premises. It certainly made sense to pay! On the other hand, there was always the risk of rival gangs from outside of the area 'muscling in' on the operation. This was exactly what appeared to be happening at The Black Horse at Illey and it was up to Davis and Scriven to return the pub into the hands of Willie Mucklow.

Lily Cole was still asleep as she snuggled in next to Scriven and draped a naked arm around her future husband. She lived with her parents and he was not supposed to be there. He had parked his car up the road and 'snuck in' when her parents were fast asleep in their beds. It was a routine that had been repeated several times and had involved Scriven throwing small stones at Lily's bedroom which rather conveniently happened to be on the front of the house. It always seemed like a good idea after a few pints in the Haden Cross, but the next morning when he had to climb down the drainpipe with a hangover, Scriven often wondered if it had all been worth it the hassle.

"Can't ar just sneak aaht the front door bab?" Scriven nudged Lily as he looked at his watch and realised it was time to get up. She looked so peaceful and beautiful as she slept and Scriven instantly remembered that the whole escapade had certainly been worth it to spend the night alongside his future wife.

"What?" She stirred before coming to her senses and hugging him tightly. "Do you really have to go?"

"Yes Bab. I've gotta meet Bill down the boxing club then we'm gewin to watch The Yeltz this afternoon." Scriven decided not to inform her of The Black Horse at Illey and his plans for later that night.

"Will ar see yer tonight bab?" She looked at him, her love filled eyes pleading for his company that night.

Scriven paused and thought about the chances of him being in jail or hospital that evening. He had done lots of little jobs for his Uncle Willie before and had used his skills as a motor mechanic to look after the family's cars, but tonight's work was a further step up into the realms of being a gangster after he had proven himself with the Gypsies. It paid better than being a mechanic and Scriven had always loved the thrill of a fight, plus he was bloody good at it! "Ar dow know bab." Scriven looked into her pretty eyes and at her shapely thigh that lay exposed on one side of the bed sheet. "Listen out fer the pebbles on the window." Scriven smiled, not knowing that she would now go to bed early and wait devotedly by the window for hours.

The Saturday passed by as Saturdays usually did. Scriven and Bill Mucklow trained hard at the boxing club before several pints in The King Edward VII pub in Halesowen and then over to the Halesowen town football club next door to watch the match. This Saturday it was just a pre-season friendly. Halesowen town, or 'The Yeltz' as they were known locally had recently been crowned champions in their first ever league title in the Birmingham and district league 1946-47 season. The club was originally established in 1873 and had joined the Birmingham and district league in 1892 with very little success in the first 50 years of existence. Both Harry Scriven and his cousin Bill were regular supporters and would go down to The Grove on a Saturday afternoon when The Yeltz were playing at home.

After the match, Harry Scriven returned to his home in Talbot Street, Colley Gate where he changed into a fresh suit and had a shave ready for the night's activities. He was relatively old to still be living at home with his parents and he spent most of his time with Bill or Lily, in the pub or over at the boxing club.

After a brief conversation with his mother and father, who were hoping their son would finally settle down and marry Lily Cole, Scriven went out to his car and started it ready to go out. The Morris Isis was old and Harry Scriven had only been a child himself when it was built in the early 1930s, but cars were a rare and unattainable luxury for most people in 1948 and his was the only car in the street. He dropped it into gear and rolled down the steep and bumpy cobbled road until he reached the T-junction on Furlong Lane at the bottom of the hill. He stopped to light a cigarette before turning right towards Eli Davis' house in High Haden Crescent which was near Willie Mucklow's home in Haden Hill.

As he drove up Barrs Road towards the crossroads on the other side of the hill, Scriven could not help but look around at the affluent, middle class houses. Lily Cole, Bill Mucklow, Eli Davis and his Uncle Willie all lived in this area which bordered Halesowen and Cradley Heath and Scriven could not help but feel slightly in awe as he too had ambitions to live in such a district. Willie Mucklow and Eli Davis had both come from poor working-class backgrounds in Cradley Heath as had Scriven's mother Eliza and he saw no reason why he should not rise up and aim high as they had.

He pulled up outside Eli Davis' house and finished his cigarette as he waited for the senior gangster to appear. Davis' wife was a rather attractive older woman in her late 40s who had a particular fondness for younger men. She could be quite flirtatious and the last thing Scriven wanted to do was get on the wrong side of the ferocious Eli! It was a lot easier and safer to simply arrive at the given time and wait in the car for Davis to appear.

As he waited he could not help but wonder again about the potential outcomes of the night's activities. Would he end up at the Police station, the hospital or both?

"Yow alright aer kid?" Davis emerged from the house and strolled purposefully down the path and got into the car alongside Scriven. Eli Davis lived in an elegant semi-detached house with big bay windows and a decorative motif that stood above the upper bay as the front of the house ascended to a point. The house had been built in the late 1920s in the typical art deco style and represented Davis' lucrative position as second in command of one of the Midlands most feared and respected criminal gangs.

"Ar, I'm ok thanks Eli." Scriven lit up another cigarette and Davis joined him in a smoke as they travelled along Halesowen Road past the Haden Cross and towards the bottom of Mucklows Hill where they continued straight towards Hunnington and Romsley. "So." Scriven removed the cigarette from his lips and exhaled coolly. "Who am we after?"

"Fella called Reg Smith." Eli Davis had done his homework and had found out from one of his regular sources that Reggie Smith and a couple of his 'heavies' had been responsible for the landlord at the Black Horse switching allegiance to The Brummie Boys gang. Smith, like Isiah Boswell, was an Aston native who had been relatively successful in The Brummie Boys gang and was often called upon by Boswell to 'break' new landlords. His speciality was interrogation and he would use whatever means necessary to bully licensees and factory owners into paying protection money to Boswell's gang. "Ar reckon there will be Smith and a couple of his goons in the Black Oss tonight."

Scriven exhaled smoke from a slightly confused looking face. "If there is three of them, why are there only two of us?"

"Dow worry Kidda… Smith ay much of a fighter. He's a bully and he can talk the talk, but that's about all." Davis exuded confidence, nothing ever phased him.

Harry Scriven shrugged and continued to watch the road in front of him. "They ay got that Mitchells an' Butlers shit have they? Ar cor drink that stuff it mecks me sick!"

Davis laughed and shook his head. "Ar bet they got Banks's Mild just fer yow aer kid!"

The Black Horse was a mid-sized pub that stood in the village of Illey, 3 miles south of Halesowen in The Black Country and 10 miles south west of Birmingham. It was a popular pub and was often filled with workers from the nearby Bluebird toffee factory in Hunnington which had been established in 1927. Harry Scriven pulled up the old Morris outside the pub and the two men entered through the main entrance which led to a large bar with several shady corners and side booths. As the pair approached the bar the room hummed with the regular Saturday night joviality and a haze of tobacco smoke formed around the ceiling like a dense fog clinging to the early morning darkness of a winter's day.

"What can I get you gentlemen?" The young barmaid spoke with an accent that was not quite as broad Black Country as Scriven and Davis and their counterparts in Colley Gate and Cradley Heath.

"Two pints of mild an' a packet of scratchun's please me wench." Eli Davis was friendly as he lent casually on the bar. It was a warm evening and he wore his suit jacket unbuttoned as he took off his trilby and placed it on the flat surface. The barmaid returned with the drinks and took payment. "Have one fer yerself too bab." Davis smiled and shot her a cheeky wink. "Could yow do me a favour please wench an gew an tell yer gaffer Eli Davis wants a word with him?"

"Who's Eli Davis?" The girl raised her eyebrows politely and handed Davis his change.

"Me." Davis' eyes turned a little colder and the girl sensed a slight urgency for her to fetch her boss. She turned on her heel and hurried over to the other side of the bar where a middle-aged man with grey hair and horn-rimmed spectacles was serving customers. She whispered in his ear and he turned and look nervously at Davis and Scriven without looking them in the eyes. He whispered something back before disappearing around the other side of the bar and off to another area of the pub where three burly looking men were hunched over a circular table playing cards.

Davis took a gulp of his beer and turned and looked at Scriven. "Nice wench." He nodded towards the barmaid and carefully eyed the bottom of her stockings that rose to a green knee length skirt that hugged her shapely figure.

"Ar seen better." Scriven laughed and peered over to try and catch a glimpse of what was going on at the circular table. The three men stood up and purposefully strolled over towards them.

"Message from the management." A tall skinny man with a pencil moustache and narrow weasel like eyes stood in the centre and regarded Scriven and Davis with eyes of contempt. "You are not welcome here. Please finish your drinks and fuck off!" The two gangsters either side of him suddenly erupted in laughter and Reg Smith, the man in the centre, smiled smugly.

Eli Davis did not laugh as he stood up straight, all six foot five inches of him and took a step closer to Smith. "Fuckin' hell mate, what yow bin atein? Dog shit?" Davis caught a whiff of Smith's foul-smelling breath and could not resist the insult. "Who the fuck am yow?"

"My name is Reginald Smith and I have been instructed to inform you that you are not welcome in this establishment." Smith narrowed his eyes even further and spoke in a loud growl so that all of the pub could hear. "By order of The Brummie Boys!" He fixed an utterly intimidating gaze on Eli Davis and waited for a reply. Davis said nothing. He looked back with cold haunted eyes that appeared to look straight through Smith and back into the darkest depths of his disturbed childhood and his chilling experiences in the First World War. Subtly, he reached behind his back and slipped on a set of brass knuckles before smashing Smith in the face with a right-handed upper-cut that connected with such force that it instantly broke his jaw and sent a mixture of teeth and blood flying into the air as Smith flew dramatically across the room and landed semi-conscious on the floor. Davis then followed up by grabbing the henchman to his left and pummelling his face into the wooden bar until he was lay bleeding and unconscious. The second henchman made a move towards Harry Scriven and the Black Country man winced as The Brummie Boy connected well with a left hook. Scriven instantly stepped back and threw up his guard in an orthodox boxer's stance. Boswell's man attacked again but Scriven quickly ducked and countered with a fierce combination of punches that caught the henchman off his guard and threw him off balance. Scriven quickly seized the opportunity and smashed his beer glass into the man's eyes. Half blinded and still dazed from the previous flurry of punches, Boswell's man was powerless to stop the next onslaught of hard straight right-hand punches that rendered him unconscious and lying on the floor next to his fallen comrade.

By now the whole pub had been shocked into silence and even Harry Scriven took a deep breath as he looked up and saw what Eli Davis did next.

"Who the fuck do yer think yow am?" Davis spat as he took the semi-conscious Reg Smith by the scruff of the neck and dragged him across the floor to a side booth where a man sat smoking a large Cuban cigar. Davis held out his hand and the man instantly handed him the smoke without question. Davis raised it to his own mouth and dragged hard causing the tip to glow fiery red. Smith muttered something incomprehensible as blood seeped from his swollen mouth and across his deformed jaw.

"Yow can tell Isiah Boswell to ram this up his fuckin' arse hole!" Davis grabbed Smith by the throat and then proceeded to extinguish the cigar directly into Reg Smith's eyeball. The gangster yelped in pain until eventually Davis raised the cigar and handed it back to the man in the booth. Harry Scriven could not help but smirk as he looked at the other two men who lay knocked out on the floor. *Eli Davis had been right, they didn't need three of them after all.*

Chapter 6

The last of the summer evening sun penetrated through the windows of the Rose and Crown pub on Halesowen Road and cast shadows from Harry Scriven's beer as he stood at the bar. He usually spent Sunday afternoon in the company of the Mucklow family but today he had been 'let off' in order to have Sunday dinner with Lily Cole, her parents and her ageing grandmother.

Lily's mother and grandmother were less than impressed with her choice of future husband. Her mother Iris knew exactly who Harry Scriven was and even though his family were wealthy (on the Mucklow side), she also knew that they were ruthless gangsters who were feared throughout the locality. The grandmother on the other hand was not quite as well informed and had asked Scriven lots of awkward questions about his employment and the prospects he could offer her granddaughter. Norman Cole however, was slowly coming round to the idea of his daughter marrying Harry Scriven. The joining in matrimony of Lily and a member of The Mucklow family offered him several benefits in business and he hoped that it would prove to be a shrewd and lucrative move. Willie Mucklow had already bought him a large whisky in the Haden Cross one night and the pair had discussed plans for the future.

After the meal, Scriven had offered to drive Lily's grandmother home in an attempt to gain a little favour with the future in laws. However, this had also been an elaborate ploy for him to sneak into the Rose and Crown pub on the way home and enjoy a few pints. As he supped he thought about the previous night's activities and how pleased he was that Eli Davis was on 'their side' and how he would never want to get on the wrong side of the huge mobster. He drained his glass and ordered another when he noticed out of the corner of his eye an old friend who had just entered the pub.

Judy Talbot was not the sort of woman you could forget easily. She was in her late thirties and had long jet-black hair and deep brown eyes that gave her an almost Romany appearance. Her cheek bones were high and her body was slim and curvaceous with the most seductive of hour glass figures. She wore a long dark blue dress which was tight and accentuated her figure and her eyes were heavily made up and complimented her seductive lipstick of deep red. Judy Talbot and her husband Charlie, who was at least ten years older than her, ran a pub in nearby Blackheath and Scriven was surprised to see her on the arm of a different man. Harry Scriven and Judy Talbot had enjoyed a long and flirtatious friendship since she had worked in the office at the garage he had worked at several years ago as a mechanic. It was a strictly platonic friendship as Scriven had also become friendly with her husband Charlie too, but deep down he had always found her extremely attractive and had often fantasised about spending the night with her.

"Hello Harry!" Judy Talbot noticed Scriven and greeted him with a beaming smile which revealed that she was genuinely pleased to see him. The man stood next to her shot Scriven a jealous and fierce look which attempted to 'mark his territory.' He was at least six foot tall, heavily built and sporting a thick and heavy beard that gave him a bear like appearance.

"Who's your friend?" Scriven enquired as he nodded towards the large man whom he figured must have been in his mid-forties.

"Oh, this is James. James Reid. We are together now." Judy smiled awkwardly and hoped that Scriven would ask no further questions.

"I see... Aer bin yer mate?" Scriven extended his right hand to shake the man's hand and Reid gripped it with the hardest and most powerful of 'bear shakes' Scriven had ever encountered. The man glared at him and muttered a barely audible greeting but Scriven gave nothing away, he would not allow his eyes to display the slightest hint of intimidation. "What happened to your ode mon Charlie?" Scriven wasn't going to comment but after Reid's efforts to intimidate him he could not resist.

"Did you not hear kid? She said she was with me now." Reid barked with a thick cockney accent and Scriven took an instant dislike to the Londoner. "I hope you never laid a finger on mar Judy? She's mar gal and I fackin' hope you never touched her!"

Scriven was tempted to lie and tell Reid that he had slept with Judy, just to wind him up, but before he could answer Judy spoke and reassured her new lover that their friendship had always been strictly platonic. Reid said nothing, he glared at Scriven and then turned to face the barman. "Where's the fackin' landlord?" The barman informed Reid that he was in fact the landlord and Reid ordered him to meet him around the back of the pub. "Ar got a bit of business ar need you to help me with." Reid snarled and the landlord nervously did as he was told and walked around to the rear of the pub. Reid followed closely behind him after warning Scriven to "keep his fackin' hands" off Judy!

Reid left the room and Scriven turned to face his female friend. "Who is that stupid bastard?" He lit a cigarette and gestured towards the back of the pub where Reid had followed the landlord.

"He's mar new fella Harry and ar love him… But he is dangerous, yow should see what he did to Charlie! He's very possessive over me. He cor bear the thought of me knowing other men before him and the only way he can deal with it is to hurt them."

Scriven knew that Judy had 'known' plenty of other men before Reid but didn't say anything. "Yow think ar'm scared of that fat southern fucker?"

"Honestly Harry, he's dangerous. He's from London and he's got all his boys up here with him… They just pulled off something big." She suddenly went sheepish and appeared to regret what she had just said. "Ar day tell yer that." Scriven raised his eyebrows in interest and decided to check on just exactly what was going on at the back of the pub. "Yow dow know who yow'm a messin' with Harry!" Judy pleaded but Scriven did not listen as he made his way out of the door and around to the back.

"This little lot is being stashed in your cellar… If any of it goes missing or if you speak to the law I will cut you from ear to fackin' ear!" Scriven watched from a concealed position behind a wall as Reid spoke threateningly to the landlord.

"But Sir, ar dow wanna get involved in anything like this!" The landlord was on the brink of tears and protested but Reid instantly knocked him to the ground with a hard, back handed slap that appeared completely effortless. Four other men stood behind him next to a cream coloured Austin van. One of the men opened the rear doors and Scriven could see that inside the van was boxes filled with expensive looking gold jewellery. Watches, necklaces, earrings, hundreds if not thousands of pounds worth. As he looked on with amazement he did not notice that the London gangsters had spotted him. Before he could move the four men grabbed him firmly and dragged him over to James Reid.

"Get the fuck off me yer bunch of bastards!" Scriven struggled and tried to raise his fists but the men were strong and outnumbered him, maintaining their hold.

"Oh look who it is!" Reid smiled gleefully on the presentation of Scriven in front of him.

"We spotted this geezer mooching around and watching us guv." One of the four gangsters spoke and nodded towards their prisoner.

"Harry isn't it?" Reid relished the opportunity and planted a solid punch into Scriven's stomach, winding him instantly. Reid hit him again and Scriven could not help but fall to the floor, clutching his ribs in agony. As he tried to get up he felt Reid strike again as the burly Londoner kicked him hard in the face sending him back down to the ground. Again he tried to get up, but more blows from Reid's feet continued to rain down all over him and he could hear the cockney mocking him.

"Fight me one on one yer gutless bastard!" Scriven managed to call through gritted teeth as he struggled again to try and get to his feet. Reid lowered his face to Scriven's but before he could speak Judy Talbot appeared from behind the wall.

"What's gewin on?" She immediately saw Scriven on the floor and hurried over to see if he was ok. "James, ar told you he was just a friend, yer day have to do this!"

Reid grunted and smiled at his beloved Judy. "Ok my Rose, we will leave your friend Harry alone." Reid spat the word friend with aggression and nodded for his four accomplices to pick Scriven up off the floor. By now Scriven had taken something of a beating and his initial reaction was to charge at Reid and try to rip him apart, but the four men quickly grabbed him and held him away from their boss. "Temper, temper Harry." Reid smiled and tapped Scriven's face in a patronising gesture. Scriven lunged forward as far as he could with his arms held by the men and tried to bite Reid's face with the ferocity of a rabid dog. Reid smirked again and tutted before switching to a more serious tone. "You saw nothing here tonight… You remember that Harry, keep your fackin' nose out of stuff that does not concern you!" He turned and held his hand out to Judy in a gentlemanly gesture. "Come my Rose, your carriage awaits." She hurried towards him but paused to take a backwards glance at her friend Harry. As far as she knew he was a motor mechanic and she knew nothing of the potential repercussions from the night's events. She smiled apologetically and then continued into Reid's arms and the couple began to walk away. "Boys, unload the stuff into the cellar." Before he departed, Reid turned to face the landlord and his eyes became threatening again. "When I come back it better still be here!" With that he wondered off into the evening.

By this time Scriven had regained his composure and upon the four men releasing him he simply picked up his trilby from off the floor and smiled sarcastically at them. He could have lashed out again but he had a better idea. He knew someone who would more than appreciate a share of Reid's stash!

Willie Mucklow sat inebriated (as he always was on a Sunday evening) in his grand living room smoking a fine cigar, drinking a glass of ruby port and listening to the smooth sounds of his favourite singer, Bing Crosby. He blew rings of smoke into the air and watched them through weary eyes as they rose to the ceiling and evaporated into the elaborate coving of his home. He was in a good mood. He had received a telephone call earlier that day from Isiah Boswell who had eventually agreed that he had been 'taking the piss' by venturing into Mucklow's turf at The Black Horse at Illey and the pair had decided to call a truce and leave things be. Boswell had much bigger fish to fry and a war would be bad for business. Willie Mucklow was particularly pleased with the outcome as he knew that Boswell's organisation was much more powerful and influential than his own, but in his mind it was always best to 'stand up' to the big boys, otherwise they would push him around whenever they saw fit. Besides, Mucklow knew that deep down, Isiah Boswell had much more respect for those that stood up to him and did not back down. He smiled to himself in smug relief when suddenly a loud knock at the door disrupted him from his self-congratulatory daze. He quickly rose to his feet in panic that Boswell had 'double crossed' him and had sent men to extract revenge for Davis and Scriven's attack at The Black Horse the previous night. Before he got to the hallway his wife had already answered the door and announced that it was "only our Harry." She looked Scriven up and down and then spoke again. "Oh dear, what happened to yow?" Willie could tell by the shocked tone of his wife that something had happened to his nephew and he instantly suspected Boswell.

"Can I have a word please Uncle Willie?" Scriven appeared in the doorway and looked almost sheepish as Wille Mucklow beckoned for him to come and sit down.

"Helen, gew an fetch aer kid some whisky." Willie placed his right hand on his nephew's shoulder in concern and told him to take a seat. "What the fuck happened?" Mucklow could feel the anger boiling over inside of him. Somebody had dared to hurt his blood and in that moment he did not care how 'big' Isiah Boswell was. If he was responsible, then he would cut the bastard's throat as he slept in his bed and to hell with the consequences.

"Some chap at the Rose and Crown. He ay local. Fella called James Reid. He's from down London way. He and some chaps gid me a bit of a lampin' but ar dow care." Scriven spoke excitedly as he thought of the valuable stash that lay in the cellar of one of the local pubs. "He stashed a shit load of fuckin' gold in the cellar, a fuckin' shed load Willie."

Willie Mucklow paused and stroked his chin in thought. "So he ay nothing to do with Isiah Boswell an that lot?"

"Naah. He's from aaht of town. Just done a 'big' job and he's taken up with a local bird." Mucklow smiled as he listened to Scriven recount the night's activities and explain exactly what had happened. "We should gew daahn there now and teck the gold for ourselves." Scriven suggested excitedly.

Mucklow shook his head and blew more smoke into the air. "No Harry. Be patient. The Rose and Crown pays us protection money so we need to protect the landlord." Mucklow closed his eyes and formulated the perfect plan. "If this Reid fella is a new face in town then he needs to learn how things work and understand that if he wants to operate around here then he needs to pay tribute money to me!" He drew heavily on his cigar and offered Scriven one. Scriven accepted gratefully and Mucklow began to speak again. "Now, we could teck all of this stuff tonight and that would be that. Or, we could give him a lampin', ar'm sure yow would appreciate the chance to get even?" Scriven nodded before Mucklow continued. "Then we tell him that he can keep seventy percent of his stash if he agrees to come into our organisation. If he's that good a robber, every time he earns we will earn too!" Mucklow smiled smugly to himself again and relished in his own 'criminal mastermind' that had helped him rise to the position he was in today. Eli Davis was just a thug, Harry Scriven too, but he (Willie) had a brain for being able to see the bigger picture. Absolute thugs were always of use to him and Eli Davis was as good as his brother, but his ability (Mucklow) to manipulate and concoct money making schemes was the reason why he was the boss, though he was more than capable of violence and thuggery himself.

Scriven smiled and enjoyed the full flavour of the rare cigar. His uncle's plan suited him well. Even if Reid didn't agree to come under the family's control, then at least he would get the chance to extract his revenge and face him in a fair one on one fight.

Willie Mucklow poured Scriven another particularly large whisky. "Gerrit daahn yer wasin."

"Fuckin' hell Willie, we gorra get up in the morning!" Scriven held his glass high and did not pull away as the amber liquid dropped into his glass.

Willie laughed and poured himself an equally generous measure. "We ay gorra do nothing kid." He took a sip of his whisky and lay back in his chair. "We know about this stash… The landlord ay gunna say fuck all. It's gewin nowhere yet. Yow have a lie in in the morning, sleep off the Scotch then gew and beat shit aaht on heavy bag daahn at the boxing club. Imagine it's that cockney Reid fucker!" Mucklow almost laughed "After that come and see me and we will set up a reconnaissance watchin' the Rose and Crown. As soon as that bastard mecks a move we will be daahn there. But relax aer kid. This is where it's at! Yow know something they dow know… One step ahead!"

Scriven nodded in agreement and then lay back and felt the hot, sweet effect of the whisky as it hit his brain and induced him into a happy mellow. He looked around the luxurious room and enjoyed the lavish décor. He desperately wanted a piece of this action for him and Lily, luxury, power and the opportunity to be the one sat there in the chair giving advice to some young upstart.

"Yow love Norman Cole's daughter dow yer aer kid?" The randomness of Willie's question stunned Scriven as he instantly sat up in his chair.

"Yes Uncle Willie. Ar do love her and intend to meck her mar wife."

Mucklow looked at his nephew slightly unconvinced. "Ok Harry. Whatever yow say. But remember this aer kid, we respect marriage in this family. Mar mother was all I had growing up and men should always respect their women. I've already had a chat with Norman Cole and if it is yower honest intention to meck an honourable woman aaaht on his daughter then fair play to yer. But just remember this aer kid, yow will respect her and do right by her!"

Mucklow's gaze turned ultra-serious and Scriven could not help but feel slightly uncomfortable. He liked women and had done since his youthful 'experiences' at the side of the cut with older girls as a child. Asking him to devote himself to just one woman was a big ask! Harry Scriven eventually looked up at his uncle and nodded, but Willie Mucklow remained unconvinced.

Chapter 7

The Waterfall pub was an old black and white building that stood halfway up the hill on Waterfall Lane, Blackheath. Opposite the pub stood an old Chapel and two days after his altercation with James Reid at the rear of the Rose and Crown pub, Harry Scriven parked his Morris Isis neatly on the pavement outside and crossed over the street and into the Waterfall. As he walked through the front door, the bar stood to the left of him and straight away he caught a glimpse of the person he had come to see.

"Hello Charlie, just the fella ar wanted to see!" Charlie Talbot looked up straight away and was surprised to see that Scriven was battered and bruised.

"Blimey H, what happened to yow? Ar dread to think of the state of the other guy!" Talbot commented on Scriven's appearance though he also had bruises himself and was suffering from a particularly nasty black eye.

Scriven lit a cigarette, narrowed his eyes in a slightly intimidating gesture before ordering a pint of mild. "Teck one for yourself and come and sit down."

Talbot pulled a pint for his friend and a half pint for himself before following Scriven over to a small circular table that stood to the left of the bar. "What can ar do for you Harry?" He appeared a little nervous as he detected that Scriven was not in the best of moods. "I heard that yow'm a working for ode Willie Mucklow now?"

Scriven offered him a cigarette and lit it for him. "Yes… Ar bin working for me Uncle Willie for a while now. He looked intently at Talbot who had forgotten that Scriven was related to the infamous Mucklow family before eventually breaking the awkward silence. "Where is Judy?"

Talbot grunted and half laughed. "Why?" He spat the word sarcastically. "Do yow wanna teck yower turn with her?" Talbot looked sadly at the wedding ring that still adorned his finger. "It seems everybody else has." He was feeling particularly bitter about his wife and he remembered how she had always enjoyed a rather flirtatious relationship with Harry Scriven. Scriven did not appreciate the comment and looked up from his drink.

"I said, where the fuck is Judy Charlie?" He raised his voice angrily and was still livid from what had happened with James Reid.

"Ar dow know Harry." A tear appeared in Talbot's eye and he looked down at the table with shame. "She left me a couple of weeks back. Went off with some flash Cockney chap… Look what he did to me!" Talbot pointed to his black eye and looked at Scriven with a face of honesty.

Scriven smiled sympathetically. "This Cockney fella, any idea where he is now?"

Talbot looked up and half smiled. "Why? Is he in trouble with Willie Mucklow?" His eyes widened in the hope that the man who had stolen his wife would have to answer to the likes of Willie Mucklow and Eli Davis!

Scriven gave nothing away and remained cold and calm. "I would just like to have a word with him that's all." He sensed that Charlie Talbot could not help him any further with his enquiries so he quickly finished his beer. "If you hear from Judy or her new fella then let me know."

"She just sodded off Harry. Left her own kids for him! What am ar supposed to tell them pair upstairs when they ask for their mother?" Talbot pointed upwards and looked desperately at Scriven.

"Do yer know anything abaaht this fella?" Scriven drained the dregs of his beer and placed the glass back on the table.

"I know his name is James and he is from London. Bethnal Green or somewhere like that. He's a villain Harry." Talbot shook his head in frustration, he knew no more.

Scriven stood up and put a comforting hand on his shoulder as he left the pub. "Dow worry Charlie. She'll be back."

As he drove back down Waterfall Lane, past the Old Furnace and the Crown pubs, Harry Scriven began to feel more and more frustrated in his unfruitful search for James Reid. The Londoner had done him wrong and his bruised and battered body ached for revenge. He turned left at the crossroads onto Halesowen Road and drove the short distance to the Haden Cross.

It was a Tuesday lunchtime and the pub was relatively quiet as Scriven passed through the main bar and into Mucklow's little room where Eli Davis and Willie Mucklow were sat indulging in beer, cigarettes and copious amounts of snuff.

"Come in Harry and sit daahn. Yow got a drink aer kid?" Willie Mucklow spoke between sneezes as he wiped the remnants of the powder from his red nostrils. Eli Davis smiled warmly and gestured for Scriven to take a seat opposite them.

"Ar went to see Charlie Talbot." Scriven took a drink of his beer and waited for a response that never came, frustrating him further. "He knows fuck all about where Reid is."

"Dow worry Harry. We got the Rose and Crown under constant surveillance, if that bastard as much as tecks a piss in there we will know about it!" Willie Mucklow was laid back and relaxed. He trusted the lad he had asked to watch the place and he was confident that Reid would return soon to collect his stash.

Scriven struggled to hide his disappointment with Mucklow's response. "Why don't ar gew an see the landlord?"

"No Harry... If he twigs that we are onto them he might gew and tell Reid. Ar dow want them to know that we know." Willie remained as calm and relaxed as ever and Davis said nothing. He was ultra-loyal to Willie Mucklow and had been since Willie and Stan had helped him get a pair of shoes as a boy.

"But what if that bastard sneaks in there an tecks his gold without us knowing? He could be back in fuckin' London by now!" It wasn't like

Scriven to raise his voice to his elders but he was determined to hunt James Reid down and inflict a vicious revenge.

"Ark at him!" Davis suddenly spoke and sought to diffuse the situation. "Dow worry Harry, we gorra' chap daahn there watching the place. If yow'm that worried, yow gew and sit outside the pub yourself! It's only daahn the bloody road. As soon as Reid mecks a move we will know abaaht it." Davis was right. The Rose and Crown was just along the road from the Haden Cross and Scriven began to relax a little. He sat back in his chair and produced a silver-plated cigarette case and lighter from his pocket. *He needed to calm down. Willie had everything under control and he would soon get even with that smug Londoner Reid.*

Several days passed and Harry Scriven was still barely managing to contain his fierce and aggressive thirst for revenge. Upon sight of his injuries that had been inflicted by Reid and his gang, Lily Cole had cried out and insisted that her fiancé find more reputable employment, however, Scriven had again reminded her that more reputable means of employment would not pay for the little extras like the car, fine suits and a plush house like Willie Mucklow! Even his cousin Billy had recently moved into a luxurious detached house that stood on the brow of the hill on Barrs Road. Billy had always had and done everything bigger and better than he had and Scriven so desperately wanted to prove himself as equal to his wealthier relatives. As he sat supping beer in the main bar area of the Haden Cross with Billy, he pretended to be excited and interested by his cousin who was raving about the upcoming birth of his first child. Of course, he was happy for his relative, they were more like brothers than cousins, but ultimately it was something else for his mother to go on at him about. He could hear her words in his mind already. *"Well, your cousin Bill has got himself a nice wife and a nice home and now they'm having a babee!"* He sighed inwardly and tried hard not to communicate his negativity to Billy.

Suddenly, Eli Davis and Willie Mucklow emerged from the side bar with their trilbies on and signalled for Scriven and Billy to move.

"Yower mates turned up at the Crown!" Willie smiled knowing that his nephew would be pleased to hear of Reid's reappearance. Mucklow's man had been sat outside the Rose and Crown in various vehicles for days and upon the sighting of Reid he had headed straight down to the Haden Cross to alert his boss. They still could not be sure that the man was Reid as Mucklow's gangster only had Scriven's description to go off, but he had described the man entering the Rose and Crown as being: "Over six foot tall, in his late forties with a big bushy beard and a pretty dark-haired woman on his arm."

Willie Mucklow entered the Rose and Crown by the front door followed closely by Eli Davis, Billy Mucklow and Harry Scriven. Upon sight of them, the landlord's heart instantly started to beat a little faster. *The scary bearded thug from the other night was already in the pub, what would Willie Mucklow say if he found out he was stashing stolen goods for rival gangsters!*

James Reid was in the pub and was sat with Judy Talbot in the far corner of the long bar room at a quiet table where they would not be disturbed. He intended to speak with the landlord later that evening and check on his merchandise, but until then he was happy conversing with his beloved and enjoying a few Irish whiskeys. As he chatted with Judy he could not help but notice that Harry Scriven had entered the room and was now staring at him with utterly menacing and intimidating eyes. At first, he could not put a name to the face, but then he remembered and realised exactly who it was. As he stood pondering Scriven's course of action, Billy Mucklow approached the landlord and announced that they would be needing 'a little privacy' and that he would appreciate a beer a piece for himself and his family. This was the least the landlord could do to show his loyalty and luckily, the bar was relatively quiet and he was able to move everyone into the lounge area that was next door. He poured four beers for Mucklow and his associates and Billy thanked him and insisted on paying for the drinks. James Reid had by now began to sense that something was about to happen and he looked on closely as

Willie Mucklow and Eli Davis sat themselves down at his table uninvited. Harry Scriven stood about two feet behind them and was more than ready to have his time with the Cockney.

"Can I help you gentlemen?" Reid sensed the importance and power of the two men at his table but his gaze gave nothing away and he remained focused and unintimidated.

Willie Mucklow took a drink of his beer, lit a cigarette and spoke when he was ready. "I hear you have a little stash hidden around the back?"

Reid took a deep breath in annoyance and looked up at Harry Scriven angrily. His eyes narrowed slightly and he turned to face Willie Mucklow. "What the fuck has that got to do with you?"

Willie Mucklow took a deep drag of his cigarette and again spoke in his own time. "I understand that you are not local Mr Reid and that maybe you do not understand how things work around here." Mucklow took another drink and kept his gaze focused firmly into Reid's eyes.

"What the fack are you talking about?" Reid was unimpressed and placed a defiant hand onto Judy Talbot's knee who was sat closely next to him. Willie smiled and relaxed back in his chair. He knew Reid's type and he knew that he would not achieve anything with words alone. He had not risen to his position as one of the top gang bosses in the Midlands on words. *Men like James Reid only understood one language.*

"Why don't yer let me have a word with Mr Reid? One on one!" Scriven accentuated the words 'one on one' but Willie raised his hand and shook his head.

"You see Mr Reid, ar'm in charge raahnd here and if you want to operate in my patch, if you want to stash stolen goods in one of my establishments then you need to 'wet my beak' a little so to speak."

Reid found Mucklow's words somewhat amusing and began to laugh. "Ok, I will bear that in mind. Now please fack off!" Mucklow shrugged a little and glanced sideways to Eli Davis. Davis had already spoken to Harry Scriven about the events of Sunday night and he knew that Reid had a particular weakness when it came to his possessive obsession with Judy Talbot.

"Yow alright Judy bab?" Davis gave her a wink and blew her a kiss.

"Do I know you?" Judy seemed surprised and looked straight at Reid in fear of his reaction. In truth, Eli Davis had never met her before, but he knew exactly what he was doing.

"Watch your fackin' mouth sunshine!" Reid was not pleased and Davis pushed himself closer to the Londoner.

"Good little whore ay her aer Judy? Great with her mouth!"

Reid erupted with anger and rose to his feet to face Davis. He could not help but notice how big Eli Davis was but he did not care. "Right, me and you, outside, now!"

Davis took another step closer so that his face was almost touching Reid's. "Good screw ay her? All the lads love aer Judy."

Reid could take it no longer, in the heat of the moment he did not care that he was outnumbered and as he punched Eli Davis in the face, Harry Scriven looked down at the floor in disappointment. *That was it. He would not get his personal revenge.*

Davis stumbled slightly to the right as he felt the impact of the highly anticipated punch. In anger, Reid had broken an important rule of boxing and had put his entire body weight into the punch leaving him off guard and unprepared for Davis' counter. With his brass knuckles firmly attached Davis grabbed Reid by the throat with his left hand and planted a firm right handed punch straight on the end of Reid's nose. The impact of the knuckle duster and the force of the six-foot five monster caused Reid's nose to disintegrate instantly and his shirt and face became decorated with fresh crimson blood. Judy Talbot screamed as Davis then grabbed her lover by his beard and pulled his head down onto the table where he pinned him with his left arm.

"Yer know mate, The Brummie boys up the road used to wear peaky hats with razor blades in." Davis smiled grotesquely and brought his face close to Reid who was powerless to move. "We used to call um

The Peaky Blinders! Lucky fer yow, ar bay no Brummie." Davis' eyes were cold and looked straight through Reid as if he was looking deep into the past. "Them Deaf n' Dummies used ter teck their caps off and slash their victims eyes until they were blind… But like ar said, I ay one of them boys." Davis smiled again revealing his black and broken teeth and pulled out a Stanley blade from his jacket pocket. "Ar dow like peaky hats, ar prefer one of these!" He slowly brought the blade down towards Reid's right eye before cutting deeply into the skin just next to it. Reid tensed with the pain but he refused to cry out in front of his woman.

"This could all be avoided Mr Reid." Willie Mucklow stood up and looked down at Reid who was still pinned to the table and covered in blood. "Yow'm operating on mar patch fella… Yow give me thirty percent of yower earnings and ar can offer yow protection in return."

"I don't need no facking protection!" Reid raged and struggled to try and free himself from Davis' intense grip. It was no use, he was stuck and as Harry Scriven looked on, anxious to have his turn with Reid, Davis grunted and lowered the blade again.

"Hey Willie, remember that bastard whose eye ar cut aaht before?" Davis laughed and looked towards his friend. Willie Mucklow laughed back and shook his head in amusement.

"Yes aer kid, yow cut part of his fuckin' eye ball aaht and med him eat it, otherwise yow were gunna teck his other eye too!" The two men laughed in disturbed amusement but both Harry Scriven and Billy Mucklow doubted the stories authenticity. Willie and Davis were tough men who had survived The First World War, *but surely they were not quite that sick?* The more they thought about it the more they began to doubt their initial reactions.

Judy Talbot screamed again as Davis again lowered the blade and cut out a small chunk of Reid's face that would surely scar him permanently. "What's it gunna be then Reid? Yow gunna work fer us or am I gunna meck yow eat yer own eye ball?"

"Hold on, hold on." Willie Mucklow suddenly became animated and he looked over at his nephew Harry scriven who he had just remembered was desperate for revenge. "Maybe ar can offer yow an alternative?" Davis pulled the knife away and eased his grip on Reid's neck slightly as both men looked towards Willie Mucklow. "Yow upset mar nephew the other night when yow and yower lads beat the shit aaht on him... Hardly seemed a fair fight did it?" A wave of excitement and adrenaline drove through Scriven as he realised that he may soon get his chance. "If yow and aer Harry gew outside onto the car park and have a fight, this is what ar'll do. If yow win, yow get ter keep all of yer stash and yow can get the fuck aaht of here and never come back." Mucklow turned to face Scriven. "If Harry knocks yow aaht then you hand it all over to me." Scriven felt flattered at his uncle's faith in him and vowed to himself that he would not let him down. Mucklow looked back at Reid and opened his arms. "So Mr Reid, what will it be?" Davis released his grip and the Cockney rose to his feet and nodded eagerly before ripping off his jacket and shirt and using them to mop the copious amounts of blood from his face.

The bearded Londoner looked like a savage barbarian as he stood shirtless and covered in blood on the Rose and Crown car park. His eyes were wide with anger and humiliation. His face, beard and body were gleaming red as his deep wounds continued to weep. Harry Scriven felt no pity for his opponent and he certainly felt no fear. He calmly took off his suit jacket and tie and rolled up his shirt sleeves and adopted an orthodox boxing stance.

"So, we meet again Harry!" Reid mocked and spat his words. "Do you really think that I'm gunna let you take mar gold?" The Cockney half laughed as he grunted, spat and screwed up his face grotesquely as he struggled to see from the constant flow of blood that covered his eyes. Scriven said nothing. He had met many Londoners during his time in The Forces and his opinion remained the same, *Cockneys always talked too much!* By now quite a crowd had gathered on the car park to watch the action and Scriven suddenly became aware of the consequences of a defeat. *He would lose all respect and his reputation as a feared enforcer working for Willie Mucklow would be in ruins. He did not intend to lose!* Reid suddenly flew forwards in a blind rage and swung his right arm wildly at Scriven, exactly as he had done against Eli Davis earlier. Scriven ducked and side stepped and could not help but feel slightly amused that Reid had not learnt from his earlier mistake. The older man was quite clearly a brawler and possessed no boxing skill and Scriven smiled to himself knowing that he could quite easily have countered and ended the fight prematurely. But he wanted to enjoy this, he wanted to savour his revenge and pick Reid off slowly, prolonging the punishment. He was also aware of the fact that Judy Talbot was watching and a chance to show off in front of her was always a bonus!

"Ha, fancy yourself as a bit of a Joe Louis do ya?" Reid sniggered as he regained his composure and made reference to one of Harry Scriven's personal heroes. Joseph Lewis Barrow, known professionally as Joe Louis had reigned as World Heavyweight boxing champion since 1937 and was nicknamed 'The Brown Bomber" on account of his African American heritage. Scriven could not help but smile at the reference as he retained his stance and waited for the next attack. Reid wasted little time as he again flew at Scriven in a wild attempt at a right hook. This time, Scriven showed less restraint as he dodged the punch with ease and countered with a combination of jabs and straights that knocked Reid off his balance and onto the ground. Feeling slightly disappointed at his lack of opposition, Scriven looked around and noticed that they were in pretty much the same spot as the other night when Reid and his men had inflicted a beating on him. As Reid clambered to try and get back to his feet, Scriven stooped and caught him with a perfect upper cut that sent him flying backwards and reeling in a pool of his own blood, struggling to retain consciousness. Scriven cursed himself, he had finished the fight too early and the words of his uncle rang through his head. *"If Harry knocks you out then you will hand it all over to me."* He knew exactly what he had to do and slowly and calmly he approached Reid who lay struggling on the floor. He looked over at Judy Talbot who looked sultry and appetising in the late summer sun and shot her a cheeky wink before pulling Reid up by his hair and hitting him with a straight right-handed punch of such power and force that the flash, loudmouthed Londoner fell instantly into a state of unconsciousness. *Even Eli Davis would have been proud of that one!* Scriven thought to himself as he turned to face his uncle. He was one of them, he was as tough as them and he continued to prove himself as a worthy member of The Family.

Chapter 8

In October 1948 the first Motor show after the Second World War was held at Earls Court, London and drew a record 562,954 visitors who were eager to see a range of new products from British car manufacturers. Most notable of these products were the Morris Minor, Land Rover, Morris Oxford, Austin A70, Vauxhall Velox and Wyvern models and the Jaguar XK120 which became the World's fastest production car.

In the Black Country, two months had passed and nothing had been heard of James Reid since that fateful day outside the Rose and Crown pub. The leaves had begun to turn a yellowish shade of brown and the gentle breeze carried the hint of a chill which served as a reminder of the vastly approaching winter months.

On a particularly chilly Wednesday afternoon, Harry Scriven and Lily Cole strolled through Haden Hill Park in an encounter that would prove poignant and haunt Scriven's future dreams for the rest of his life. Haden Hill house was built in 1878 by George Alfred Haden-Best next to the original Tudor building known as Haden Hall. Haden-Best had inherited the estate from his uncle, Frederic W.G. Barrs in 1877 and his original plan had been to demolish the old hall, however, his elderly Aunt still lived in The Hall and when she died in 1903 he had abandoned his plans to abolish the Tudor building and the two buildings remained side by side. Haden-Best lived in the house with two local girls who would go on to become his adoptive daughters. Emily Bryant and Alice Cockin had been the children of two poor families and when Haden-Best took them into his home he brought them up as his own and gave them a wealthy upper-class lifestyle. Following Haden-Best's death in 1921, the entire estate and its vast grounds were put up for auction and sold to Rowley Regis Urban and District Council on the 14th of October 1922 for use as a public park.

"The trees always look so beautiful at this time of year dow they Harry?" Lily Cole snuggled in close to her fiancé as they walked hand in hand through the park grounds and amongst the fallen leaves and whatever conkers remained after not being salvaged by the local children. Scriven looked up at the trees that swayed slightly in the autumn breeze and took a moment or two to take in the rich colourings and appreciate how they appeared to glow in the lukewarm sun. Despite the nature of his employment and his aggressive persona, Harry Scriven had always possessed a softer, sensitive side which cultivated a deep love for rich landscapes, scenery and especially music. He rarely displayed this for fear of 'looking saft' amongst the company of the somewhat Neanderthal Willie Mucklow and Eli Davis so he simply grunted and nodded his head in response to Lily's observation. "Just think Harry, this time next year, we will be wed!" She pulled herself even closer to him and felt reassured when she felt his hand tighten its grip on hers in an affectionate gesture.

"Yes bab." He smiled with genuine happiness. He truly did love Lily Cole. He had finally found a girl that he wanted to settle down with. Not because it would please his mother, or The Mucklows, but because it was his chance to have his own home with a girl he loved and to even have his own children. Scriven had felt quite jealous when his cousin Billy had announced that he and his wife Mary were expecting their first child. He genuinely liked children and desperately hoped that one day he would also become a father and in Lily Cole he could not think of a woman he would rather spend the rest of his life with. "Mrs Lillian Scriven. Has a ring to it dow it bab?" For a second he felt silly for making such a comment, but then he remembered that even Eli Davis had fallen in love and got married at some point.

Lily Cole could not contain her happiness and giggled with joy. "It's so nice to see you getting on with my Mom and Dad too!" Scriven had been making an effort with the 'in laws' lately and had joined them socially and at their home on several occasions where he had conducted himself in a satisfactory manner. They had also met his own parents

Horace and Eliza and Lily's father Norman had been particularly impressed to find out that Scriven's father was not a gangster and was in fact an honest hard-working man like himself. *There was hope for Harry yet!* So he thought.

The couple strolled up, down and around the park for hours. Happy just to exist within each other's company, speaking excitedly of their future dreams, hopes and plans. As the autumnal sun began to fade, shadows cast against the gold and amber leaves and the chill that haunted the wind increased its grip and turned Lily's cheeks an even rosier shade of red. It had been a perfect afternoon and neither of them wanted to leave the company of their beloved.

"It's getting cold Harry. Ar suppose we better get gewin." Lily spoke first and Scriven could not help but feel a little disappointed that she had suggested an end to their afternoon together. His throat was dry and the pub beckoned, but for the first time in his life, he was in no hurry to rush off.

"Just 5 more minutes bab." They strolled for a further thirty minutes and by now the sun had faded beyond the grand structure of the old Victorian house and the cold of night had set in. For some reason he could not quite understand, Scriven had a persistent and gnawing feeling that this would be his last time spent in the company of his petite and beautiful Lily. *They were due to be married and had a whole lifetime together to look forward to!* He disregarded his premonitions as ridiculous and the pair began their slow walk back towards the car. *They had both never been happier and this was just the beginning of their time together!* As they walked, Scriven's feeling of finality became stronger, though he could not have comprehended at this time just how accurate his notion would become.

A wholesome and innocent period of his life was rapidly moving away from him, a time that he would spend the rest of his days longing to return to, a distant memory that was pure and decent and could have steered his whole life's pathway in a different direction. The autumn wind cried a little pity at the pathetic sight of the lovers. The snap of the air and the peaty, smoky smell of the night would be an eternal reminder that would prove both tragic and heart-breaking, the consequences of which unforeseeable at this time. In the grand scheme of life and death, this day was not relevant, this love was nothing any different to that of countless lovers around the world. But for Harry Scriven it marked the end of one life and its potential and the beginning of another which for him would quiet literally prove to be the difference between Heaven and Hell.

Chapter 9

Ye Olde White Lion pub, known locally as 'Staffords' on account of the landlord George Stafford, stood halfway up Windmill Hill on Colley Gate High Street which lay between Halesowen and Lye. The road was named after two windmills that once stood on the summit of the hill and throughout its 350-year history, Ye Olde White Lion had not always been used as a pub. Amongst over things, the pub had been previously used as an undertakers and tales of the building being haunted were well known amongst the staff and customers. In 1903 a young girl had died in the pub of Scarlet fever and subsequently the room where she passed had been kept intact as a shrine and sealed off. Since then, many ghostly occurrences had been reported, however, when Harry Scriven entered the pub after his afternoon walk with Lily Cole at Haden Hill Park, the only spirits he was interested in was Irish whiskey!

Billy Mucklow had been spending a lot of time in 'The Lion' recently. He had a quiet secluded table in a far corner of the bar and when Harry Scriven entered the pub, Mucklow called him over and gestured to a circular tray that contained a packet of pork scratchings, two pints of Banks's Mild and two measures of Irish whiskey. The pair had often socialised in the Colley Gate area on account of Harry Scriven's now deceased paternal grandfather. He was of no direct blood relation to Billy Mucklow, but Mucklow had never known a living grandfather on either side of his family and Scriven's grandfather had been a kind man who many years ago had taken it upon himself to be a grandfather to both boys. He had kept an old shed at the rear of Scriven's Talbot street home and here the two young cousins had spent many happy hours playing Pirates, Cowboys and Indians and various other games. The boys had also got their first tastes of beer amongst the pubs of Colley Gate and Halesowen with their grandfather and quite often they would still meet up there for a drink, especially when they wanted a little privacy away from the prying eyes of Willie Mucklow and Eli Davis.

"How bin yer aer kid?" Bill Mucklow spoke in a broad Black Country accent but had served in the British Army as an officer during World War 2. He had a particular talent for being able to alter his way of speaking to suit the audience. For example, in the officer's mess he always spoken The Kings English, but back home amongst his family and friends he reverted to his traditional tongue.

"Yeah saahnd mate. Yow said you wanted ter see me?" Scriven recalled that Billy wanted to speak to him about something specific, but the romance of his afternoon with Lily Cole had somewhat disrupted his train of thought. He sat down and nodded a thanks to Billy for the drinks.

"Yes mate, but this is strictly confidential right?" Billy spoke in a hushed whisper and raised his eyebrows and pointed his finger in an authoritarian way.

"Yes Captain!" Scriven joked sarcastically but it was lost on Billy, he had more important matters on his mind.

"Yow'm like a brother to me Harry. I need your advice." Mucklow pulled out his cigarette case and offered one to Scriven before taking one for himself. Scriven accepted the cigarette, casually lit up and nodded for Billy to finish what he was about to say.

"The ode mon is thinking of packing it in… Retiring." Mucklow lit his cigarette and allowed the statement to sink into Scriven's mind.

"What? Why?" Scriven was surprised. His Uncle Willie was only in his early 50s and in Scriven's mind he was much younger. He kept forgetting that he and Billy were rapidly approaching their 30s and were not kids anymore. The War should have taught him that! *All the more reason to settle down with Lily Cole,* he thought to himself. The thought of settling down with a wife was no longer a concern for him and the mental image of a happy family home with Lily and his future children made him feel immensely happy. *But how would he provide for them if his Uncle Willie was calling it a day?*

"Dow worry Harry." Billy raised his hand confidently and blew smoke across the table. "Dad wants me to teck over." He took another drag of his cigarette and enjoyed the moment. He was going to be the new boss! "The ode mon wants to move up Clent. Reckons my mother deserves it after all these years of worry." Bill was right. Since her marriage to Willie Mucklow at a young age, Bill's mother had endured one worry after another. Willie had not always been a wealthy man and in the early days she had had to look after the family home in Cradley Heath and her young son Billy whilst her husband was out with Eli Davis, raising hell, building their criminal empire and scrapping in the streets. She never knew if he would come home hurt, end up in a jail cell or wind up murdered by a criminal rival or dangle on the end of a rope! As Willie got older and became more powerful and successful, this worry only got worse. Then along came The Second World War where her only son's survival hung in the balance as he fought viciously and bravely on the beaches at D-day, across Europe and into Germany. Then, when he returned from The War, he was quickly drafted into the family business. All she could do was 'keep house' and ensure that her famous Sunday lunches were on the table every week. The more Scriven thought about it, the more he could understand why his uncle was considering early retirement. *He was certainly wealthy enough, so why continue to put his wife through the worry?*

Scriven nodded in agreement and pushed his arm forward to shake his cousin's hand. "Congratulations aer kid. Mecks sense fer yower mother." Mucklow shook his hand warmly and nodded.

"We just have one problem mate." He looked down at his cigarette and watched it glow and burn with a sense of dread.

"What?"

"Eli Davis." Bill Mucklow shook his head before raising his cigarette to his mouth again. "He woe be happy abaaht the ode mon gewin an he ay gunna teck orders from me!"

Scriven began to feel a slight sense of dread and started to worry about what Billy was insinuating. "What yow thinking Bill?"

Mucklow looked up and caught a glimpse of Scriven's expression. "Oh dow be saft Harry! Nothing like that! The guy is family." Scriven felt relieved, for a minute he had thought that his cousin was suggesting that they permanently 'erase' their adopted uncle Eli. "He's a fuckin' liability Harry. Last night he glassed a barman in The Neptune on Powke Lane cus he thought the guy had shortchanged him!" Scriven nodded sympathetically, Eli Davis was definitely getting worse. "The ode mon had to gew daahn there and sort it out. Eli was so pissed he couldn't even stand up! The poor bastard he glassed needs a new fuckin' face!" It was incredibly sad and somewhat ironic that after being rescued from the drunkard violence of his father as a child, Eli Davis' life had headed in a very similar direction and both Scriven and Billy Mucklow felt disappointed at the sadness of the situation, but neither one of them could offer a solution.

"Ar wanna meck money, not enemies!" Bill Mucklow shook his head in frustration. With the exception of Eli Davis, Bill Mucklow was the toughest and most accomplished man of violence around. But he had seen and done deeply disturbing things whilst in military action in Europe and now all he wanted was to earn his fortune with as little violence as possible. It was bad for business, but then it was also necessary and he was cold and numb to it. He was more than capable of turning off his emotions and doing WHATEVER needed to be done. His policy was to strike as hard and as extreme as physically possible, but only when necessary. This way, he could create fear and respect which would deter people in their ways and thus prevent the need for further bloodshed. "If folks fall out of line then of course they need teaching, but that barman had done nothing wrong. Is he gunna trust us now?" Mucklow shook his head again and drained his whiskey. "It's happening all too often mate, an if ar'm in charge then it cor happen with the plans I've got!" A hint of a smile crossed his lips at the mention of his plans and Scriven felt intrigued.

"What plans Bill?" Mucklow smiled again and produced a second cigarette case from his inner jacket pocket.

"Have a look at them." He threw the case onto the table and watched as Scriven opened it up and took out a large cigarette that looked very different from anything Scriven had ever smoked before. It was big and clumsily rolled and when Scriven brought it to his nose he noticed a strong and herby aroma that instantly made the hair inside his nostrils stand on end. It wasn't an unpleasant smell but Scriven felt an almost immediate headache.

"Ron… A little privacy please." Mucklow put up his right hand and clicked his fingers at the barman who immediately came over and showed the two men into a small room at the back of the pub where they would be undisturbed. Bill Mucklow patted him on the back and handed him a 10-shilling note before ushering him out of the room and closing the doors. "Give it a try mate." Bill tossed him his lighter and Scriven placed the oversized 'cigarette' into his mouth. "Yow will fuckin' love this Harry, mecks yer wanna love everyone, not fuckin' glass the bastards!" He rose the light to the marijuana and lit it as Scriven inhaled deeply. A rich, sickly sweet aroma filled the room and Scriven instantly erupted into a fit of coughing. He could smoke with the best of them but he had never tasted anything like this before! Bill Mucklow burst out laughing as he took the joint from Scriven and placed it in his own mouth.

"What the fuck is that shit?" Scriven eventually found his voice as he coughed and spluttered from his first exposure to cannabis.

"It's an 'ace' mate." Mucklow continued to giggle and laugh as he took a long drag and savoured it in his mouth before slowly exhaling, his eyes upwards in a state of calm and euphoria. "I'm just blastin' the weed!"

"Where you get them from?" Scriven watched his cousin carefully, the smell intoxicating his brain and leaving him with a feeling of inner mellowness. He had heard about how some of his favourite musicians, American jazz cats like Charlie Parker and Miles Davis would smoke 'aces' and that it would induce them into a state not unlike being 'pleasantly half drunk.'

"Ar got talkin' ter this fella." Mucklow took another drag of his 'ace' and spoke slowly and in a mellow tone. "A darky, he just come off a boat from Jamaica. Bostin' bloke." The term 'darky' was a widely used term to describe people of colour and neither Billy Mucklow nor Harry Scriven were remotely racist. Scriven's boxing and musical idols were mostly black and the rarity of black people in the U.K. gave them a special kind of status, a coolness and Harry Scriven felt excitement at the prospect of doing business with such exotic friends. Billy Mucklow also had a particular fondness for ladies of colour and one of his regular 'bits on the side' was a mixed-race lady of the night who was known to move in high social circles. Of course, his father did not approve of extra marital activity so this remained a very private aspect of Billy Mucklow's life.

"Who's that then?" Scriven took his turn with the ace again and was beginning to enjoy the effect as it mixed with the beer and whiskey and cast romantic and pleasurable feelings of relaxation within his mind.

"A chap called Robert Murray. He wants to gew into business with us Harry… We will meck a fortune!"

On the 22nd of June 1948, the British ship HMT Empire Windrush brought a group of 802 migrants to the port of Tilbury near London. The Empire Windrush was a vessel that was used to carry British Army personnel and was en route from Australia to England via the Atlantic when it docked in Kingston, Jamaica to pick up servicemen who were on leave. An advertisement had already been placed in a Jamaican newspaper offering cheap transportation on the ship for anyone who wanted to come and work in Britain. Upon arrival in the U.K. the migrants were temporarily housed in Clapham in south west London, but Robert Murray had not wanted to hang around and had made his way to the midlands where he had met Billy Mucklow. The pair had hit it off straight away and formed a bond and friendship that would last for many years. The suggestion was that Murray would bring in the marijuana and Bill Mucklow would provide the security and protection for the operation. Willie Mucklow was fiercely against this and had wanted absolutely nothing to do with the business, but he had recognized the potential profits involved and this had caused him to ponder his own retirement. The deal would actually go on to be quite short lived as Billy Mucklow would draw the line at bringing 'harder' drugs into the country a few years into the future. But by this time, Mucklow and Murray had built up a mutual respect that would ensure that they would always remain friends.

As Mucklow explained the finer details of his potential arrangement with Murray, Harry Scriven could feel himself drifting further into a deep inner calm as if he was physically floating. "Wow Bill, these things am bostin' ay they?" He had hardly listened to a word his cousin had had to say. "Who wants ter fight when yow'm on these! They meck yer wanna love everyone!" He nodded his head enthusiastically in time to 'Nature boy' by Nat King Cole which was playing on a small radiogram in a corner of the small but brightly lit room. Both Scriven and Mucklow adored American music, Jazz, big band and the popular singers of the day such as Bing Crosby, Nat King Cole and Billy Mucklow's personal favourite Frank Sinatra. The music scene in Britain had been pretty sterile and Scriven and Mucklow had much preferred the rich authenticity of the American sound as opposed to such British acts as George Formby.

"Ar want yow to meet somebody Harry." Bill Mucklow spoke suddenly and interrupted Scriven's intoxicated appreciation of Nat King Cole. Before Scriven cold ask who, Mucklow disappeared back into the main bar before re-emerging with a young man who looked no older than 21 years of age. He was short and quite skinny but he radiated an absolute confidence and swagger that Scriven found instantly intimidating. "This lad was the Army boxing champion, well until he got kicked out and put in jail for punching a sergeant!" Mucklow and the lad burst out in laughter, but Scriven, even in his current state was unable to see what was funny. "He's gunna' work for me, once we figure out what to do about Eli, this lad will watch our backs for us. Best young boxer in the country. With a reputation like that, we woe have to do fuck all cus they will all be shittin' their pants!" Mucklow put his hand on the lads back and looked excitedly at Scriven. "Harry, ar want yow to meet Dickie Hickman!"

By the time Scriven and Billy Mucklow had reached the Haden Cross, they had 'smoked their minds out' and were giggling incoherently. The drive over had been eventful as Scriven had driven particularly slowly, though to him and Billy it had appeared to be a 'white knuckle ride' and Scriven felt proud that he had managed to make the journey without crashing the car! Dick Hickman had not ventured into the Cross with them as Eli Davis and Willie Mucklow would be there so instead, he had been dropped off on the way at his home in Old Hill.

Scriven and Bill sat at a table with Willie Mucklow and Eli Davis in their private room and every so often Mucklow senior would shake his head in disapproval at his son and nephew's drunkard and 'stoned' behaviour. "What the fuck is that smell?" He would shout and Scriven and Billy would again erupt into tears of laughter. Just then, there was a loud knock at the door and one of Mucklow's thugs put his head around and began to speak.

"There's someone here to see Harry boss."

"Who is it?" Willie Mucklow hated being disturbed.

"Some wench. Looks tasty but some fuckers gid' her a lampin." The young thug moved aside and in walked Judy Talbot, heavily made up and looking good, but her right eye was bruised and slightly swollen. Billy Mucklow jeered excitedly at the sight of her and nudged Scriven on the arm with the suggestion that Scriven's luck was in.

"What can ar do fer yer bab?" Scriven smiled and went slightly red through the effects of the marijuana, unable to keep his swaying head completely still.

"I want a private word with you Harry."

Billy Mucklow jeered again and Scriven began to laugh, not noticing the sideways glance Judy shot Eli Davis. Scriven stood up and followed Judy out through the packed bar to a small patch of ground that stood near the car park at the back of the pub. She lit a cigarette and blew smoke into Scriven's face seductively before sultrily passing him the lipstick stained 'fake' and inviting him to put it into his own mouth. She stood directly in front of him, her lips glowing red and her heavily made up dark eyes glaring at him with a mixture of lust and hatred. She had long dark hair, a heaving full cleavage and the scent of rich expensive perfume that attracted Scriven and awakened in his senses a raw and deep desire to have her right there and then.
    "Who gid yer that?" Scriven held onto his desires and pointed to Judy's injured eye. "Was it Reid?"
    "Dow mention that name!" Judy's eyes flickered with anger and for a woman well into her late 30s Scriven found her totally irresistible. "Reid fucked off after yow gid him that beating. My ode mon Charlie gid me this." Scriven said nothing. *After what Judy had done with James Reid, she was lucky her old man had taken her back at all!* But there was never any doubt of that, she was much more attractive than her older husband and he had been grateful that she had returned to him and their children. "Ar wanna thank you Harry, for getting rid of that Cockney bastard and allowing me to return home to my children." She instantly dropped to her knees and undid Scriven's flies as he pushed his head back in ecstasy and enjoyed what she had to offer! He looked up at the starry night and could hear 'A nightingale sang in Berkley square' by Vera Lynn playing loudly inside the pub. He suddenly remembered that his unlocked car was nearby on the car park and he quickly pulled Judy to her feet and ushered her over to his car where he led her to the back seat and continued to have his 'wicked way' with her in every single way that his lustful, high on marijuana mind could imagine.

    About half an hour later, Harry Scriven wandered back into Willie Mucklow's side bar with a smug, intoxicated grin of contented satisfaction. Billy Mucklow burst out laughing again and stood up to shake his cousin's hand. "Fair play aer kid! Yow'm a fuckin' legend!" Willie Mucklow said nothing. His disappointed eyes fixated upon a small clock that stood on top of the fireplace. Eli Davis said nothing either. He sat back in his chair and looked down at his half empty pint of beer, hiding his sense of satisfaction and anticipation.

Chapter 10

The Three Musketeers starring Gene Kelly and Lana Turner was released in October 1948 and would go on to be one of the most popular films of the year. It was a technicolour adventure film based on the classic 1844 novel Alexandre Dumas and Harry Scriven most certainly would have taken Lily Cole to see it at the pictures had it not been for some rather unfortunate events.

Lily Cole had always been a 'Daddy's girl' and it made her immensely happy that her father had slowly began to accept her husband of choice. The day after her autumn walk with Harry Scriven around Haden Hill Park she did as she often did and carried a lunch of tongue sandwiches, a tomato and a bottle of beer to her father's scrap yard on Garratts Lane, Old Hill. Norman Cole had instructed his three young labourers to go and grab their lunch before settling down in a small pokey office that stood in a small brick building at the front of the yard. Inside was an old Victorian desk with four chairs and an old coal burning stove that his workers would use in the winter to keep warm. The previous year had been The Great Winter of 47 which had been one of the coldest British winters in history. The fire had not seen any action yet this year though. Coal was expensive and Norman Cole could not afford to heat the building in late October! The truth was that he most certainly could afford it, but his miserly ways had helped him to build his business and he hated the thought of spending money on things that were not necessary. Besides, he had a wedding to pay for!

"Dad, it's bloody freezin' in here! Why dow yer get the fire gewin?" Lily laughed as she sat in the office eating her lunch with her father.

"That weddin' of yowers ay gunna' pay for itself is it?" Cole tossed his eyebrows and smiled at his daughter. He could see how happy she was and even if Harry Scriven was not his ideal son in law, the man made his daughter happy and that was all he could wish for.

"Ar'm sure yow can afford it Dad!" Lily laughed again but before Cole could answer there was an almighty crash just outside the office and both Norman Cole and his daughter instantly rushed outside to see what the disturbance was.

"Hello Norman." Eli Davis stood in the middle of the yard with two young vicious looking thugs either side of him. He was dressed in black with a long three-quarter length Crombie jacket and a dark coloured trilby hat that cast a shadow across his amused and evil eyes. In front of him was Norman Cole's youngest employee Dennis Hill. Hill was just 17 years old and had worked hard and with loyalty to Norman Cole since he had left school at the age of 14. The lad was absolutely infatuated with Cole's only daughter Lily and had not gone for his lunch with his fellow workers in the hope of catching a glimpse of the object of his adolescent desires. He lay on the floor screaming and crying in utter agony as Davis and his thugs had pinned him to the ground and dropped a huge piece of scrap metal onto his leg. Norman Cole instantly rushed forwards to try and help him but Davis raised his hand and struck him hard across the face with a back handed slap that sent him straight to the ground. "No Norman. Ar want a word with yow!"

Lily screamed at the sight of her father on the ground and tried to help him but one of the thugs grabbed her around the waist and held her as Dennis Hill continued to yelp in pain.

"He needs help!" Cole protested and pointed towards Hill but Davis was not interested. He and his two associates had purposefully dropped the metal onto the young man's leg and they were in no hurry to remove it.

"Willie Mucklow wants his money Norman. Yow know how it works mucka." Davis spoke loudly deliberately so that Lily could hear the entire exchange.

"What money? We have an agreement?" Cole was confused and the chilling cries of his young employee distressed him even further.

"It appears your agreement is null and void… The sooner yow pay up the sooner we can lift this shit of yower kid's leg mar mon."

"What do yer mean null and void? Mar daughter Lily is marrying Mr Mucklow's nephew?"

"It appears not." Davis took great pleasure in announcing this as loudly as he could and Lily Cole was confused. Eli Davis had never liked Norman Cole and it had gråted on him that the scrap dealer had been allowed to get away with not paying his dues to the family. Arranging that 'bit of business' with Judy Talbot on the car park of the Haden Cross had worked in his favour and had shown Willie Mucklow that Harry Scriven was not ready to marry Lily Cole. Willie Mucklow had not been impressed and had subsequently ordered Davis to collect from Norman Cole. Of course, this was news to both Lily and Harry Scriven who upon being informed of his Uncle's decision had headed straight for the scrapyard.

"Yes he is!" Lily Cole was still struggling to break free. "We are getting married next summer!" Lily hesitated slightly and started to worry. *What had happened to Harry?*

"Why dow yer ask him for yourself bab?" Davis spoke sarcastically as Scriven's car screeched to a halt in the middle of the yard. The front door flung open and Harry Scriven flew out in an utter rage.

"Put mar wench daahn you fuckin' bastard!" He rushed towards the thug who was holding Lily and knocked him to the floor with a hard right hook. With the rage that was boiling within him, he wanted to stay in that spot and continue to beat and stamp on the man who had touched his woman, but he had more pressing issues to deal with. Bill Mucklow had been in the car with Scriven and had now walked over to his cousin to ensure that he did not go too far. The whole time, the poor and tragic Dennis Hill still lay in absolute agony.

"Uncle Eli, what the fuck is gewin on?" Bill Mucklow spoke with such authority that Davis was taken aback in surprise. Bill had never spoken to him like that before and he did not like it.

"Just following yower ode mon's orders Bill." Davis shrugged and then rose his voice to speak again. "After aer kid Harry fucked that wench on the car park last night, it appears that Willie Mucklow dow think they should be married anymore."

In that awful moment, Scriven looked deep into Lily's eyes and saw her soul break. In them, he saw no love, no recognition, just hurt, pain and a look of total utter devastation that would haunt him forever. She turned away, unable to ever look at him again. She looked at Dennis Hill and then back to her father. "Pay him."

"You bastard!" Scriven screamed and threw himself forwards as if to attack Eli Davis, but Bill Mucklow grabbed him and wrestled him back.

"I told you what my father's thoughts were on loyalty between a man and his wife Harry. Uncle Eli is family, he is following orders like we all do. You fucked this up Harry, not Eli, or me, or my father. You." Scriven froze and in that moment he looked at Davis, then back at Lily and Norman and then at his cousin. "We are your family Harry." Mucklow spoke again and Scriven silently cursed at the two-faced irony of his cousin. *The previous night he had laughed hysterically and congratulated him on his conquest, now he was preaching to him about morals!* He turned back towards Lily and could not take his eyes of her broken figure. Inside he wanted to rip Eli Davis' head off and beg Lily for forgiveness, but as he watched her, utterly devastated and sobbing, he stood routed to the spot, unable to move, powerless through his devotion to his family. For this, she hated him even more. *Maybe she would have forgiven him? Maybe they could have found a way to work things out? But why wouldn't he move? Why couldn't he choose her over them? Surely she meant more to him than this?* Tears descended from her eyes and trickled across her pretty face as the love of her life continued to freeze and do nothing. Norman Cole collected whatever he could from the cash box inside the office and Davis and his thugs helped him to remove the metal from Dennis Hill's shattered leg.

As Billy Mucklow led him into the car, Harry Scriven kept his eyes upon his beloved until the last moment and as Mucklow started the engine and reversed out of the yard he pressed his head to the glass and continued to stare. Too ashamed to speak, apologise or even wave farewell. It was not even the shame of his activities with Judy Talbot that tore at him, it was the guilt and shame of not being able to make the right choice and speak out against those that were closest to him. He would never see Lily again. The Cole family sold up and moved away for good. Harry Scriven would spend the rest of his existence regretting this day and clinging to the memory of that last autumn walk together, not fully understanding quite how much he had lost and the true implications of his actions.

Chapter 11
1953

A small boy sat on the stairs and stared obsessively at a tall, well-lit Christmas tree that adorned the large hallway of his Wolverhampton home. It was Christmas Eve and the grand 1920s detached house in which he lived with his mother and stepfather was filled with guests. Occasionally, a well-meaning relative or family friend would attempt to engage him in conversation or comment upon his activity. But he remained focused, mesmerised and oblivious to the outside world. To those around him, he appeared unusual, odd, weird, strange rather than rude. "The things this family have done for that boy! With him being illegitimate an all!" One guest had commented. "He dow know he's born, livin' in a posh house like this!" Another guest had not so subtly observed. But still the boy remained fascinated with the elaborate tree that stood before him. Every so often, he would freeze with utter terror and frantically check the space around him, his face turning back and forth with a twisted look of shear horror and then he would return to the comforting presence of the tree that he had helped his mother to decorate. *That had been a happy day, he had had his mother all to himself all day and he had actually spoken to her, smiled and been happy...* BUT THEN, he shuddered, *he could not think about it, if he thought about it then he would 'get accidents' and Mommy would be cross at him for the mess in his pants.* He looked over and saw his mother, she wore a sparkly dress and her golden hair hung long across her snow-white face. *She must be a Princess!* He thought to himself.

    She caught her four-year-old son's gaze and smiled warmly at him. She did worry about him. He would rarely speak and if he ever did it would only ever be to her or her father. He would regularly soil himself and every time she watched him closely, she could sense that he always appeared to be in fear of something. It tore at her maternal instincts and the fact that she was unable to do anything to help her offspring ripped her heart into a million pieces. He was constantly checking the space around him, shivering, icy cold, as if he was haunted, possessed by some evil spirit that tormented him endlessly. She had tried to speak to her husband about it, but it was always brushed off. Not that her son was really any of her husband's concern. He was not the boy's father and she was thoroughly grateful to the man for taking her in and marrying her with an *illegitimate, bastard child.* She did not love her husband. There was something about him she did not like or trust, but his family were wealthy and she kept telling herself that she should be grateful. She forced a smile as she looked around at the *vile, loathsome* guests who constantly judged her and her child. Her own family were not permitted to be there and she would have to wait until Boxing Day to see them. But her husband's family where there, even though he had not arrived home yet. He had been called to business and she knew that this probably meant that he had gone with a gang of thugs to inflict a vicious beating on somebody. *Why did she always attract men like that? Men who were so insecure and obsessed with themselves that they had to hurt others, Men who were obsessed with dominance and violence.* She allowed her mind to wonder into past memories for a brief moment, but she stopped herself. *Men could wallow in their self-pity, their attention seeking drama and constant search for reassurance, but never women, they had to keep house and look after the children!* As her eyes glanced around the large living room at her guests, she paused at the sight of her father-in-law, whom she utterly detested. He was a short and overweight man with wiry, dirty looking curly hair. He was often found sitting around and never moved quickly, but then Brian Tanner did not have to move for anybody. He was the gangster king of Wolverhampton and was feared throughout the town. She had heard many horror stories about her father-in-law, stories that she did not doubt were true, but she chose not to listen to them. His family had taken her in and accepted her son and as she kept telling herself, she must be grateful! *Her son's blood family were certainly no better!* Brian Tanner had actually shown some kindness towards her son and had even insisted that the lad call him 'Grandad Brian.' But her son had refused to speak and she remembered how he would not even acknowledge the man. *If only she could get to the bottom of what was wrong with the child!*

The boy remained on the stairs when suddenly he heard a muffled bang outside the house. He instantly froze with terror. *He knew that noise anywhere, he listened out for that noise daily, a sign that the nightmare had begun, the slamming of a car door, the ghost!* He bit into his lower lip with such intensity that he drew blood and he felt a sinking feeling as his entire little world was descending into darkness. He could not see the Christmas tree anymore, he could not see his mother anymore, all he could see was fear.

The front door opened and in walked Cedric Tanner. He was short and overweight like his father and was of around thirty years of age. He had an extremely round face with small black eyes that were both piercing and somewhat disturbing in appearance. The child clambered frantically upstairs at the sight of the man and straight into his bedroom. He shut the door and pulled a large teddy bear in front of it before darting under his bed where he would remain, hands covering his 4-year-old ears and his eyes tight shut. *He must hide, he must be quiet, he must not move, or the ghost would find him…*

The little boy eventually fell asleep, drenched in his own urine and filth. He awoke a few hours later and upon realisation of his own wetness and soiled clothing he immediately worried that his mother would be upset. *If only he could get to the bathroom and clean himself.* Slowly, shivering and still terrified he crawled out from under the bed and approached the door. In the cold icy darkness he watched his breath as it arose from his mouth and ascended into the shadowy blackness of the lonely room. He put his hand upon the door handle and summoned up the courage to slowly turn the handle and allow the light from the dimly lit landing to cascade into his bedroom as he opened the door. It was still and quiet and not a soul moved, he looked left and right several times until he was quite satisfied that he was alone and then he ran as fast as his tiny legs could take him over to the bathroom. Once inside he locked the door and he was safe! His mother had told him that he was never to lock the door in case he was to get locked inside, but deep down he wished that he could get locked inside, away from the horrors and truly disgusting physical pain that he endured outside. *It was rude, it was naughty, it hurt.*

      The bathroom was cold and damp and smelt of soap, but at least he was safe. He sat himself upon the toilet and looked down at his soiled trousers with shame, but then he heard a sound. The door handle began to move and the small boy felt a pang of terror and then with absolute horror he watched as the latch began to open as whatever was on the outside manoeuvred the door back and forth to loosen it. By now, the little boy could not breathe with panic and dread, the door opened slowly and there in the eerie, silent darkness of the doorway, stood the ghost…

Chapter 12

Norman Cole's Christmas did not begin until Boxing Day. It was only then that he was allowed to see his only daughter and his grandson Michael and he worried incessantly about them. Since they had left Haden Hill 5 years previously, the Cole family had moved into a newly built 3-bedroom semi-detached house in Woodsetton which stood between Sedgley and Tipton. After the move, Lily Cole had spent the first few months feeling utterly devastated over the collapse of her engagement to Harry Scriven, but then she had met a man from Wolverhampton who quickly brought the young, attractive blonde under his control and moved her into his home. Norman Cole disliked Cedric Tanner even more so than he had Harry Scriven and objected profoundly to his daughter's new relationship and subsequent marriage. As a result, Cole and his wife were all but completely cut off from their daughter and her son, but Lily loved her parents immensely and she made sure that she visited them as often as her strict and overtly possessive husband would allow. The Cole family were not welcome in Cedric Tanner's home and if Tanner had his way he would be using physical violence against Norman Cole to 'teach him some respect' for his insult of not approving of their wedding. Luckily for Norman Cole, Lily commanded just a little influence over her husband and for this reason Cedric Tanner and his all-powerful father Brian allowed Cole to remain unharmed. What Cole found hardest to come to terms with was the fact that he knew deep down that his daughter did not love Cedric Tanner and that she felt bound to him for his taking her in alongside her illegitimate child. *Lily was old enough to look after herself, but Michael was a massive worry.* The little boy was particularly odd and refused to speak to anyone other than his mother and Norman Cole.

As Lily sat inside the house chatting to her mother, Norman stood outside in the relatively mild winter air and watched his grandson as he played with a small tricycle Cole and his wife had bought him for Christmas. Whenever the boy came to their house, he would always arrive rigid, afraid and as if something was extremely wrong. Within half an hour of being around 'Grandad Norman' he would begin to ease and slowly 'come out of his shell.' This would continue until his mother would announce it was time to leave and the small child would suddenly become rigid again.

"Wow Michael, that's a fast un ay it!" Cole smiled with joy at the rare sight of his grandson playing happily.

"Yes grandad, its super-duper fast!" The boy zoomed past and then suddenly stopped dead in the middle of the yard. "Grandad?"

"Yes Michael?" Cole strolled over to his grandson and dropped to his knee to address the child on the same level.

"Is this bike fast enough to get away from the ghost?"

"There ay no ghosts Michael!" Cole laughed at his grandson's comment. "Who told yow abaaht ghosts?"

"There is a ghost at my house." Michael's face suddenly changed and his happy smile was replaced with a look of pure terror.

"What's wrong Michael?" The child's sudden change in mood alarmed Cole greatly and he placed a comforting hand on the boy's back.

"The ghost hurts me Grandad." Tears appeared in Michael's eyes and he began to shiver with fear. "He makes me do rude things." As the little boy continued to recount more of his ordeals in greater detail, Cole quivered with anger and tried hard to hold back vomit as tears of distraught sadness began to flow down his cheeks. He eventually composed himself enough to speak for the sake of the boy.

"Michael, you must show me who the ghost is, and then we can make him stop." The little boy nodded with a little confusion, he had never seen his grandfather cry before and he began to worry that he had done something wrong, but then a small glimmer of hope arose within his young mind. *Would grandad Norman save him from the ghost? Would it all stop?*

Norman Cole said nothing to his wife or daughter. In his anger and haste for retribution he grabbed his jacket and the keys to his 1951 Morris Minor and lifted his grandson onto the back seat. He knew that Cedric Tanner was spending Boxing Day at his parents' house in Tettenhall Wolverhampton and a burning rage inside of him needed to sort this out there and then. He got into the front seat and pulled out the choke before starting the engine. He reversed quickly out of his drive in Masefield Avenue , Woodsetton and shot down the road to the tune of the Morris Minor's 'raspy' four cylinder engine.

The Christmas period of 1953 was unusually mild for the time of year and as Norman Cole raced through the streets of Woodsetton, Coseley and Wolverhampton he struggled to see on account of the afternoon winter sun that blinded him at almost every turn. He was shaking with rage and was so distraught at what his beloved young grandchild had had to endure that he almost crashed his car on several occasions. If he had of been thinking rationally, he would have confronted his daughter with her son's sickening revelation first or returned to his home town to seek assistance from Willie Mucklow. But through his anger and heartbreak he could not see the danger in what he was doing in single handily going to confront the Tanner family. As he drove, he kept the image of Cedric Tanner in his mind and imagined how he would punish the man he had already disliked but now hated more than he ever envisaged he could hate anyone. He could not be sure that it was Cedric who was in fact the ghost, but somewhere deep down inside of him knew that he was the one. He just needed Michael to confirm it. As he sped on he passed cars, houses, shops, churches and people who were all at home enjoying the festivities of the season. For Norman Cole there was no such thing, he was living a real-life nightmare.

He reached the large town house in Tettenhall, slammed on the brakes of the Morris Minor and flung open the front door. He released his grandson from the back seat and strolled purposefully up the garden path. "Don't be afraid Michael. Just nod when you see the ghost and we will sort this out once and for all!" The glimmer of hope within the young Michael Cole began to grow. *Would Grandad Norman stop the ghost? Would everything be ok now?*

Norman Cole hammered on the front door aggressively and a young maid answered. "Can I help you Sir?" The girl was no more than 17 years old and was nervous of Cole's threatening manner.

"Where is he?" Cole barged past the maid and into a large hallway with an elaborate dining room off to the right. "Cedric? Where is he?"

"I'm afraid the family are out at a public house at the moment. Yow cor just come in here Sir!"

Cole looked into the dining room and the thought of that *sick bastard* sitting down to eat at such an elaborate table infuriated him even more. He launched into the dining room where the table was meticulously set out for a Boxing Day meal and proceeded to utterly destroy it. He turned over every chair and drew blood from his own fists as he smashed his way through the expensive cut glass and table ornaments. The maid panicked and quickly withdrew herself into the kitchen but Michael stood and watched with a curious glee. *Grandad Norman was strong! Grandad Norman would save him from the ghost!*

As Norman Cole's 66 year old body began to tire from his efforts and aggression, he did not notice that Cedric Tanner had returned early from the pub and had entered the house alone. He was instantly drawn to the almighty sound of Cole's destruction and he rushed into the dining room.

"Norman! What the hell do you think you are doing?"

Cole instantly turned to face his overweight son in law and noticed as he turned that Michael was now nodding frantically and with fear at the arrival of the ghost. "You sick twisted scum!" Cole narrowed his eyes and set his sights upon Cedric Tanner. "You've been interfering with mar grandson and when ar tell mar daughter yow ul' be finished!"

"Oh dear…" Tanner spoke in a patronising tone and looked over at Michael with a look of lascivious annoyance. "You naughty boy. I thought it was our little secret. I will have to deal with you later."

The exchange between Cedric Tanner and the young boy enraged Cole yet further and he could not contain his rage any longer as he rushed towards his grandson's abuser. Unfortunately for Michael, Norman Cole was not a man of violence and Cedric Tanner quickly stepped aside and caught the older man off balance with a hard right-hand punch. Cole instantly fell to the floor and cracked a rib and as he tried to get back up, Tanner continued to rain down kick after agonizing kick as young Michael watched on, his hopes of salvation fading fast. Eventually, when Tanner was quite satisfied that Norman Cole would not be able to get back up, he removed his black silk tie and secured it tightly around Cole's neck. "Michael." He demanded the name with a sick and perverted pleasure. "Watch what happens to your grandfather!" Tanner then proceeded to garrotte the life out of Norman Cole as the young boy watched on, barely understanding the events, but somehow he now knew that his hopes of salvation were being crushed before him. He did not quite understand the finality of his grandfather's predicament, but the images and sounds would remain with him forever as he slowly watched his beloved grandad Norman die.

As he passed, Norman Cole kept his eyes upon his grandson until the last. In that moment, he thought not of his life, not of his only daughter and not of his wife, but of his utter horror at not saving his grandson Michael who's soul was now lost to the evil that had taken his own life from him.

Once he was quite sure that Cole was dead, Cedric Tanner turned to face Michael, his black eyes bulging with a mixture of depraved sexual lust and sheer anger. He slowly and ceremoniously undid his leather belt and his expensive silk trousers loosened around his rounded waist. He removed the belt and whipped it hard off the floor to scare the child and signal his intent. Michael looked helplessly at the floor as Tanner moved closer to the terrified boy. "You should not have opened your mouth young man!" He grabbed the child by the hair and used his belt to whip him hard across the buttocks with the buckle. Michael yelped at the pain but he knew that it was nothing compared to what was about to come.

"What the fuck is gewin on in here?" To Michael's relief, Cedric's father Brian suddenly marched into the room and was alarmed to find his dining room destroyed, a dead man on the floor and his son in the middle of the room with the young boy. Cedric Tanner immediately felt ashamed at the sight of his father and released the boy. "I thought we had cured you of all that Cedric!" Brian Tanner was immensely disappointed. His son had displayed signs of this sort of thing before and Brian had had to pay for the silence of parents of previous victims. Brian Tanner had hoped that since marrying a 'normal' young woman his son had 'cured' himself of 'perverse and unnatural' desires. *How wrong he had been and now he would have to pick up the pieces yet again.* Brian Tanner loved his son more than anything on earth and he would do WHATEVER was necessary to protect him. Whilst Cedric was sent upstairs to take a bath, Brian Tanner arranged for some of his associates to arrive and remove Cole's corpse. They placed him inside of his Morris Minor and drove him out to a remote location near Kinver Edge before setting the car alight and thus destroying any evidence. The fact that they drove the car into a tree first would cause the Police to believe that Cole had simply had an accident and perished in the subsequent fire. Initially, Tanner senior had ordered the men to kill the boy and place him inside the car alongside his grandfather, but the mobsters had protested heavily and Brian Tanner had eventually changed his mind on the grounds that the child was probably too traumatized to speak and incriminate his own son. He then proceeded to give his son a severe 'talking to' about his conduct and informed him that under no circumstances was he to ever touch the child inappropriately again. Unfortunately for young Michael Cole, Brian Tanner vanished mysteriously just a few weeks later in January 1954 and no other living person knew or would know of the torment he would continue to suffer at the perverted hands of his Stepfather Cedric Tanner.

Chapter 13
1973

The late afternoon November sun hung low in the sky but offered little warmth. A long white and blue 1961 Vauxhall Cresta PA took over a substantial section of the Haden Cross car park. Its elaborate 1950s American style tail fins and immaculate chrome cut a sharp appearance in the autumn sun against the drab 1970s boxes that surrounded it. A 1972 Morris Marina stood alongside it looking remarkably ordinary in contrast as did a virtually brand-new Austin Allegro which was parked opposite.

Lent against the Cresta's long bonnet was a young man of 24 years of age, coolly smoking a cigarette whilst constantly watching the pub. His hair was neither long nor short but was somewhere in between with a sharp side parting that was typical of the times. A pair of expensive looking aviator sunglasses covered his intense staring eyes and his chin was slightly darkened from several day's worth of stubble. He was about 6 foot tall with broad shoulders which were clad with a black leather blazer and an open neck white shirt with the top three buttons undone revealing a gold chain.

He savoured the last dregs of his cigarette before throwing it to the floor and stubbing it out with his black leather cowboy boot. *Where the fuck is this guy?* He thought to himself. He was due to meet a potential business associate on the car park but the man was late. He checked his watch again and took out another cigarette as an attractive older woman leaving the pub caught his eye. She was about 40 years of age with long red hair. She carried a little extra weight, but to the young man she still looked incredibly good and when she flashed him a cheeky smile he could not help but give her an approving nod as he exhaled smoke into the autumnal air. He thought about making a move but then he caught sight of a large man in his early 40s who had just emerged from the pub.

"Yower name Micky aer kid?" The man approached him, his eyes looked unintelligent but worldly wise.

"Who want's ter know?"

"Ar'm Barry, Barry O'Leary, we spoke on the phone." O'Leary put out his hand and the younger man shook it.

"Micky, Micky Cole… I heard you were looking for new guys?"

"Not me, the boss. He's inside but he's in a fuckin' foul mood. Sent me aaht here to check yow out." O'Leary lit a cigarette and lent against Micky's Vauxhall Cresta to face him. Micky grunted and blew smoke into the big man's face.

"Well ar wanna see the boss. Ar wanna know who ar'm gunna be workin' for."

"Who said yow'll be workin' for anyone kid? Ar'm second in charge raahnd here so yow better learn some fuckin' respect!" O'Leary gritted his teeth and pushed his face into Coles. "Now ar heard that yow'm a useful fella to have abaaht? But I also heard that yow'm a bit of a loose cannon? A fuckin' psychopath?"

"Who told you that?" Cole took off his sunglasses and revealed cold, haunted eyes that almost caused O'Leary to regret his aggressive stance.

"Some face from over Coseley way. Said yow started aaht workin' for Cedric Tanner?" At the mention of the name, O'Leary saw a change in Cole's eyes. They went from cold and staring to murderous and evil as his pupils widened and his stare intensified. "The boss ay gunna be happy abaaht us workin' with one of Cedric's boys!" Micky Cole took a deep breath and moved his face so close to the older man that O'Leary could smell the whisky and marijuana on his breath.

"You can tell your boss that I AM NOT one of Cedric's boys…" Cole spent the next ten seconds considering whether or not to bite O'Leary's face off. "Cedric Tanner is an utter BASTARD." O'Leary moved backwards slightly and took a drag of his cigarette.

"Be careful kid, yow cor gew abaaht sayin' stuff like that." Cedric Tanner was the undisputed underworld king of The Black Country. His father had vanished in 1954, Willie Mucklow had long since retired and his son Bill Mucklow had been sent to prison in 1955. When Isiah Boswell died in the late 60s, Tanner's only potential rivals had been some night club owning brothers from Aston, Birmingham, but they were more interested in running night clubs and did not consider themselves to be gangsters. Of course, the Kray twins from London had briefly tried to return to the Midlands in the 60s, but in 1969 Reginald and Ronald Kray were sent to prison for life so Cedric Tanner and the framework of his father's old organisation literally had a free reign.

After a tortured and troubled childhood, Micky Cole had eventually gone to work for his stepfather Cedric Tanner. His mother Lily had disapproved and had not wanted her only son to get mixed up in gangland, but he had been expelled from several schools and had got into countless amounts of trouble with the local Police. He had severe emotional anger issues that his mother could just not understand though she always put it down to genes from the boy's biological father. Cedric Tanner saw potential in his stepson's borderline psychotic thuggery and quickly recruited him into his organization as a teenager, however, this had recently come to an end with the death of Micky's mother from cancer and the angry young man had disappeared off the radar for a while.

"Ar say what ar fuckin' want!" Micky threw his cigarette onto the floor and lent back against his car. O'Leary nodded and half smiled.

"The boss will like you kid. Yow'm a lot like him!" Barry O'Leary was impressed with what he had seen so far. Since the mid-50s and the disappearance of Harry Scriven and the imprisonment of Billy Mucklow, his organisation had been in decline and they were desperately in need of some new 'muscle' to help them get back on track. But Barry O'Leary was still not quite convinced. *This Micky Cole could certainly talk the talk and was pretty intimidating, but was his bark worse than his bite?*

"So, am yow gunna' invite me in for a drink or what? It's fuckin' freezing aaht here!" A slight warmth returned to Cole's eyes as he rubbed his hands together and O'Leary could not help but feel a little relieved.

"It ay as easy as that kid. The boss is kinda' paranoid." O'Leary's boss was particularly paranoid due to his overuse of cocaine, but this was something Cole could identify with as his own daily existence relied heavily on a cocktail of various narcotics and alcohol. "Let me talk to him and ar will give yer a call mate." Before Cole could answer, a bright yellow Ford Escort Mexico with the 1598cc crossflow engine pulled onto the pub car park at speed. 'My Coo Ca Choo' by Alvin Stardust was blasting out of the stereo at such a volume that when the driver wound down his window to speak, neither O'Leary nor Cole could make out what he was trying to say. The driver was in his early 20s and had long shoulder length hair. Next to him sat a moderately attractive girl in an exceptionally short mini skirt and knee-high boots whom the driver was eager to impress. He turned down the cars stereo and spoke again.

"Oi, move that fuckin' heap of shit ahht of mar way! Ar wanna park!" The man pointed aggressively at Cole's aged Cresta PA and both Cole and O'Leary figured that he was trying to 'show off' for the benefit of the girl. Barry O'Leary gave a sly smile and looked at Micky Cole. Here was the perfect opportunity for him to gauge Cole's worth as a potential gang associate. Was he all mouth? Or was his contact from over Coseley right when he described him as an absolute 'nut job!' The opportunity was not lost on Micky Cole either as he turned to face the Ford Escort and approached the car, noticing the girl's long shapely legs instantly.

"Hello baby." Cole put his head to the passenger's side window and winked at the girl. "Yow gorra' bostin' pair of pins bab. What yow gewin abaaht with a dick head like this for?" The girl could not hide the fact that she was flattered and suppressed a slight giggle. Her male companion saw red and rushed out of the car.

"Get away from mar wench yer bastard!" The man walked around the back of the car and stood next to Cole who was still hunched over the window and enjoying an eyeful of the girl's inner thighs and cleavage. "Ar said get the fuck away from her before ar loose mar fuckin' temper!" Cole winked at the girl again and stood up. He felt O'Leary's eyes upon him and he thought he saw the pub curtains twitch as if someone from inside was also watching. He casually looked left to divert his opponent's attention before smashing him in the right eye with such force that the socket ruptured and the man fell back against the car. Before he could move, Cole hit him again with his other fist and broke his nose. In that moment sheer adrenaline, aggression and pent-up hatred shot through Cole's veins like the hard drugs he was accustomed to. But there was no buzz like this, not from cocaine, not from alcohol and not from sex. He opened the front door of the car and grabbed the driver's hair in one swift move before holding the man's head against the B pillar of the car and slamming the door hard shut on his head. He then pulled him semi-consciously out of the doorway and sank his teeth into the man's ear. Part of it came off in Cole's mouth and he tasted the salty iron of the man's blood. He jerked his head back angrily and spat the piece of ear and gristle onto the floor. By now the girl was screaming hysterically and her boyfriend was on the floor trying to cover himself as best he could whilst muttering a desperate protest. Micky Cole noticed that one of the man's hands was exposed on the floor so he instantly raised his boot and used his heel to stamp the fingers into the concrete floor, disintegrating the finger nails and almost certainly breaking bones. Barry O'Leary looked on impressed. This guy would be a perfect addition to the crew, but he didn't want things to get too out of hand. Of course, they paid the cops to look the other way, but it would be hard to explain a dead body and an hysterical girl on the pub car park!

"Hey tough guy. I think you proved your point!" O'Leary put a hand on Cole's back and the younger man turned to face him, his mouth gruesomely grotesque as blood and remnants of his victim's ear covered his lips and chin. The driver used whatever strength he had left to crawl around the back of the car and into the driver's seat where he turned the key in the ignition and drove away as fast as he could in fear for his life.

"Yow better fuck off in case the cops show up!" O'Leary smiled and nodded approvingly. Come back here on Friday night at 7. We may have a bit business for yer."

"Then do I get to meet the boss?" Cole wiped the blood from his face with a clean handkerchief and put his aviator sunglasses back on.

"Maybe. Just maybe." O'Leary shrugged and turned to go back into the pub as Micky got back into his car and drove off. As he drove up the hill towards Old Hill he watched the pub in his rear view mirror grow smaller and smaller. His plan was slowly beginning to come together.

Chapter 14

Showdown by Electric Light Orchestra was a top 20 hit for the Birmingham band in October 1973 and was taken from their forthcoming album On The Third Day which was due to be released in the November of the same year. When Micky Cole entered The Haden Cross on Friday 26th October 1973, the ELO record was playing loudly on the pub jukebox and Cole thought that it was somewhat fitting for his first meeting with his new boss.

He had been told to arrive at 7 o clock, but he had a particular habit of arriving early and as he stood at the bar and ordered a pint of Harp Lager with a Johnnie Walker chaser, he noticed that the old clock on the wall read five to. He took a long gulp of his beer before 'downing' the whisky in one and then lighting a cigarette. He felt the soothing effects of the whisky and nicotine and took a few seconds to take in the surroundings of the Haden Cross. He had never been inside the pub before but the whole place felt eerily familiar, as if he was surrounded by ghosts and reflections from a bygone era or a previous life that was for some reason relevant to him. Since his horrific experiences as a young child, Micky Cole had developed a highly intuitive and receptive sensitivity that he could not quite understand. The hairs on the back of his neck stood on end and he felt chills as if the very walls of the Haden Cross pub retained memories of events that were particularly important to him. He dismissed his experience as utterly ridiculous as The Ballroom Blitz by The Sweet burst out of the juke box and he noted the presence of two incredible pairs of legs standing at the other end of the bar.

The first girl was tall with dirty blonde hair and was wearing a pair of tight white-hot pants. She didn't have the prettiest face in the world, her eyes were slightly too close together, but Cole had certainly seen a lot worse! Next to her was a shorter girl in an orange mini skirt who had large, pretty brown eyes, freckles and shoulder length dark hair. He figured that they were both of a similar age to himself and he took an immediate preference to the shorter girl, but he was not fussy. He had a beautiful girlfriend waiting for him at home, but to Micky Cole, variety was the spice of life! He noticed that the ladies were giggling and looking over at him so he checked his watch and figured that he may as well chat to them for a while whilst he waited for O'Leary and his new boss to arrive.

"Hello ladies." Cole smiled and shot the girls a cheeky wink as he approached them. Deep down, he was an incredibly sensitive and nervous soul, but his excessive use of narcotics, alcohol and an overwhelming notion to hide his inner self gave him a somewhat 'cocky' and overconfident edge which in reality could not be further from the truth. In his short life he had seen and experienced things that no human should ever have to and he had contemplated suicide throughout his life. In his mind, his one purpose was to wreak vengeance upon those who had been responsible for the things that had happened to him and he would not find true peace until these aims had been achieved.

"Hello." The girls spoke in unison and giggled. Despite it being relatively early in the evening, they had already consumed several gin and tonics and were intent on enjoying their Friday night after a gruelling week at work in a Black Country factory. They had enjoyed their fish and chips from Ivan's in Old Hill at home and now they were out looking for a good time. The taller girl seemed the more confident and she took an instant liking to Micky. "We ay seen yow in here before?"

Cole shook his head and took a cool drag of his cigarette. "Nah, ar never been in here before bab. Yow pair come here often?" The girls laughed at the corniness of his line and smiled.

"We always come in here on a Friday night." The favoured brunette with the big eyes answered the question and Cole met her gaze with an intense lustful stare.

"Why do you come here? What's so special abaaht this place?" The girl raised her eyebrows and pouted.

"This is where the bad boys hang out!" She snatched the cigarette from his fingers and took a long seductive drag.

"We like bad boys." The tall friend in the hot pants interrupted the intimacy of the moment. "Am yow a bad boy?"

Cole laughed and inhaled smoke as the brunette pushed the cigarette back into his mouth. "No, ar'm a fuckin' angel bab." The girls laughed and Cole began to wonder about his chances of having them both together!

"When we were kids, this place was well known for the bad guys!" The big-eyed brunette spoke again and Cole was genuinely interested.

"Oh yeah, who were they?"

"Billy Mucklow used to be king raahnd here back in the day. He was always in this pub with his gang and mar Dad always told me to stay well away!" The brunette smiled and gazed deliberately into Cole's eyes.

"Yeah, that's why we started comin' here, cus it's naughty!" The tall blonde deliberately interrupted the ambiance between Cole and her friend and slowly turned and pushed her shapely buttocks into Coles crotch, her tight hot pants pushing closely into his most intimate area. *She wasn't going to let her mate get away with this one!*

"Where is Billy Mucklow now?" Cole's face changed a little and his voice became serious.

"Fuck knows, ar think he went to jail when ar was about 7!" The tall girl answered again and Cole's eyes narrowed, he loved a girl with a dirty mouth.

"Micky!" Barry O'Leary suddenly arrived from out of a door at the side of the bar and spotted Cole instantly. The two girls knew exactly who O'Leary was and that he represented the latest incarnation of 'bad boys' at the Haden Cross and they were impressed.

"Well, yow must be a bad boy if you know him!" The big-eyed brunette lent in closer to Cole and rested her exposed kneecap just below his crotch. He knew that his luck was in but he also knew that he had been invited back to the pub for a reason. He winked at the girl and turned to face O'Leary, *he would have to wait and see if the girls were still there waiting for him later!*

"Mr O'Leary." Micky smiled and downed the last of his lager. O'Leary laughed.

"Please mate, call me Barry." O'Leary clicked his fingers and gestured to the barman. "Another beer over here please, an one fer yourself!" Cole shook the second-generation Irishman's hand and looked around for the boss.

"Where's the gaffer?"

"Boo!" A voice behind Cole sounded in his ear and he instantly turned around to face his new employer. He was about 5 foot 9 with well-kept mousy brown hair that was beginning to turn grey. He wore an immaculate black suit with a matching black shirt and a snow-white tie. The man exuded both utter confidence and a nervous paranoia and when Cole looked into his eyes he met a stare that was equally as intense and intrusive as his own. Cole raised his arm to shake the boss's hand and the boss gripped it tightly. "Hello Mick… Barry has told me so much about you." The boss was in his mid-fortiess and had a cheeky swagger which like Micky Cole masked his mental instability.

"It's an honour to meet you Mr…?" Micky did not know his new employers name, but he hoped that the man would eventually be able to help him on his own personal quest.

"Hickman, Dickie Hickman, but yow can call me Dick." Hickman smiled at Cole and quickly downed his rum and coke. "Let's get some more fuckin' drinks boys!" Hickman turned to the barman and clicked his fingers, O'Leary had already ordered drinks but Hickman wanted more! One minute he was cool and calm, everybody's friend, the next minute he could be raging and ready to slit some guy's throat. He was extremely volatile and as he had moved into middle age he had become notably worse. The barman hurried with the drinks and brought them over. Hickman thanked him and then turned to face Cole, his expression changing somewhat. "Barry here tells me that yow used to work for Cedric Tanner?" Hickman spat the name with content. In reality, Dickie Hickman was of no threat to Cedric Tanner. The man was in a league above, but Hickman loved his own sense of self-importance and clung to the notion that Cedric Tanner was a direct rival to his own criminal 'empire.' The reality was that since he got out of prison just a few years previously, in the absence of Harry Scriven and Billy Mucklow, Dickie Hickman had tried to claim the Mucklow family's legacy as his own. But he was living on past glories and trying to live up to a reputation of 'glory days' long gone. He existed, he had a small hub of criminal activity that was more than enough for him to survive, enough for him to dress in fancy suits and pose inside Billy Mucklow and previously his father Willie Mucklow's room inside the Haden Cross. In Hickman's mind, Micky Cole was the new muscle in town who would help to put him and his small band of followers back on the map. Cole bit into his lower lip as Hickman waited for an answer and thought carefully about his reply.

"Yes ar used to work for Tanner." Even the mention of the name made Cole's blood boil with anger. "Is that a fuckin' problem? Ar dow work for him now." Hickman laughed.

"No mate, Barry said yow were touchy about the whole Cedric Tanner thing kid." Hickman continued to laugh and Cole struggled to hide his annoyance. "Look kid, ar respect your decision to want to come and work for me!" Hickman took out a miniature cigar and lit it. "Yer see Mick, ar'm Mr Big around here, the boss, number one. I'm the best fuckin' leader this gang has had since ode mon Willie Mucklow back in the 40s!" Barry O'Leary looked away. He knew exactly how Hickman had felt about Willie's successor Bill. He had absolutely worshipped the guy, but the problem was, Dick had never gotten over what happened and what his idol Bill Mucklow had done to him back in 55. He also knew that things were very different now to how they had been in the heydays of the early 50s.

"Yow with us tonight or what kid?" Hickman suddenly noticed that Cole was still distracted by the two young females who had moved over to the other side of the bar. Cole smiled and raised his right hand in apology. "Fair play aer kid, ar'd give em both one meself!" Hickman tapped Cole on the back and joined him in 'eyeing up' the leggy pair. "Which one yow want Mick? Ar dow care. If they'm still here when we get back from our business we will teck a bottle of Mateus Rose over to em! They will be on their backs in no time!" Hickman waved to the girls, downed his drink and looked at O'Leary. "Bazza, yow can gew home with Pam and her 5 friends!" Cole spat his beer back into his glass in laughter. *Dickie Hickman was lively and a genuinely funny guy, nothing like the paranoid loose cannon he had been warned about.* Hickman looked at his watch. "We got time fer coke. Yow want some Mick?"

"Ar'm happy with the beer and whisky to drink thanks Mr Hickman." Cole nodded towards his drinks, hoping that he had made the wrong assumption.

Hickman burst out laughing again. "No yer silly bastard, not coca fuckin' cola!" Hickman lent in closer and sniffed. "The white powder, Charlie, a fuckin' line!"

Cole raised his eyebrows and smiled excitedly. "Now yow'm talkin' mar language!" The pair went off to the gents together to snort a few lines of cocaine. The men seemed very much alike and had hit it off straight away, instant friends with a common goal that they would soon discover. Barry O'Leary looked the other way. He was old school and had been brought into this life back in the early 50s when he was a lost and aimless teenager fresh out of Borstal. Billy Mucklow had given him a job and Bill's cousin Harry Scriven had been his mentor, his role model and the first person he had ever looked up to. His parents had been violent alcoholics and the Police had beat him throughout his childhood. Barry O'Leary really looked up to and respected Bill Mucklow and Harry Scriven and he longed to return to more 'moral' times. *Sure, they had been vicious gangsters, but the world was a safer place with them around and they had both lived by strict moral codes. Sure, they could drink up their own body weight in beer and whisky and in later years they even enjoyed the odd joint, but Billy Mucklow and Harry Scriven were real men who would never have allowed cocaine in one of their pubs.* O'Leary sipped on his bitter and looked around the crowded bar. It was nothing like it used to be back in the day and he felt completely out of place. He often wondered why he was still there. He had heard that Billy Mucklow and Harry Scriven were now living it up in Spain somewhere and he made a mental promise to himself that one day he would look them up and go out there. *It would sure beat sitting around this place listening to 'Dickman' thinking he was 'Don Vito Corleone' from the Godfather, Hickman's favourite movie which had been released the previous year. Billy Mucklow always said that Hickman 'watched too many pictures' and he was bloody right!*

About twenty minutes later Hickman and Cole returned, their noses were red and their mouths displayed crazed almost disturbing grins. O'Leary knew of the extreme violence both men were capable of, as were Billy Mucklow and Harry Scriven. The difference was that the latter two were rational thinkers and were not out of their minds on drugs! Hickman contemplated more drinks but on inspection of his watch he announced that it was time for them to move on.

"Where we gewin then?" Cole drained the last of his lager and looked at the boss.

"We gorra' sort aaht some fuckers. They owe me money on a dope deal." Hickman pulled a long black Crombie overcoat from off a hat stand and gestured for the other two men to follow him out to the car park. Once there he tossed O'Leary the keys to his 1966-mark 10 Jaguar and nodded for Cole to get in the back alongside him. "Yow come in the back Mick, ar got some more Charlie!"

Micky Cole sank into the soft leather seats of the large luxurious Jaguar and felt like a king amongst the wood and sumptuous interior. Hickman emptied another line of cocaine into his hands and he eagerly snorted it all up, enjoying the instant buzz and rush of adrenaline. He sank back into the seat and Hickman handed him a cigar and lent over and lit it. "Thanks Mr Hickman."

"Please kid, call me Dick." Hickman lit a cigar for himself and tapped on the back of the passenger seat signalling for O'Leary to get moving.

It was a short drive, up the hill, over Haden Hill cross and then left into Harcourt Road where they entered a council estate that had been built in the 1960s. They followed the road through the estate for about half a mile until they came to a relatively modern pub, the Bull Terrier. O'Leary turned the Jag into the car park and both Hickman and Cole enjoyed the buzz of the cocaine and the anticipation of violence as they got out of the car. Hickman led the men into the pub and kicked the door open dramatically to signal their arrival. Micky was not impressed with Hickman's lack of subtlety but he followed unquestioningly. The pub was about half full and everyone in there turned their faces away in fear upon sight of the men. Dick Hickman still had a fearsome reputation locally and tales of his acts of cruelty were well known and stretched right back to the early 50s. A young woman at the bar smiled nervously and asked the men if she could help.

"Three bitters, three double Bells and three Hamlets on Tony Swift's tab." Hickman's face was straight and intimidating. The woman did not argue. Tony Swift was a drug dealer who lived on the estate and owed Hickman money. "Where is Swifty?" Hickman demanded menacingly as the woman poured the drinks. Several customers left the pub in order to avoid any trouble and most of those that remained went through to the room next door.

"Ar dow know Mr Hickman, he ay bin in tonight." The woman stuttered and both Barry O' Leary and even Micky Cole felt a little sorry for her. Cole was a ferocious thug, but his closeness to his late mother had given him a respect for women, though his vile treatment at the hands of his stepfather had made him open to and accepting of all sorts of violence towards men. After what his stepfather did to his grandad Norman when he was young child, Micky Cole never took the risk of telling his beloved mother of his abuse in case the same thing happened to her. Now that his mother was dead and he was grown, he had his own plans for Cedric Tanner!

Hickman picked up an empty glass from off the bar and slung it at a large mirror that hung at the back of the bar. He pulled out a flick knife and slammed it down hard on the bar.

"Ar know that yow'm his bird, an if he ay in here before 11 them ar'm gunna cut that fuckin' dog ugly face of yowers so bad that he woh ever wanna fuck yer again!" The woman tensed in fear and almost wet herself. She struggled to regulate her breathing and nodded. Barry O'Leary looked on in despair. *If Billy Mucklow and Harry Scriven could see what had become of their old firm, they would be mortified. But who was he to judge? Hickman still took old man Willie Mucklow and Eli Davis out for a drink on a Sunday afternoon and he bought Willie's wife flowers on her birthday, what did Billy Mucklow have to do with his aged parents?*

The scared woman went over to the other side of the bar in the room next door and Hickman watched her intently, ensuring that she was not trying to escape! She bent and whispered a message to a local who was a mutual friend of hers and Tony Swift. She told him of her predicament and that she needed him to fetch Tony and his brothers straight away. The man nodded and set off casually across the bar and out onto the estate to find the drug dealer.

Cole sat on a stool at the bar next to Hickman and O'Leary. He lit his Hamlet cigar and hoped that Swift would make an appearance soon as 'Life on Mars' by David Bowie began to play on the juke box. He was not a huge fan of David Bowie but he did like this song. "I hate this fuckin' shit." Dick Hickman was clearly not impressed with the music and he looked at Cole and O'Leary in anticipation of their opinions. He had literally gone from a raving thug who was eager and more than willing to cut an innocent women's face off to his cheeky, smiling, one of the lads, self in less than a minute.

"Tay mar cup of tay Dick." O'Leary sipped his whisky and offered his opinion.

"Yer cor beat ode Frank!" Hickman lit his cigar and made reference to Frank Sinatra. O'Leary said nothing but he knew that Hickman was mimicking his old boss Billy Mucklow, the man that they were never allowed to talk about! Billy Mucklow had been a passionate Sinatra fan and O'Leary knew that despite Hickman's supposed hatred of their old employer, deep down he truly missed the man who had once been like a messiah to him. Bill Mucklow had brought Dick Hickman into the gang in the late 40s when his father Willie took early retirement along with his ever-faithful stepbrother Eli Davis. Mucklow junior had overseen the most lucrative and successful period in the family's history from 1948 onwards, but a fallout with London gangsters in 1955 saw him go to prison for a long stretch alongside his protégé Dickie Hickman. From the moment Hickman got out of prison at the start of the 70s, Billy Mucklow's name was never to be mentioned, but it was obvious to everyone that Hickman still idolised the man.

About twenty minutes later the front door swung open and in walked three unsavoury looking men. In the middle was a tall man in an afghan coat, his fingers covered in tattoos and sovereign rings. He was in his late 30s and was balding with a rather pathetic 'comb over' pulled over the top of his head.

"Yow wanna see me Dick?" Tony Swift was unintimidated by the situation and the two men either side of him produced cricket bats from under their long Parka coats. The man to the left looked mean and angry but the man to the right appeared slightly nervous and apprehensive. Hickman stood up from his bar stool and stubbed out his cigar in a green Banks's ashtray.

"Tony... Yow know why ar'm here aer kid." Hickman was relatively friendly in his manner, the knife remaining on the table next to his beer, whisky and cigars. In his younger days Hickman was an exceptionally skilled boxer who had boxed at a professional level and could have been a serious contender if it had not been for his obsession with being a gangster!

"Ar dow appreciate yow threatening mar wench!" Swift allowed a tone of annoyance to enter his voice.

"Ar dow appreciate yow not payin' me mar fuckin money!" Hickman suddenly flew forwards and straight into Swift's face. "Now pay up now or ar will deliver on what ar said!"

Swift gritted his teeth angrily and was not impressed. "Fuck you Dick!"

"What, yer mean yer dow wanna see that ugly slut over there cut up like a piece of meat?" Hickman laughed cruelly. "If she was half decent ar would av let yow off with a blow job a piece for the lads! Now give me mar fuckin' money now!" The comment infuriated Swift, his face erupted with anger and he shoved Hickman with such force that the shorter man nearly fell over, but Hickman's eyes suddenly changed as the mixture of cocaine, alcohol and adrenaline drove through his veins like a raging fire. He lunged forwards and executed a ferocious and precise boxing combination of punches. Although not as fast as he once was, the onetime boxing legend quickly knocked Swift to the ground with a flurry of technique. The two men either side tried to intervene but Cole and O'Leary had now dived into action alongside their leader. O'Leary smashed a chair off the nervous looking man's head and then continued to throw clumsy punches and kicks until the man covered his face and scurried into a corner to cower away. The second brother stood bat in hand and glared at Cole without a hint of fear. He clumsily swung the bat in Cole's direction and the younger man dodged it easily. The same routine repeated a couple of times and Cole sensed his opponent was tiring. As the man swung the bat again, Cole quickly dodged and lunged forwards to grab him. He punched him hard in the stomach and the man dropped the bat to the floor. Cole quickly stooped and picked it up before swiping it across the man's head and sending him into a semi-conscious state. *This was it, his big chance to prove his worth and get into Hickman's good books!* What happened next would remain in the memory of all that were in the Bull Terrier pub that night for a very long time. Both Dick Hickman and the half dazed Tony Swift, who lay upon the floor looked on with a mixture of horror and in Hickman's case amusement as Cole lay the semi-conscious brother across the table and pulled down the man's trousers! He then pulled back the handle of the cricket bat and firmly rammed it upwards and into the man's anus. The man jolted across the table and let out a harrowing yelp of pain as Dickie Hickman exploded in laughter. "Right then yow bunch of bastards, any other fucker tecks a swing at me and ar'm a gunna shove it up there arsehole too! Now pay up!" Cole brought his face down to Tony Swift and gave him a look that Swift daren't argue with. He handed over the vast majority of the money that was owed and he escaped the same fate as his brother! Micky Cole was not in the habit of hurting women and he was pleased with himself. *His decisive action had eradicated the need for Dick to take a knife to Swift's Mrs's face and he may even be able to make it back to the Haden Cross before the big-eyed brunette left!* Hickman was more than pleased too, he had employed a man after his own heart and he had found a new best friend!

Chapter 15

"And now, the end is near, and so I face the final curtain!" Dick Hickman lay back in his chair, listening to music and singing along with the lyrics as he relaxed inside the Haden Cross. It was well past midnight and everyone had left apart from Hickman, Cole and the barman who was anxiously waiting for them to leave. My Way had been a major hit for Frank Sinatra and had been released in early 1969. In the UK it became the recording with the most weeks spent inside the top 40, spending 75 weeks there from April 1969 until September 1971. Sinatra had recorded the song in just one take on 30th December 1968 after fellow singer Paul Anka wrote alternative English lyrics to the original which had been in French. By all accounts, Sinatra and Anka had been at a dinner with some gangster pals from the Mafia when Sinatra (in Anka's words) announced "I'm quitting the business. I'm sick of it; I'm getting the hell out." This conversation inspired Anka to rewrite the original French song from the prospective of Frank Sinatra to mark his potential departure from the music business. Despite the song's great success, Sinatra would grow to hate it, but to Dick Hickman it was his favourite song. Sinatra's music reminded him of happier times and often he would sit alone in the side bar, after hours with a large Scotch, cigars, the comforting sound of Sinatra's voice and his precious memories.

Hickman suddenly stopped singing and threw his empty glass across the room as if he was throwing it at an invisible spirit entity. He had been upbeat and happy after the successful trip to see Tony Swift, though the two young ladies had long gone when they returned, but after copious amounts of alcohol and other substances his mood was partial to sudden changes at any time. Micky Cole was not afraid.

"Mick, why the fuck am yow here?" Hickman looked at the floor and shook his head before taking the half empty whisky bottle from off the table and drinking straight from the bottle. "Ar mean, ar'm a fuckin' looser… Look at me, who the fuck am ar tryin' to kid?" Hickman almost became teary eyed as he wallowed in the maudlin morbidity of his self-pity. Cole took a long drag of his cigarette and sat up. The time had come.

"I think you can help me with something Dick… I think we could help each other." Cole's eyes were deadly serious and Hickman was almost intrigued, *but Cole was just a kid, 22, 23 years old?*

"What's that then mate?" Hickman laughed and passed the bottle to his young associate.

"Revenge." Cole's tone was straight to the point. He poured more whisky into his glass and placed the bottle back on to the table.

"What?" Hickman grabbed the bottle again. "Yow want me to gew up against Cedric Tanner cus he fiddled with yer when yow was a kid?" Hickman emitted an insensitive laugh and Cole bit into his own lip and restrained himself mentally, he needed Hickman. "Sorry kid, I ay all that! Ar'm just some washed up has been trying to adjust to life outside of prison." Hickman looked at his reflection in the window with an embarrassed self-loathing. Before Cole could explain any misconception Hickman spoke again. "Three years ar bin aaht of jail an ar still ay got used to it… 15 years, 15 fuckin' years of mar life!" The rage began to build intensely inside of Hickman as he watched himself in the reflection with utter hatred. He clung to the whisky bottle tightly and then suddenly drove it hard and straight into his own face. Blood and whisky instantly discoloured his shirt and tie and he shook violently for about 20 seconds as Cole looked on. Cole had spent most of his life with a similar disposition though he had little sympathy, only an understanding and acceptance of what to him was completely normal behaviour. Hickman wiped the blood and whisky from his eyes and turned to look at his new friend. "A lot has changed since 1955 Mick."

"All the more reason for revenge." Cole sipped his whisky a little slower as the remainder of the bottle was dripping a scarlet mess from Dick Hickman's face. How many hours he had spent watching blood drain from his own wrists, the scars there as a shameful reminder. "I ay talkin' abaaht Cedric Tanner… I will sort that on my own, believe me!" Cole grinned a wicked, evil grin and Hickman began to feel intrigued again as his routine self-loathing was slowly passing.

"Who then?" Hickman lit a cigarette and waited for a reply.

"Harry Scriven…"

Hickman winced at the sound of the name and he could feel the anger begin to build again. "We do not mention that name!" Hickman instantly tried to push the name from out of his mind.

"Harry Scriven and for yourself, Billy Mucklow." Cole spoke the names with no fear and looked at Hickman in anticipation. Hickman closed his eyes, breathed deeply and remained silent for well over a minute.

"Why?" Hickman eventually opened his eyes and focused his gaze on Cole. Cole took a drink and adjusted his position in his chair.

"Because Harry Scriven is my real father…" Cole took another drink and waited for a response. Hickman smiled and nodded, the bloody cuts on his face making him look menacing in the dimly lit room. *He knew that the kid reminded him of someone, he hadn't been able to quite put his finger on it, but now it was obvious. Micky was a 'chip of the old block,' a thug, a gangster, a genuine Mucklow, of course he was Harry Scriven's blood!* "That bastard fucked off and left mar mother on her own and because of that I had to grow up being bounced around by Cedric Tanner!" It was Cole's turn to get emotional, it came out of nowhere but tears were in his eyes and Hickman actually felt compassion. Cole's eyes narrowed again as he regained his composure. "I heard that yow were livid with Bill Mucklow, so I figured we could team up and take them both down?"

"Who told yer I was angry with Bill?" Hickman found it physically difficult to say the name.

"My mother before she died. She never got over Scriven. She read all about the trial in the papers back in the day. I know because she saved them and I found the cuttings in a shoe box. Inside were love letters, an old black and white photograph of the two of them together alongside some keep sakes of mine when I was a baby." Cole became choked again at the thought of his deceased mother but he did not embarrass himself. Hickman wiped more blood from his brow and looked at an old 1940s clock that had stood on the mantel piece for many years.

"Bill Mucklow was like a fuckin' god to me kid." Hickman smiled again and settled back into his chair and lit a cigar. "I looked up to that man, fuck I loved him more than my own father!" A salty tear fell from his eye and trickled into an open wound. "Back in 55, we did a job, a robbery… Me, Bill, Harry and some kid called Cooper. It was fuckin' beautiful, we took fuckin' thousands of pounds worth of jewellery right from under the noses of some London firm." Hickman enjoyed the memory and looked aimlessly into thin air as if the invisible spectre had returned. "Anyway, we pissed off a lot of people, the wrong fuckin' people. But Bill day give a fuck, he wor gunna give the stash back! Fuck em he said." Cole could tell by the way Hickman spoke about his old employer that he still had a lot of admiration for the man. "Me and Bill, we went off to New York to try and sell the gear we had nicked. Was fantastic. Big bars, clubs, fancy Italian dinners with these mob guys… We thought we were gunna' get whacked but they were decent lads, was amazing. They laid on whores and booze and everything. God what a time!" Hickman became animated and spoke enthusiastically. "They paid us well for the stuff we had nicked from the London firm so we set off back for England with these fuckin' cases full of money, ar mean fuckin' shed loads! Anyway, we get back to England and Bill disappears with all the cash. The next thing I know, Bill's been arrested and the Cozzers are after me! So ar'm on the fuckin' run ay I? Fuck knows where the money has gone and every copper this side of fuckin' London is after me…" Hickman's mood appeared to be changing slightly. "So they eventually grab me in this whore house in Birmingham, fuckin' Boswell's lot grassed me up ar'm sure of it! So, we gew to court, an there he is…" Tears began to flow freely from Hickman's eyes and he shook his head with the pain of the memory. "Fuckin' Billy Mucklow, my hero, my god, my master, the man I would have followed to the end of the world, grassin', giving evidence against me! All to protect himself and keep fuckin' Scriven's name out of it." Hickman wiped his eyes again and held his head in his hands. "Bill got out in 68 and headed straight to Spain." Cole suddenly looked up with great interest, now he was getting somewhere with regards to finding out the whereabouts of his biological father! Hickman remained utterly miserable and continued his story. "I stayed in jail until 1970 and guess what?" Hickman shook his head again and tried to make sense of things as he had been trying to do for the last 20 years. "Harry fuckin' Scriven escaped to Spain in 1955, marries some Spanish whore and opens a fuckin' casino! By the time Bill got out there in 68 they were fuckin' millionaires! Yow hear a lot of things in prison Mick… What did I get? Ar did the job too, all I got was longer porridge whilst them pair am livin' it up! It ay fuckin' fair!" Hickman beat his fist down hard on the table but instantly felt better for getting the story from off his chest. He had not spoken to anyone about it in 20 years and the fact that Cole also had a motive to destroy Scriven and Mucklow made him almost feel like 'a problem shared was a problem halved' but the pangs of anger still bit hard at him. His hero had done him wrong and he had paid a high price. What hurt most of all was that he was utterly lost and helpless without Bill Mucklow and he still longed more than anything to be able to return to simpler, happier times. Micky Cole could tell how bitter and angry Hickman was and he knew that he would be able to use this to his advantage.

"So let's do it. Let's fuckin' kill the bastards! They fuckin' deserve it!" Cole's eyes were deadly serious but Hickman began to laugh hysterically.

"Fuckin' hell kid, yow wanna' murder a lot of people, Harry Scriven, Bill Mucklow, Cedric Tanner? Yow'll need a fuckin' army to take down those guys. Yow'm a tough kid, ar'll give you that, but those men are all hard bastards, as hard as they come." Hickman was beginning to regain his realistic sense of normality.

"That's why I need your help Dick." Cole waited for a response that didn't come. "Well at least just tell me where ar can find Scriven in Spain?" Cole's enthusiasm impressed Hickman, but *he was still just a kid*. Hickman stood up and walked over to the window. The wind had got up and it had begun to rain. It tore at the windows and howled hauntingly across the old room as Hickman looked out into the dismal night sky.

"Let's just see what happens aer kid… Yow come an work for me for a bit and we will see what happens.

The next day was cold and miserable. Dark clouds hung in the sky and every so often there would be short burst of rain. Lucy Price walked up the road that led to her 4-bedroom detached home in Cotwall End Road Sedgley. Her husband Davey Price worked for the much-feared Cedric Tanner and served as his right-hand man and second in command. He was only young, but Tanner was particularly fond of him and above all he was obedient and a capable thug. His wife Lucy was in her early to mid-20s, of average build with a pretty face, blue eyes and light blonde hair. She wore lots of make-up, a black leather skirt, red heels and a matching black leather jacket. She pushed her hands deep into her pockets and shivered with the cold, not noticing as she neared the house the Vauxhall Cresta PA that was parked opposite and stalking her every move.

Micky Cole sat in the driver's seat of the Cresta PA and watched the young woman with mixed feelings. He had smoked several cigarettes whilst waiting for the woman to return and had swallowed a cocktail of pills, but as usual, upon sight of her he had frozen and worried about the necessary task he so very much did not want to carry out. *He must do it sometime soon!* He thought to himself. *She was as guilty as the others and sooner or later she would need to be punished.* He closed his eyes and allowed the painful memories to ascend upon his tortured and twisted mind.

They had been just 16 years old and Lucy Harris, as she was previously known, was the love of Micky Cole's life. She sat behind him at school and had felt sorry for him despite his angst and aggression towards his peers and teachers, she actually saw something deeper in him and the pair fell into adolescent love. The memory of his feelings for her filled his mind alongside memories of his mother and a tear emerged from his left eye. Lucy Harris had been perfect, sweet and innocent. Apart from his mother she was the only decent thing in his life at that time and she most definitely had the potential to save him from a life of crime, substance abuse and violence. He lit another cigarette and could feel the tears flowing down his face. He closed his eyes, lent back in his seat and drifted back to a hot summer in the mid-1960s.

It was August 1965 and Cole had taken Lucy down to the side of the 'cut' and produced a cheap engagement ring and asked the young girl to marry him. He knew that they were only 16, but lots of people married young. His intention had been for them to get engaged and then marry when they both turned 18. What happened next would go on to torture him endlessly. As he blew smoke across the lonely interior of the car he allowed the memory to become vivid in his mind.

He looked nervously into the eyes of his blonde beloved and summoned up the courage to produce the cheap ring he had saved up to buy. In that moment, the school loner, recluse and 'damaged angry child' bared his soul to her, revealed his true feelings and lay completely and utterly at her mercy. His mother, teachers, doctors and other medical professionals had never been able to unlock the inner person behind the anger and the hate, but in that moment he was willing to give himself to Lucy Harris, fully and unconditionally. Maybe the young girl was nervous, maybe she did not mean to be quite so insensitive, but her reaction was unforgiveable. At first, she laughed, cruelly and mockingly.

"Mick, ar came here today to tell yow ar'm breaking up with you. Dow be so bloody saft." She continued to laugh and before he could get his thoughts together the ever so smug Davey Price appeared out of nowhere. Price was older

than himself and worked for his stepfather Cedric Tanner which made him untouchable. His face was mocking and overtly confident as he walked over and grabbed Lucy around the waist, lowering his hand to cop a feel of her buttocks.

"Lucy's with me now fag boy." Davey laughed and spat used chewing gum onto his shirt. In that second he looked at Lucy, his unrequited love met with cruel giggling eyes. If it was ever possible for him to feel even more broken than he already was, now was the time. "Do you know why we call him fag boy Lucy?" The blonde giggled and shook her head. "Cus he's a dirty little shirt lifter... Mr Tanner told me that. Right ay it fag boy?" Lucy continued to laugh harder and harder as he turned away sadly and began to walk, his torment continuing as both Davey and now Lucy taunted him and chanted "Fag boy, fag boy." The ring he had bought with money his grandmother had given him remained on the floor, unnoticed and unappreciated.

Lucy Harris went on to marry Davey Price and as he rose up through Tanner's organization he would continue to bully and torment Cole, knowing that his closeness to the boss would protect him from any attempted violence. What he did not understand was that Micky Cole was definitely one to hold onto a grudge and slowly and surely, the bitter and severely twisted young man continued to develop his deeply disturbing plans for revenge. He watched Lucy disappear into the house and then started up the engine to leave. *It was vital to his plans that when the time was right she would suffer, as would the others. Only then would he be able to truly find peace and put himself out of the insufferable misery that continued to warp his mind.*

Chapter 16

She wore black lacy underwear that looked alluring against her tanned coffee coloured skin. Micky Cole lay back on his red leather sofa and smoked a joint as he watched his mixed-race girlfriend move around their flat in her knickers. As he watched and smoked, an incense stick burnt a sickly aroma into the room that blended with the marijuana to create a relaxed and sweet-smelling haze. Cole was not a fan of television and on a small table next to him stood a portable record player that was currently blasting 'Child in time' by Deep Purple. The songs eerie entrance chords featuring Jon Lord on Hammond organ contributed to the brooding atmosphere of the room and Cole enjoyed a rare moment of relaxation.

"Yow gewin ahht today bab?" Cathy smiled at him lovingly. It was only 8:30 in the morning and smoking 'weed' and listening to this sort of music was somewhat early even by Micky Cole's standards. It was never too early for whisky, cocaine or even Quaaludes, but after being in a relationship with Cole for well over 12 months she had begun to understand his habits and routines. Smoking joints was a 'chilling' activity and was usually saved for later in the day.

"Ar dow know, ar'm just enjoying the view." Cole winked and returned the smile. After what had happened during his youth with Lucy Harris he had promised himself that he would never get close to anyone again, but Cathy Richardson was different. He still tried hard to keep his distance emotionally, but the longer they spent together the more difficult this had become. She had had a similar upbringing to himself and therefore she did not look at or react to his past with pity or disgust. She understood it.

Cathy Richardson had been brought up on a tough estate in Dudley. Her father was a black Jamaican who had impregnated her white mother when she was just 18 before swiftly disappearing. Not only did Cathy's mother have to deal with the early 1950s prejudice of her being a single teenage mother, but also the fact that her child was black in an overtly racist society. Even her own parents disowned her but the fact that she was a particularly attractive woman meant that she was not out in the cold or 'on the shelf' for long. Cathy's mother quickly fell in with a white man who was slightly older than herself who took her in and eventually married her. The fact that she had a half black child was frowned upon by the man but his own lack of personality or good looks meant that he was willing to accept the 'shameful' step child in order for him to obtain a wife who was substantially more attractive than himself. The couple eventually had 'good wholesome white children' of their own and Cathy was constantly aware that these children were her parent's priority. Her stepfather treated her with a great deal of content at times, though mostly he was just indifferent and constantly regarded her with a look of irritation and distaste. However, when Cathy started to mature into an attractive teenager, she began to attract unwelcome attention from her stepfather that would eventually result in her running away from the family after her mother had refused to believe in any wrongdoing from her husband. After a brief period being groomed for prostitution in Wolverhampton by Cedric Tanner's criminal organization, this was where she first met Micky Cole. He was a little older than her and had appeared slightly different to the other gangsters she was around. He was confident and chatty with women, but she could tell that this was a front and that he had an inner sensitivity and vulnerability that defied his tough macho gangster persona. She knew that he had a reputation for violence, but he was a good-looking lad with intense blue eyes that always seemed to hang onto her gaze a little longer than he should have. They quickly became an item and Cathy no longer had to worry about a life on the streets.

    She was tall, slim with curves in all the right places and had a stunningly beautiful face with immensely pretty brown eyes. Her hair was jet black and long which after spending hours with an iron was usually straight, though often, like today, it was in its natural curly 'afro' style.

He watched her bend over the chair whilst tidying the flat and as ever he liked what he saw. She really was a potential distraction to his vengeful plans. Part of him longed to leave the past in the past and move on and enjoy his life with Cathy, but a monster inside of him could never let that happen. He understood that he was a slave to the monster and that he would never be free from it until he did what he had to do. He often wondered about what would happen to Cathy. He never worried about himself, he assumed, even hoped that he would be killed in his quest for revenge. It was a preferable option to spending life in prison, *but what would happen to Cathy?* She was blissfully unaware of the true extent of his plans and she hoped that one day maybe they would marry and start a family. Micky Cole could never think like that, not until the monster inside of him was truly slain. He continued to eye Cathy with a mixture of cautious love and pity. *Was he putting her in danger?* He pondered the question for a few minutes before concluding that without him she would be walking the streets of Wolverhampton and Walsall selling sex.

He stood up and moved over to the window of the rented tower block flat. Micky and Cathy had moved to The Riddins Mound council estate about 3 months previously when Cole's mother had died. The estate was built near Halesowen Road railway overbridge in the 1960s and stood between the town of Old Hill and the more affluent area of Haden Hill where Bill Mucklow and Harry Scriven had previously lived. From out of the window in its elevated position he could see the autumnal sun slowly rising and casting shadows across the town of Old Hill. He knew that this area had significance to his biological father's family and he figured that this would be the ideal place to base himself as he began to make enquiries as to the whereabouts of him. He also knew that his mother and her family were originally from the area too so it made no sense to remain at his old address in the vicinity of the Tanners whom he despised with a passion. He sucked on the last dregs of his joint before stubbing it out in a cheap ashtray he had drunkenly taken from some pub when there was a sudden knock at the door. Cathy shrieked in shock. She was barely dressed and quickly disappeared into the bedroom to cover herself up. Micky Cole was not used to visitors, not many people knew of his most recent address and he approached the door cautiously. "Who is it?"

"Me… Dick, yer saft bastard." Cole recognised the voice of his new employer Dickie Hickman and promptly opened the door.

"Sorry mate, I ay lived here long so ar gorra be careful." Cole gestured for Hickman to come in and as he walked through the door the smell of incense and marijuana hit him instantly.

"Fuckin' hell mate, what yow bin smokin' in here aer kid?" Hickman coughed and joked and looked up to see Cole's girlfriend Cathy emerge from the bedroom. She wore knee high leather boots, a ridiculously short tartan skirt and a mustard polo neck jumper that was tight and celebrated her generously proportioned breasts. Hickman was instantly impressed but he wanted to keep Cole on his side as a more than useful thug so he had to be tactful. "And who is this sexy piece?" As usual his mouth ran away with itself. Cole took no offense in the comment and replied in good humour.

"This is my girlfriend Cathy… Cathy meet Mr Hickman, my new boss." Cathy outstretched her right hand to shake Hickman's. She had met many men like this before, middle aged gangsters with their sharp suits, fancy cars and violent dishonest intentions. She truly hoped that her Micky would not end up like this! Hickman looked her up and down again and kissed her on the cheek whilst copping a cheeky feel of her bottom.

"Ar got a bit of work for yer aer kid." Hickman looked down at Cole's attire. He wore a house coat and was barefoot. "Best get dressed son."

Hickman's Jag was parked in the street outside the tower block. "Get in aer kid. Yow can drive." Dick Hickman opened the passenger door and handed Cole the keys.

"Where we gewin?" Cole started the car and enjoyed the majestic rumble of the straight 6 engine as he teased the accelerator pedal. Hickman put his finger to his lip to shush him and turned the radio up to hear the song. 'I left my heart in San Francisco' by Tony Bennett was another one of Hickman's favourites and he attempted to sing along as the big saloon roared off up the street. It was clear to Micky Cole that Hickman's mental state was prone to extreme highs and desperate lows and that he was dangerously unstable. "I need to know where ar'm a driving mate." Cole revved the car aggressively and enjoyed the power of the vehicle. Hickman used his right arm to point the way until the song finished and he tuned the radio down.

"We'm gewin' to Tanhouse. A chap there owes me money." Hickman lit a cigarette and continued to direct them through the streets.

"Where's that?" Cole had heard of the notorious estate, but he had been bought up mostly in the Coseley, Tipton and Sedgley areas of the Black Country so he was not overtly familiar with his new surroundings.

"It ay far aer kid." Hickman blew smoke across the cabin, he had plans. "There's a chap there, a fuckin' drug addict. He owes me money." Hickman grinned menacingly. "Ar told him that if he day pay me this week ar would teck one of his fingers." Hickman pulled a pair of lethal looking pliers from his pocket and laughed. "Billy Mucklow showed me how to use these things back in the day." Cole could not help but think that Hickman was somewhat obsessed with Billy Mucklow. "I remember one time, me an yower ode mon held this bloke down whilst Bill wound his fingers through one of them ode fashioned mangles." Hickman erupted into laughter at the memory. "And then, when we were done, I asked the poor bloke which hand he used to jerk off with!" Hickman roared in laughter at his own story and Cole smiled, but one aspect of Hickman's story from the old days bothered him.

"What do you mean, my ode mon?"

"Harry Scriven, he's your ode mon ay he?" Hickman spoke about the men he supposedly hated in good humour and Cole was confused. Hickman's feelings regarding his old associates were mixed and extremely deep routed. There really was a fine line between love and hate and Cole began to wonder if he had made the right choice in teaming up with Dickie Hickman.

"That bastard may be my biological father, but he ay mar fuckin' ode mon! He fucked off before I was born and as a result I got fucked over, literally!" Cole resisted the urge to slam the brakes on and put Hickman's head through the window. Hickman quickly changed the subject.

"Ar want yow to do it Mick." Hickman suddenly interrupted Cole's thoughts and his expression completely changed.

"Do what?" Cole turned the wheel and looked at Hickman.

"Cut the chap's finger off." Hickman watched Cole closely to gauge his reaction.

"Ok." Cole shrugged and continued to watch the road in front of him, unaware that he was being scrutinized.

"Ar bin thinkin' a lot abaaht what yow said the other night Mick." Hickman looked out of the window and pointed to where he wanted Cole to park the Jag. "Hopefully it will still be here when we get back!" Hickman wasn't joking. Tanhouse was a residential area of Halesowen situated in the west of the town near the border with Stourbridge and had been built in the 1960s. It consisted of three multi storey tower blocks, Kipling House, Byron House and Chaucer House. When the flats were first built the residents praised them as they offered a higher standard of living conditions than the older properties from which they had been rehoused. However, decline soon set in and the area became one of the most troubled estates in the Midlands with frequent problems with drug abuse, burglary, vandalism, graffiti, car crime and violence.

The man Hickman wanted to see lived high up near the top of Byron House and just the thought of the long climb up the stairs was an annoyance to him, but there was also another purpose to today's visit and as the two men began to climb the stairs Hickman elaborated further on what he had begun to say in the car. "I cor gew on like this Mick. Ghostin' abaaht this shite hole, chasing after druggies through corridors and stairways that stink of piss!" Hickman sniffed and gestured to their surroundings. "All whilst Billy Mucklow and Harry Scriven am livin' it up in Spain on money ar went to jail for!" The anger was rapidly creeping back into Hickman's voice and Cole genuinely worried that the older man had brought them there so that he could throw himself off the top of the flats. "Did yow mean what you said Mick? Abaaht killin' Bill and Harry? Or was that just the drink talking?"

"I've never been so serious about anything in my life mate." As they neared the top of the tower block Cole looked out on a grand view of Colley Gate, Cradley Heath and further into the Black Country as he watched black smoke belch furiously into the air from the vast array of huge chimneys. There was a constant thundering of heavy factory hammers and an industrial smell that clung to the very fabric of the air in which they breathed.

"The thing is Mick, yow wanna kill a lot of folks, yow'm a very angry young man and what ar wanna know is just how fucked up am yer? Do you have what it takes to murder someone or am yow just full of bull shit?" Hickman threw his cigarette to the floor and stopped and nodded as they came to a doorway that was high up in Byron House flats. "Oi Carter, open up, it's the big bad wolf!" Hickman hammered on the door with his fist and waited for a response. He loved being the bad guy, the pantomime villain, the old cloak and dagger.

"Yow ay gunna hurt me Mr Hickman am yer?" A muffled voice replied, it was weak and sounded lost.

"Just open the fuckin' door before ar lose mar temper!" Hickman screamed and soon a key began to turn in the lock.

Inside the flat was an utter disgrace. There was not a single piece of furniture as all of Carter's possessions had been sold to fund his drug habit and all that lay in a corner of the foul-smelling room was a filthy old blanket that was surrounded by empty vodka bottles, syringes, excrement, urine and cigarette butts. "Fuckin' stinks in here Carter." Ollie Carter cowered on the floor as Dick Hickman stood over him, his black leather gloves and long black Crombie coat making him look threatening and menacing within the unlit, sub humane room. "Yow got mar money Carter?" Carter began to sob and got on his knees and began to beg as Hickman had hoped he would.

"Please Mr Hickman, please, ar got nothing." The lad sobbed and Cole almost felt pity for him. Drugs were a dangerous game and he knew that from personal experience. Carter was younger than himself. Cole thought that he was probably about 21 years old and he wondered about the circumstances that had led to the squalor of his current situation. Hickman looked over at Cole without sympathy or compassion and nodded. Cole responded by kicking Carter hard in the chest so that he was winded and fell sideways onto the floor. The man was particularly thin and extremely weak. Hickman passed Cole the pliers and watched as his young associate pinned Carter to the floor with his right foot and pulled the man' submissive hand out and held it in place. He applied the pliers to Carter's little finger and shoved the levers together forcefully and then yanked at the bone. Carter let out an inhumane, blood curdling scream that echoed throughout the filth ridden room as Cole continued to yank and twist at gristle and bone. Hickman was impressed by Cole's eagerness, but it was obvious that he had never done it before. Billy Mucklow had been particularly skilled with a pair of pliers and had taught Hickman the 'trick of the trade.' The finger eventually came loose and dropped to the floor in a bloody mess as Carter lay barely conscious. Cole looked up at Hickman and raised his eyebrows. *Had he done enough to convince his new boss that he was capable of killing Harry Scriven?*

Hickman looked at him coldly and produced a carving knife from his pocket. "Let's see if yow'm up to it kid… Slit his fuckin' throat." The druggie heard the instruction and he managed to utter a protest. Cole looked down at the man and pondered his dilemma. He genuinely did not want to kill the lad, but he needed to prove to Dickie Hickman that he was capable. *He would have to try and call his bluff.* He looked back at the middle-aged gangster, shrugged and held out his hand for the knife.

"Ok. Whatever you say." He coldly took the knife and shifted back over to Carter who was sobbing with the pain of his severed finger and at the prospect of his impending execution. The young man looked on with terror as a thousand thoughts went through his mind. He thought about how he had ended up in this predicament, he thought of his siblings, he thought of a girl he once knew and he thought of his mother. *His entire short life he had been one big let-down and disappointment and now he was to pay the ultimate price.* Cole grabbed him by his filthy matted hair, pulled back his head and brought the knife to his throat.

"Cut him!" Hickman commanded, his eyes cold and full of indifference. Cole pulled back the knife and applied a small amount of pressure to the side of Carter's neck. The knife turned crimson with blood and Cole was on the verge of casting the knife aside. *This man did not deserve to die and he was not prepared to murder him to simply prove a point to Dickie Hickman.* "Stop… That ul' do." Hickman's words were an absolute blessing and Micky Cole worked hard to not show his relief. He let the man's hair go and Carter pulled away with his life still intact. Hickman began to laugh hysterically and then produced a tube of pills from his pocket and emptied them onto the floor. "Here Carter, have these on the house kid. But meck sure yow pay next time or ar'll teck another finger." Hickman reached into his pocket again and produced a clean handkerchief which he tossed to Carter. "Put this on yer hand and gew and see a doctor. Tell em yer caught it in a door." He gestured to Cole with his head for them to leave and the two men went back out into the corridor. Cole secretly hoped that the kid would be ok, but he continued to maintain his cold and tough persona in front of Hickman. "Yow really am a vicious bastard ay yer aer kid." Hickman smiled as they began their long descent of the stairway. "Looks like yow got yourself a partner."

Chapter 17

Micky Cole sat in the driver's side of the stationary Jag and watched the red and brown leaves flutter around in the autumn wind. It was only 6 o'clock in the evening but it was already dark outside. Cole's girlfriend Cathy had very little contact with her family, but she always made a point of visiting once a year on her mother's birthday with a card and some cheap chocolates. Cole always sat outside and waited in the car, he was not welcome in there and he also knew that if he ever caught sight of Cathy's stepfather he would find it very hard to keep his cool and not seriously hurt the man. After what he had put Cathy through as a child, Cole had often considered putting her stepfather on his list of people to get even with, but she was a much better person than he was and would never condone such violence. He often wondered how Cathy would react to his life plans and what she would do if she knew of the extreme violence he was capable of and enjoyed as part of his career.

The Wrens Nest Estate in Dudley, known locally as 'The Wrenna' was largely built between 1935 and 1939 to rehouse families from town centre slum areas. The estate had a tough reputation and became notorious for its levels of depravity and crime. Cathy Richardson had spent her childhood on the estate and her mother, stepfather and half siblings still lived there. On this night, she had insisted that Cole brought her over to visit in Hickman's Jag as she liked the idea of 'bettering' her own family who had treated her so badly. Cole had initially had reservations about parking the luxury vehicle in such a tough area and even though he was to wait with the car, the last thing he needed was to get arrested for fighting off potential vandals and thieves. But as so often was the case, all Cathy had to do was flutter her pretty brown eyes and offer 'other incentives' in order to get her own way.

Later that evening, Cole and Cathy were due to pick up Dickie Hickman and his lady friend and accompany them to The Regis Club in Old Hill. Hickman loved to make a big entrance and to have one of his associates drop him off at the front door so that he could emerge from the back of his Jaguar wearing a perfect suit whilst accompanied by his notoriously attractive lady friend. His organisation may have been on the decline, but he still liked to look the part. Micky Cole had also dressed for the occasion, he wore a black suit, a white shirt with oversized collars and an off-white tie. As he sat in the Jag in the middle of one of the Midlands biggest slum areas, he checked his watch and wondered what was taking so long. *Fuck it, who cares if Hickman is late,* he thought to himself and pulled out a cigarette. He waited for another 5 minutes and then Cathy eventually emerged, walking slowly up the garden path in her high stilettos, short black dress and with her black hair long and straight. *What was she doing with him? She really could be model.* He thought to himself as he slung the cigarette out of the window and started the engine, the flash car was wasted on Cathy's family as they did not emerge from the house and into the night air.

"Everything alright bab?" Cole asked as Cathy got into the car alongside him.

"Yeah, just something was a bit weird." Cathy could not quite make up her mind as to whether she was pleased or concerned.

"Why?" Cole drove away from the Estate and accelerated hard towards the main road, enjoying the sound of the engine.

"It's my stepdad Roger." Cathy shook her head in confusion. "Somebody as given him a bit of a lampin." She was surprised by the occurrence. Roger Richardson had never been involved in anything remotely dodgy in his entire life. He did not drink or smoke and he certainly never went into a pub to socialise. *Where did he get that black eye?* She didn't really care. The man had ignored her throughout her childhood and then forced upon her his unwanted attention when she had got a little older. She shrugged and then a thought entered her mind. "Yow ay had a gew at him have yer Mick?" She turned to face her boyfriend whom she knew hated Richardson on account of the way he had treated her as a child.

Cole laughed as he drove. "Is he crippled and in a fuckin' wheelchair?"

"No." Cathy shook her head and smiled; she should have known that Micky would have done a much more thorough job! It was certainly odd that someone had given Roger Richardson a minor beating, but neither of them was about to lose any sleep over it and they certainly would not allow it to ruin their evening.

Micky Cole pulled up the Jag outside Hickman's terraced house in Highgate Street Old Hill. Next to his house was a double entry that previously led to several houses that were demolished before the Second World War. They had been pulled down due to them having had no safe rear exit and the residents had had to be relocated to Victoria Road. Even though they were late, Hickman did not emerge straight away and Cole looked up at the full moon and thought about his first beer of the night. Eventually the front door opened and Hickman came out first, loud and brash with a huge cigar hanging out the side of his mouth. His lady friend was behind him but she had turned around to lock the front door and Cole could not quite make her out through the darkness of the night. He was intrigued as he had often wondered what the great Dickie Hickman's woman would look like but he was still none the wiser. He would have to wait until they arrived at the club.

"Micky aer kid... An his bostin' wench, yow pair am late!" Hickman looked at his gold Rolex that had once been a present from Billy Mucklow and joked. Cole smiled and nodded.

"It's her fault!" Cole rose his thumb to point at Cathy who was sat alongside him in the front of Hickman's Jag and they all laughed.

"Ladies have a god given right to teck their time getting ready." Hickman's lady friend spoke and Cole noted that she seemed very confident and friendly enough. He had expected her to be some nervous, timid wreck who was covered in bruises and treated like a punch bag by her psychologically imbalanced other half, but on first impressions she appeared to be nothing of the sort. Her voice was husky and sexy and Micky Cole was intrigued.

On arrival at The Regis Club, the doormen groaned inwardly as Cole opened the door for his boss and Hickman made his grand entrance. Every time he came to the club he would get drunk and high and cause trouble. Violence was guaranteed. Cole held the door open for Hickman's lady friend as his employer made his way towards the front entrance to the club and he noticed that she was the same attractive red-head he had noted leaving The Haden Cross on his first visit to meet Barry O'Leary a few weeks previously. She wore a figure-hugging red leather dress that accentuated her slightly oversized rear end and Micky Cole found it instantly mesmerising. He reckoned that she was probably in her mid to late 30s and when she turned and flashed him the same provocative smile she had given him when he first saw her outside the Haden Cross he couldn't help but blush a little. Luckily for him, Cathy missed the entire exchange and as she made her way around from the passenger side of the Jag he took her arm and watched the doormen closely as they eyed her perfectly formed, long, tanned legs.

The foursome took a table to the left of the bar and Hickman clicked his fingers and ordered champagne. The barman quickly scrambled into action and Hickman relaxed in his chair. He was suave and overtly confident and Cole found it hard to understand how this was the same man who could quickly switch from this to a suicidal, paranoid, borderline psychotic lunatic in seconds.

"My darling, this is a new friend of mine." Hickman smiled at his lady friend and gestured towards Micky and Cathy. "Meet Michael Cole and his lovely bird Cathy." Hickman's lady friend smiled warmly at the couple and extended her elegant right hand for them both to shake. "Mick, this is mar wench Suzy. Suzy Miller." The name meant nothing to Cole but Hickman had told her exactly who his new young friend was and the attractive older woman had been looking forward to meeting him for a while. She lit a cigarette and blew smoke provocatively across the table before placing her right hand high up on Cathy's exposed thigh and whispering in her ear.

"Why dow we gew and dance? Leave the men to talk business." Cathy turned and smiled and the pair went off to the dance floor to dance to Cum on feel the noise which had been a hit for local band Slade that very year. The drinks arrived, were poured and Hickman 'necked' his champagne in one swift movement and without sophistication.

"So." Hickman placed the empty glass back down on the table, belched and lit another cigar. "We'm gewin after them then?" His eyes were pure evil and Cole was reassured by his enthusiasm. "I've dreamt of doing them pair for the last 20 years aer kid. Ar cor bloody wait!" Hickman spoke eagerly of the execution of Harry Scriven and Billy Mucklow and Cole could not help but share his enthusiasm.

"Where are they?" Cole took a sip of his champagne and waited for a response.

"In Spain mate."

"Yeah everyone knows that, but where exactly in Spain?"

"Ar dow fuckin' know." Hickman sucked on his cigar and burst out laughing whilst Cole struggled to retain his composure. *He had put his trust in this buffoon, cut off some poor kid's finger and almost slit his throat and this washed-up piece of shit didn't even know where Harry Scriven was!* He struggled to stop himself from grabbing Hickman by the head and smashing his face repeatedly against the table and in his mind he repeated the action several times. His expression gave away his feelings and Hickman suddenly stopped laughing. "Put yer face straight aer kid, ar dow know where they am, but ar can find aaht no problem." Hickman glared at Cole and blew cigar smoke into his face. "Yer see mar wench over there?" He pointed to Suzy Miller who was dancing closely with Cole's girlfriend Cathy. Cole nodded and took a longer drink of his champagne. "Well her mother Irene used to be Harry Scriven's bird." Hickman raised his eyebrows smugly. "The dirty bastard even fucked Suzy too!" Hickman tensed at the thought of Harry Scriven and Suzy together and he tried to push the image out of his head. Suzy Miller had been just 20 years old when she had fallen head over heels in love with her mother's partner after he had saved her from the evil clutches of the sadistic sex offender and cold-blooded murderer Jimmy Danks. Hickman knew that deep down Suzy longed for Scriven to return to her and that she still loved him after all these years and this just gave him more determination to want to kill the man. "Suzy or her mother will know where they am." Hickman nodded confidently. "If not we will go to the demon king, the man who knows everything about every underworld figure this country has ever produced!"

"Who's that then?"

"Cedric Tanner. Tanner knows everything." Hickman knew that the mention of the name would have an effect on Cole but he mentioned it anyway. Cole drained his glass and said nothing. He was still thinking about Suzy and his biological father. *The guy had fucked both the mother and the daughter.* He didn't know whether to be impressed or disgusted. Hickman looked at the floor and then suddenly looked up and changed the subject. "Yer see that bald fucker sat over there in the suit?" He nodded towards a well-dressed man in his 50s who was sat at a table on his own with a large whisky.

"Yeah, I see him." Cole looked over at the middle-aged man and wondered about his significance.

"That's Bert Hackett… Him and his brothers have owned this club for years." Hickman knocked back another glass of champagne and closed his eyes to recall a memory. "Ar remember when Billy Mucklow and Harry Scriven came daahn here an knee capped the fuckers with a pistol!" Hickman smiled and then laughed at the memory. "Bill stuck a bullet a piece in the brother's knees and then he told ode Bert he'd teck a piss on his grave if there was any more trouble… They day fuck abaaht in them days kid, ode school." Hickman smiled, full of admiration and hero worship. "That was on Christmas eve 1954 aer kid. Nobody fucked with Billy Mucklow, Harry Scriven and me raahnd here mate." Hickman continued to have nostalgic thoughts and Cole began to wonder again about the suitability of his accomplice. Did he really want to kill Billy Mucklow? He was obsessed with the guy. The man was his utter messiah. The more he thought about it the more he began to understand Hickman's obsession. Billy Mucklow had made him into the man he was today, he was his god, his inspiration, his biggest influence, but when Mucklow stood in that witness box and stabbed him in the back in 55 he damaged the man so deeply and in ways that nobody else could ever understand. The obsession continued and the only way for Hickman to exorcise his demons and truly be free was to literally kill off the ghosts that haunted him so frequently.

They drank more champagne, smoked cigars and ogled each other's woman before returning to their homes at the end of the night. As Micky Cole dropped Hickman and Suzy off at their Old Hill terraced house the two men wished each other good night, shook hands and promised to meet for drinks the next day. The next day was Sunday and it had long been a tradition for the whole gang to meet at the Haden Cross, drink vast amounts of beer and eat Pork Scratchings from dinner time onwards.

It had always been traditional for the original Mucklow gang to meet at the Haden Cross at 12:00pm on a Sunday and this was a tradition that had continued. Willie Mucklow had moved away and rarely attended but Eli Davis, who was now in his early 80s, occasionally popped in for a drink and even more so since he became a widower a couple of years previously. Despite his supposed hatred for Billy Mucklow, Dickie Hickman continued to make an effort and keep an eye out for Bill's father Willie in his son's absence. *The family had always been good to him and it wasn't the old man's fault that his son had ratted him out!* In truth, Bill Mucklow had been given no choice but to give evidence against his associate as he had come under pressure from notorious London gangsters Billy Hill and The Kray twins. The Flying squad had tried to fit Hill up for a jewellery robbery that had been committed by Mucklow, Scriven and Hickman, so in order to protect himself and his family, Bill Mucklow had had to plead guilty and thus incriminate Hickman in the process. Hickman had not been aware of Hill and the Kray's intervention and had put up a plea of not guilty which was therefore of contradiction to Mucklow's guilty plea. As a result, Mucklow got a slightly shorter sentence and Hickman was left with eternal resentment. The fact that Bill Mucklow was also a distinguished war hero who had served with distinction as an officer in World War 2 also helped him to get a more lenient sentence, though he still spent over 12 years behind bars.

On this particular Sunday neither Willie Mucklow or Eli Davis were present in the pub and Dick Hickman and Barry O'Leary stood waiting for their newest associate Micky Cole to arrive.

"Where is he Dick?" O'Leary had already finished his first pint and was glancing down at his watch. "It's nearly fuckin' twenty past!"

"Ar know mate." Hickman was anxious. He had been informed by the barman that a visitor from out of town had been looking for them the previous night whilst himself and Cole were at The Regis club and he needed all the backup he could get as the barman had apparently told the visitors that Hickman and his associates would be in the next day at 12! *Hickman had no idea who this visitor could be, he had pissed off enough people in his time and then there were the big time London mobsters they had robbed back in the 50s!* He sipped his beer and smoked a cigarette to ease his nerves. *He would feel a lot better if Micky Cole was there to back him up.* He was a desperately paranoid man and his mental illnesses were getting worse by the day. He suddenly looked up and to his relief in walked Cole with a slightly sheepish look on his face.

"Sorry lads, was busy with the Mrs." His sheepish look turned into a grin and both O'Leary and Hickman had little doubt as to what he had been up to. Hickman took a long calming drag of his cigarette and decided not to let his frustration become obvious. Micky Cole was a loose cannon just like himself and at that moment in time Hickman needed him on his side in anticipation of their mysterious visitor. Cole was completely unaware of any annoyance and was immediately distracted by the presence of the leggy, dirty blonde he had previously spoken to on the other side of the bar. He contemplated walking over but she was already with a male companion and he was hoping that Hickman would shed some further light on the whereabouts of Harry Scriven. He turned back around to face his associates and took a long gulp of The Harp Lager that had been stood standing on the bar for the last twenty minutes.

Before Hickman had chance to explain that they were expecting a visitor, a black man in his mid to late 50s entered the pub and immediately spotted the three well-dressed thugs. He wore an expensive fur coat, brilliant white shoes, a black leather cap and was absolutely dripping with flashy yellow gold. He had a small moustache and Cole thought that he looked like a considerably tougher version of Sammy Davis Junior. He strutted over with utter confidence and swagger and Micky Cole thought that he was possibly the absolute coolest man he had seen in his life and he instantly felt in awe.

"Hey, look who it is." The man patted Hickman hard on the back and smiled to reveal immaculate white teeth. "Big bad gangsta boy." The man spoke confidently and Cole got the impression that he was mocking Hickman. "Where da fuck is Billy Mucklow man?"

O'Leary winced and spoke quietly. "We dow mention that name anymore Bobby." Both O'Leary and Hickman appeared to know the man and O'Leary at least seemed genuinely pleased to see him. Hickman said nothing, he forced a smile and gestured towards their visitor.

"Mick, may I introduce Mr Robert Murray, probably the world's biggest drug dealer." Murray burst out laughing, his laughter was raucous, high pitched and relatively friendly. Hickman ordered their guest a large rum and stubbed out his cigarette. "So where ya bin Bobby?"

Murray nodded a thanks for the drink and took a sip. "Well, since Billy Mucklow decided he didn't wanna deal with no white powder back in the early 50s, I went north. First to Stoke on Trent, then on to Liverpool man. Stayed there for the first part of the 60s, all those white boys takin' dope with their shitty white boy music." Cole nodded enthusiastically. He hated The Beatles with a passion and his stepfather Cedric Tanner had played their records in the house when he was a young teenager. Murray smiled again. "You wanna hear Rock n Roll go listen to Chuck Berry and Little Richard man." The more Murray spoke about music the more Micky Cole agreed with him. "Then after that I went up to Glasgow where I've been for the last 8 years." Murray pulled a face of distaste and shook his head. "Ahh, dat town is bad man… Too many flashy angry men running around trying to kill each other." Murray looked at Hickman and smiled, he made his point. "You would fit in very well there Dickie." Apart from Hickman, the other men laughed and Murray took another sip of his rum. "Me and Billy Mucklow always used to say that violence was very bad for business. Yer can't make money if you is dead man! Glasgow is full of angry white dudes who just fight for no reason." Murray looked at Hickman again and winked. "Remind you of anyone boys?" Murray had been close friends with Bill Mucklow in the 50s and had never taken to *Mucklow's 'pet'* Hickman.

    Hickman ignored the mockery and saw a business opportunity. He lowered his voice and looked serious. "Billy ay in charge no more Bobby. Ar'm the boss now and ar'm open for business… I deal in everything and anything, maybe we could cut some kind of deal?"

    Murray sucked his teeth and looked upwards. "No man, I'm semi-retired… Got more important things to deal with."

    "What could be more important than making money Bob?" Hickman was confused.

    "Family Dick. Family." Murray downed the remainder of his rum and lit a cigar. "You know, Billy Mucklow was always like family to me." He knew exactly what he was doing and he could not resist the opportunity to wind Hickman up. *He could not take the angry little man seriously. To him he was and always would be Billy Mucklow's vicious little stupid side kick.* "Back in the early 50s Bill was my brother from another mother." Murray took a long drag of his cigar and his expression became more serious. "When I first came to this country in the 40s, the only thing a lot of people saw was the colour of my skin. Billy Mucklow and his cousin Harry weren't like that, they didn't just see colour man." Murray laughed again in his raspy Jamaican accent as Hickman, O'Leary and Cole listened intently. "They didn't judge me by the colour of my skin, they knew I was bad man and they knew that they was bad too and we all knew that we wanted to make a fuck load of money." Murray continued to laugh but suddenly stopped and glared at Hickman with serious eyes. "Them mother fuckers didn't wanna start Word War 3. They was businessmen, gentlemen, old skool gangstas…" Murray lent on the bar, looked away and then returned his gaze back to Hickman. "I'm disappointed they not here man."

Hickman shrugged and looked away. He certainly wasn't afraid of Murray, but business was bad and a contact like Robert Murray would be very useful. "Anything we can help you with Bobby?" Until now, Murray had not paid much attention to Micky Cole, but he suddenly became very aware of him out of the corner of his eye. *He felt like he knew him from somewhere and he felt slightly wary of the man. He was not like Hickman, he could read him like a book, loud, mouthy, angry, a predictable wannabe gangster.* In fact, the more he thought about it he was surprised that the man (Hickman) was still alive! The other man, the one who remained in the corner of his eye was different, there was a familiarity to him but he was potentially dangerous. He smiled again and diffused any potential tension, though he needn't have worried. What Murray did not realise was that although Cole was friends with Hickman, ultimately he shared his viewpoint about the man, though he also knew that Dickie Hickman was very dangerous and that he needed him in his quest to track down Harry Scriven.

Murray thought for a few seconds and then decided to come clean with his intentions. He had originally wanted to speak with his old friend Billy Mucklow but since this was not possible he thought that he might as well try his luck anyway.

"I'm looking for my little girl boys." The three men were surprised by the sentence and shook their heads in confusion. "You see, back in the early 50s, when I was workin' with Bill and Harry, I was seeing this sexy bit of stuff from over Dudley… Anyway, I got this chick pregnant." A look of sadness came over Murray's eyes and he looked down at his empty glass. "Boys, the biggest regret of my life is that I fucked off and left her alone to raise my kid… I later found out that I had a daughter but I never went back… I think about her all the time. Ghosts man. Whatever you do in dis world, will always come back to haunt you." Micky Cole's ears suddenly pricked up as it occurred to him that *this man could possibly be Cathy's father? She had been born to a single mother in Dudley in the early 50s. The more he thought about it the more plausible it became.* Murray rummaged in his pocket as if looking for something and began to speak again. "Anyway, I went back there the other day. I found the chick who I got pregnant all them years ago. She said that me girl was not there and then some white dude she is married to now ordered me to leave." Murray eagerly accepted another drink. "So I give this dude a bit of a slap, you know, make dat mother fucker talk man. They tell me that me girl has come over Halesowen way." Murray took a long sip of his large rum. "Well I know that is round here so I thought I might ask my old pal Billy, but he ain't around." Micky Cole began to breathe deeply, *should he say something? Was it his place to say something? What would Cathy want? This was obviously the reason why Cathy's stepfather had bruises the other night. It was up to Cathy whether or not she wanted to meet her real father.* In that instant he did not think about or even realise any similarities to his own situation with Harry Scriven, though these thoughts would eventually play on his mind in the coming weeks. Murray was genuinely upset about missing out on his daughter's childhood and had suffered in silence for all of these years. Micky Cole did not even consider it at this point, but it would later occur to him (especially after Murray's favourable account of Harry Scriven and Billy Mucklow) that maybe his own father had similar thoughts? Before Cole could think anymore, Murray produced an early colour photograph from out of his pocket and held it up for the men to see. "I got this picture of her, its a few years old I think." Murray had taken the photograph from

Cathy's mother's house and even though it was a few years old it clearly depicted Cathy in her early teens. Cole said nothing but Hickman recognised her straight away.

"Hang on a minute Mick, that's yower wench ay it?" Murray frowned and turned to look at Cole. Cole shrugged and replied.

"It does look like her yes." He returned the intense glare and waited for a reaction.

"You been ploughing my daughter man!" Murray's eyes were livid and the Jamaican tried to compose himself. Micky Cole was not afraid of anyone and he moved closer to Murray in a threatening gesture and opened his eyes wide.

"Me and Cathy have been together for a long time, we live together. Ar saved her from that shitty family of hers and I also saved her from a life on the street." Cole gritted his teeth and squared up to the tall, well-built Jamaican. "Whilst yow were fuckin' abaaht playing wild west up in fuckin' Glasgow or wherever the fuck yow said you had been… So dow come raahnd here playing the devoted father!" Cole banged his pint glass upon the bar and felt the anger rise inside of him. "I think yow owe me a fuckin' beer mate!" He was fully aware that Murray was probably armed and carrying a gun somewhere, but he really didn't care. He fixed his stare on the older man and prepared himself. Murray remained silent for all of 20 seconds and then smiled and extended his right hand for Micky Cole to shake.

"If what you say is true, then I owe you a lot more than just a drink man!"

Chapter 18

Harry Scriven's footsteps crunched in the icy white snow as he moved swiftly through the dark frozen forest he knew so well. The leafless trees whispered his name and he was no longer sure if he was following someone or if he was the one being followed. All he knew was that the shadowy figure of a faceless woman moved through the trees in front of him and he felt an overwhelming desire to reach her. As he followed and longed to call out to her, his mind explored the possibilities of who the woman could be. *His mother Eliza? His Spanish wife Antonia? Irene Miller?* Deep down he hoped that it would be the one woman he had truly loved and had regretted leaving so many years ago. *Was it her? Could it be?* His heart pounded and the hairs on the back of his neck stood on end. The shadowy figure suddenly stopped and, in that moment, Scriven wanted more than anything else in the world for it to be his beloved Lily Cole…

She slowly turned around and met Scriven with a wicked and overtly sexual smile, her total magnetism and her lascivious eyes did not disappoint him, though it was certainly not Lily Cole… Of all the women Scriven had known, it was Suzy Miller that had aroused the biggest physical effect on him. She had made him grit his teeth with animal lust and utter desire, she was the devil, she was temptation and she was pure filth. Suzy Miller personified the wicked lust that was within him, a lust that had tarnished his entire life. Lust for sex, lust for money, lust for power and above all, lust for violence.

As he drew nearer to the red headed beauty, he could smell her cheap perfume that had tantalised his senses all of those years ago, but she suddenly vanished into the dark misty night and Scriven was left routed to the spot in a place he had been so many times before. The smell of perfume was suddenly replaced with the stench of rotting flesh and even though the woman had disappeared he could sense that he was not alone. In front of him lay a hole, a shallow grave that he had helped his cousin to dig many years ago and as he leant over to look, as he always did, he knew that the worst was still to come. He suddenly stopped himself from looking and stood still.

"Hello Harry." Scriven recognised the raspy high-pitched voice straight away, but he could not look to see, he could not look behind him. He gritted his teeth, as he always did. He would not allow himself to be afraid, *he was Harry Scriven, he didn't give a fuck!* The bravado was false and as usual he tried to hide his fear with anger and intimidation. It did not work. "Look in the hole Harry." Brian Tanner had been dead for nearly 20 years and when Scriven eventually turned around to face him he was greeted by the same newly dead walking corpse he had helped to bury back in January 1954. His face was dark purple and grotesquely distorted, his fingers were missing from when Bill Mucklow had removed them in a gangland torture and his jaw was broken from where Scriven had punched him across the room. Scriven stood and stared. Tanner's eyes were dead, but they still mocked him, they laughed at him as they had 19 years previously, shortly before he died. The stench was unbearable. "Look in the hole Harry." The corpse spoke again and Scriven slowly and reluctantly turned around to look, as he always did. He felt confused, the hole was not empty as it usually was. There was another corpse, one that was too far deteriorated for him to recognise, but he knew that it was Lily Cole. Her rotting skeletal face glared at him, even though her sockets were eyeless and black. Remnants of her once golden straw like hair hung around her head and a rat suddenly emerged from a crack in her skull. Harry Scriven was not even aware that his previous and much-loved fiancé had even died and as he turned back around to face Brian Tanner for answers, the dark, misty air revealed that the dead man had gone. At this point another voice sounded from close by in the trees and Scriven shivered as a rat scuttled across his expensive Italian shoes. He instantly recognised the voice and with horror he realised that the worst part of his nightmare was soon to ascend upon him.

More rats poured from out of the shadows and as Scriven desperately tried to wake himself up and return to normality, he could feel the rodents scurrying over him, tearing at his clothing, slowly beginning to make their way further up his leg.

"Hello Harry." The broad Tiptonian accent sounded again and Harry Scriven was under no illusions as to who this man was. "Ar said ar'd be seeyin' yer again day I Harry." Scriven was powerless to stop himself from looking up into the trees, the fear of knowing what was there but not actually being able to see it was too much. With his usual mix of fear, regret and almost remorse he looked up to see the truly horrific spectre of Jimmy Danks. He stood crucified, though not on a cross. Danks' soul was truly black and there had been nothing remotely holy about the man. It was unclear as to what exactly he was nailed to, but Scriven's attention was automatically drawn to the fleshy hole where Danks' face had once been. Scriven vividly remembered pouring acid into Danks' wounds after he had used a hammer and chisel to remove parts of his jaw and he also remembered the blood curdling noises Danks had made as he lay nailed there and was tortured, though not to death. That had come a few hours later once Scriven had removed his eyes with a stubby screwdriver and left him to be consumed alive by the dozens of rats that had come from the nearby cut to feast upon his living flesh as he lay powerless and nailed to the floor of his Tipton home. Despite the horror, Scriven could still not feel remorse. Jimmy Danks had been a truly evil man and had deserved everything that had happened to him. As he continued to look on into the gaping depths of Danks' face, he stood defiantly in stubbornness, unable to accept that what he did to Jimmy Danks was wrong as the rats rose further up his body. They appeared to grow in number as they slowly pulled him down into the hole in the ground that had originally been dug for Brian Tanner. He kept his eyes upon Danks until the last, staring, *he would not plead, he would not show remorse* and as the last grain of soil fell upon his face he lay alone in the darkness against the rotten corpse of Lily Cole.

    Scriven awoke… His nightmare had been vivid and utterly hellish and as he gasped for air and frantically searched the room for signs of normality he struggled to regulate his breathing. Nightmares and panic attacks such as this were of a regular occurrence for Harry Scriven and often his Spanish wife Antonia would simply sigh, turn over and go back to sleep in annoyance. She had tried to talk to him about them, about his past and what was causing his bad dreams, bouts of paranoia and anxiety, but he had always been reluctant to speak and she eventually gave up asking. It was not that she didn't love him at all, he was a fair bit older than her, he was bald and slightly overweight, but he had been good to her. He was genuine and had rescued her from an awful relationship with the son of another English gangster Isiah Boswell. Scriven had also taken her to the deserted village of El Acebuchal where she had spent her childhood and watched her father and brothers taken away to be killed during the Spanish civil war and he had then returned to marry her once he had made his fortune in England. In her own little way, she did care about him, but not enough to wake up every other night and ease him as he lay drenched in sweat and gasping.

    Scriven hurried through the dark Spanish villa he owned in the Sierra mountain range that stood above Torremolinos and Marbella in the Costa Del Sol where he had lived for the last 18 years. He burst into the large terracotta kitchen and felt around desperately for the light switch. The lights flashed on and Scriven felt instant relief. He grabbed a bottle of tequila from the cupboard, a glass and his cigarettes as he moved out onto a vast terrace that overlooked a large turquoise swimming pool.

    After the jewellery robbery in 1955, Harry Scriven had escaped to Spain with the money Billy Mucklow and Dickie Hickman had made from selling their haul to the Italian-American mafia in New York. Mucklow and Hickman went to jail and their fourth accomplice Chad

Cooper had been tortured to death by the sadistic and twisted Tipton thug Jimmy Danks on behalf of the London mob from which they had stolen the jewels. Though, shortly after, Scriven had heavily punished Danks for his crime as an act of vengeance when he turned up at his Tipton home before moving to Spain. Once he arrived on the Costa Del Sol, Scriven built a hotel and casino complex in the resort of Torremolinos and over time built his empire and became a very wealthy man. By the time Bill Mucklow got out of prison in 1968 and came over to Spain, the pair were able to finally retire from a life of crime and live the high life in the Andalusian sun. But all was not always well with Harry Scriven, he suffered with bouts of anxiety and paranoia as the ghosts of his past crimes constantly returned to haunt him. Bill Mucklow did not have such anxiety and Scriven often wished that he was blessed with the same arrogant and defiant sense of entitlement that Bill had.

As he sat, drank tequila and smoked cigarette after cigarette, he looked up at the same Mediterranean sky that had captivated him all those years ago on his first visit to Spain, but only now he had become accustomed to them after living under the same skies for the last 18 years. He was 55 years old and as the years passed it seemed as if no amount of wealth, luxury or Spanish sun could protect him from the ghosts of his past crimes. He often thought about the final words of Jimmy Danks who had vowed to 'catch up with him in hell.' He also recalled an encounter with a retired army officer who had informed him of the same thing during a botched robbery at a large house in Himley. He blew smoke into the air and tried to relax, but it was no use. He fully understood the eternity of his situation and as he moved through the autumn years of his life, he could feel the sands of time slipping away as he grew closer to his judgement and the costs of the crimes that he had committed. Little did he know was that plotters many miles across the ocean in his hometown were planning to come for him and punish him for a deed of which he was not even aware. His paranoia and anxious anticipation was entirely profound and as he tried to make sense of his morbid dreams, Harry Scriven was beginning to feel afraid.

Chapter 19

Merry Xmas Everybody by Slade was released on the 7th of December 1973 and was the Black Country band's sixth and final number one single in the U.K. Within the first week of release, the disc sold over 500,000 copies and Polydor records had to make special arrangements for 250,000 extra discs to be sent over from Los Angeles in addition to the 30,000 copies a day that they were receiving from manufacture in Germany. The band's lead singer Noddy Holder had apparently written the lyrics whilst drunk at his mother's house on The Beechdale estate in Bloxwich and had later presented them to bandmate Jim Lea. The pair crafted the final composition together and the band recorded it at The Record Plant in New York in the summer of 73. Cathy Richardson had been lucky enough to obtain a copy of the single on the first day of its release and had subsequently driven her boyfriend Micky Cole close to madness by constantly playing it over and over again. She had also bought a Christmas tree and had been the talk of her neighbours by putting it up early and decorating the flat in which she and Micky lived. It had been traditional to not put Christmas decorations up until Christmas Eve and although some families extended the festive season by putting their trees up the week before Christmas, the idea of putting the tree up in the first week of December was relatively unheard of. But there was a reason for Cathy's festive, feel good state of mind.

It had been a week and a half since Cathy Richardson had been introduced to her biological father Robert Murray and words could not emphasise just how happy the experience had made her feel. Her mother's side of the family had given her nothing but misery and when Murray turned up with Micky the night after she had agreed to meet him, she had instantly fallen in love with her father. He was charming, he was generous and above all he was extremely remorseful. He had explained his reasons as to why he had left her mother and expressed an overt desire to try and make things right and make up for lost years. Micky Cole was not quite as convinced and as trusting as she was and he remained sceptical, but Cathy was an adult and was more than capable of making her own decisions.

As he sat on the sofa listening to Merry Xmas Everybody (again) on the record player, he stared aimlessly and hypnotically at the small Christmas tree Cathy had decorated in a corner of the flat. Since childhood he'd had an obsessive fixation with Christmas trees and he recalled a distant memory of helping his mother to decorate a grand tree in their home. The reason for his love of Christmas trees was down to the fact that his stepfather Cedric Tanner hated Christmas and would insist on turning off the Christmas lights to save electricity every time he would arrive home. The young Michael Cole had come to understand that the glow of the lights meant that his stepfather was not around and he could feel safe. Christmas however, did carry other much more painful memories.

One particular Christmas stood out in Cole's memory and that was the year that he witnessed the murder of his beloved grandfather Norman when he was just 4 years old. Cedric Tanner had always assumed that Micky Cole was too young to remember what happened, but he remembered well. He could have gone to the Police and informed them of what he saw, but the Police did not feature in his own personal plans for revenge.

Cole was due to meet Dickie Hickman at The Spring Meadow House pub on Halesowen Road, Old Hill at 7:00pm and as he glanced at his watch he was disappointed to realise that it was only 6:05pm. He peered through to the bedroom and saw that Cathy was on the phone again to Robert Murray, *the world's greatest dad!* He did not want to sit and listen to Noddy Holder sing Merry Christmas Everybody again so he pulled on his leather jacket and set off down the stairs of the flats and through the estate towards the pub.

As he walked he thought about Cathy and how happy she was about the arrival of her long lost father and how it had been a strange coincidence that the man happened to be a onetime associate of his own biological father. For a few seconds he allowed himself to think that maybe his own father was not all that bad? *Robert Murray had spoken well of Scriven and Mucklow. What if Harry Scriven turned up full of remorse and begging for a second chance as Murray had done with Cathy? Could he allow himself to be happy? He had the woman he loved, did he really need to destroy everyone who had ever done him harm?* As he neared the pub his mind and painful memories had caught up with him and he had recalled the true horror of his childhood and the people who were to blame for what had happened to him. There was only one thing for it… People would have to die.

The pub had a small bar and as Cole sat down with a pint of Harp Lager, he wondered why Hickman had chosen such a venue for their meeting. They could not meet in the Haden Cross as what they were to discuss was very sensitive and there were people in the Haden Cross who were still loyal to The Mucklow family and would betray their plans. In the Spring Meadow House the bar was tiny, packed full of local workers and a noisy fruit machine that Cole found particularly annoying. He had seen the pub many times on his travels, it was next to A.B. Jones' shop but he had never been inside. As he drank he noticed that none of the regulars were paying any attention to him, they were all caught up in their own conversations and on numerous occasions Micky Cole caught himself listening in on what was being said. It was mostly about work, their wives and the plight of West Bromwich Albion Football Club. Cole had never really followed football, but his stepfather Cedric Tanner was a massive supporter of Wolverhampton Wanderers so Cole had made a point of always claiming he was a 'Baggies' fan as 'The Albion' were bitter rivals of 'The Wolves.' He lit a cigarette and settled back into his chair, he still had a few minutes until Hickman was due to arrive and he remained confident and devoted to the cause of tracking down Harry Scriven and murdering him for abandoning his mother.

Hickman was on time. He arrived in the pub at 6:55 and was immediately recognised by some of the locals who quickly glanced nervously away and made sure they kept their distance. He had a notorious reputation locally and tales of his past and present brutality were widespread.

"What yer drinkin' aer kid?" Hickman walked over to where Cole was sat and pointed to his glass which was two thirds empty.

"Lager please Dick." Cole raised his right hand in thanks and waited for Hickman to return from the bar with their beer. Hickman suddenly became profoundly serious and lowered the volume of his voice.

"Yow still wanna go through with this Mick?"

"100 percent." Cole was still resolute and Hickman was pleased. "So where in Spain are they?" He took a drink of his lager and then pulled out his cigarettes and offered them to Hickman.

"Ar got me own fakes mate." Hickman shook his head and lent in a little closer. The last thing they needed was for some local to alert Mucklow and Scriven of what they were planning. "Suzy dow know fuck all. But to be honest, ar dow think she would tell me even if she knew where they were." Hickman shook his head again over the lack of loyalty from his lover. "The slag probably still loves the bloke!"

Cole shrugged. He had moved to the area in order to try and get close to Dickie Hickman in the hope that he would lead him to his father. *Had he wasted his time?* He thought about it for a minute and decided that he probably had not. *If Mucklow and Scriven were as tough as their legendary reputation's suggested, then he would need all the help he could get whilst taking them down.* "So what we gunna do?"

"We ask the one fella who knows everything! Mr Big himself." Hickman looked away, knowing exactly how his young accomplice would react.

"Who?" Cole asked, even though he already knew the answer.

"Cedric Tanner." Hickman looked Cole directly in the eyes and waited for his reaction.

"Fuck that... Besides, what makes yow think that he will tell us even if he does know?"

"Because ar know what happened to his ode mon Brian Tanner."

Cole raised his eyebrows curiously. Brian Tanner had tried to make an effort with him when he was a young child, but he had suddenly disappeared not long after Cole's grandfather Norman was killed. "What happened to him?"

Hickman tapped his nose and smiled. "Dow worry aer kid. Yow'll find aaht. Ar will arrange a meeting with Cedric and you will find aaht then."

Cole grimaced. "I ay gewin' near that sick fuck."

"Yow still scared of him kidda?" Hickman asked the question genuinely.

"No." Cole lied. "But if I see him ar'll fuckin' kill him." Tanner had messed with his head in unimaginable ways and Cole had it set in his mind that his next encounter with Tanner would result in his abuser's death, besides, he had other business to settle before he dealt with Cedric Tanner.

"Well, yow'm gunna' have to grin and bear it...Tanner's our only hope of finding aaht where Scriven and Mucklow are without arousing suspicion." In Hickman's mind there was only one way.

"Why dow we just fly out to The Costa Del Sol and ask around?"

Hickman laughed. "It's a fuckin big place mate. Besides, the more people who know we are lookin' for them the more people there are to point their fingers and grass us up once the job is done."

Cole had never thought about what would happen once the job was done until recently. Up until now his sole purpose in life had been to track down and punish those who had damned him and his mother and once that was over he had planned to either take his own life, go to prison or more than likely both. However, in recent months his feelings towards Cathy Richardson had continued to develop and he had begun to feel that there was more purpose and potential happiness in his life than ever before. His day-to-day existence was no longer based primarily on alcohol, drugs and violence. He took a drag of his cigarette and thought about the future. *Maybe he could have his cake and eat it? Maybe he could enjoy a happier existence once he had gotten even with Lucy, Price, Tanner and Scriven?* He turned back to face Hickman and nodded reluctantly. "Fine, lets gew and see Tanner. But dow expect me to look at him!" Micky Cole sighed. His plans for Cedric Tanner would have to wait until after he had revealed to them where they could find Harry Scriven.

Chapter 20

The Chateau Impney stood in the Worcestershire town of Droitwich Spa which lay approximately 18 miles south of The Black Country. The elaborate Gallic styled building was built between 1873 and 1875 by the local industrialist John Corbett who was originally from Brierley Hill but had relocated to Droitwich when he purchased a disused salt workings in Stoke Prior. He brought many innovations from the Industrial Revolution to the business and quickly transformed the salt works into the largest in Europe making him vastly rich.

The Chateau Impney was built as a gift for Corbett's half French wife Hannah Eliza O'Meara who had been raised in Paris. Unfortunately, Hannah would eventually leave her husband and when he died in 1901 the house was let out to a number of wealthy families from the Birmingham area. The vast property would then go on to fulfil a number of purposes from Motor speed hill climb location, exclusive hotel and restaurant, Casino, night club and music venue. By June 1972, the 66-bedroom hotel was reopened after an extensive refurbishment and it became a plush and luxurious complex for wealthy Midlanders to relax and spend their hard earned finances. Cedric Tanner was one such customer and The Chateau was the ideal location for him to relax in the Worcestershire countryside away from his criminal empire. He would play golf with wealthy associates at the ultra-respectable Droitwich Golf Club, sip Champagne and enjoy fine food at the Chateau's a' la carte restaurant Angeliques's and he would entertain rent boys and prostitutes in his suite, dependant on whatever mood he was in.

As Micky Cole pulled the Jag onto the car park of The Chateau Impney, he spotted Tanner's white Rolls-Royce Silver Shadow straight away and a mixture of fear, loathing and utter hatred passed through his spine. When he was a child, his stepfather had driven a Rover P4 followed by a P5 and then several Jaguars, but Tanner had continued to rise up in the world since then and was now the absolute boss of an empire that stretched across the entire country. Whilst many of the old school gangsters were shunning the sale of hard-core narcotics, Tanner had seized the opportunity and after his father Brian had mysteriously disappeared in January 1954, he was free to take the family business in whatever direction he chose. By the end of 1955, the Mucklow crime family had ceased to exist and with no rivals and morals Cedric Tanner had built his vast empire with the sickeningly violent tactics he had learnt from his loathsome father.

    Brian Tanner had been notorious for not respecting any limits or boundaries with regards to hurting civilians, families, grandparents or even children. He did not care who he harmed as long as he achieved his aims and this had ultimately led to his downfall. Tanner junior was not much different, only he had become so wealthy and so powerful so quickly that he had become untouchable.

    Micky Cole parked the Jag and as he and Dick Hickman emerged from the car dressed in their finest black suits he flashed the key to the Jaguar and nodded towards Tanner's Rolls-Royce with a wicked grin.

    "Dow fuckin' think abaaht it aer kid." Hickman shook his head forbiddingly. "We've gorra keep the fucker on our side… Just stay quiet and leave the talking to me." Hickman shut the car door and remembered how Bill Mucklow used to give him the same advice before big meetings with men such as Isiah Boswell. *"Shut yer cairke ole Dick. Ar bay avin' yow shouting yer mouth off in theyur!"* Hickman could hear Mucklow's voice clearly in his mind and mixed emotions flooded through his head as he suddenly realised that they were there on this day plotting the murder of his former employer. Then he remembered the years spent locked up in prison whilst Harry Scriven was living the highlife on the money he was in jail for! His blood began to boil again and he felt reassured.

The two men went in through the main entrance of the Chateau and were greeted by a grand spiralling staircase and a large Christmas tree that glowed and sparkled as a focal point to the lavish and extravagant setting. A dark featured man with a strong French accent stood behind a desk and as the two thuggish looking men approached the reception he already knew exactly who these men were there to see.

"We're here to see Cedric Tanner mate." Hickman leant against the desk and turned to look around the grand room.

"Of course." The Frenchman spoke with a mild annoyance. "Follow me please gentlemen." Cole and Hickman followed him down a small staircase into a fine restaurant area which was newly decorated in lavish velvet and rich wood. At a far table sat Cedric Tanner with 4 burly looking men in suits standing in his vicinity. They all regarded Cole and Hickman with suspicious eyes and Cole thought he recognised some of them as they were led closer to the table.

"What is that vicious little bastard doing here?" Tanner recognised Micky Cole instantly and suddenly became wary.

"This is aer kid Mick. He works for me now Cedric." Hickman was not afraid of Tanner and he would not go out of his way to accommodate the man's ego.

"That's Mr Tanner to you Dick!" Tanner gestured for Hickman to sit at the table opposite him but raised his hand to stop Cole. "You sit over there Michael." Tanner pointed to a chair at an adjacent table. "If he moves, grab him!" The middle-aged gang boss turned to face his bodyguards and then regarded his onetime stepson as if he was a 'bad smell' within the room. His black eyes looked like small pieces of coal frozen in snow and an intense and horrific fear shifted through Micky Cole as he looked on. He had not seen Tanner since his mother's funeral and *he simply could not breathe easily or rest upon this earth until that man was dead. He was terrifying, he was loathsome, he was 'The Ghost' and he was quite simply the lowest form of humanity Cole could envisage.* Tanner was a predatory paedophile who preyed upon anyone who was of benefit to him and he would use them for his own sexual or financial gratification.

Micky would not show fear as he had done for so many years. He sat down at his designated chair and stared at Tanner with total intensity as he imagined the countless acts of sickening violence he would love to perform on the man should they be alone. *But for now, he would have to wait.*

"So… What can I do for you Dick? I heard you're very good at stitching mail bags?" Tanner took a sip of his champagne and the 4 bodyguards sniggered their approval as he made fun of Hickman. He clicked his fingers and a waiter appeared. "Get a beer a piece for these two. Champagne would be wasted on these Neanderthals."

Hickman ignored the insults and began to speak. "I need to find out where Billy Mucklow and Harry Scriven are Cedric." Hickman lit a cigarette and refused to give in to Tanner's intimidation.

"What the fuck has that got to do with me?" Tanner was confused and annoyed. *His time was valuable and why was he wasting it with this washed up has been?* "Did you drop the soap one too many times in prison Dick?" The bodyguards sniggered again.

"Ar'm sure yow would love that Cedric. Right up yower street." Hickman could not help the dig back and the bodyguards struggled to stop themselves from laughing. Tanner was not impressed and he was feeling apprehensive about the presence of his 'damaged' stepson.

"Why should I give a shit about Bill Mucklow and Harry Scriven? I heard that they are doing very well in Spain, which is more than can be said for you." Tanner was patronising and was losing his patience.

"I wanna sort them both aaht. Permanently. Hickman blew smoke across the table.

"I can understand that Dick, after what they did to you." Tanner shrugged and lent in a little closer. "Did you drop the soap then Dick?" The four bodyguards laughed, fully aware of their employer's sexual persuasions.

"Surely you would want them dead too Cedric?" Hickman ignored the mockery and adopted a more serious tone.

"Why should I care?" Tanner pointed for the waiter to put the beers down on the table and looked back at Hickman.

"Well you know that Harry Scriven is Micky's real father dow yer?" Hickman took a gulp of his beer. He eyed the bodyguards and felt confident that he and Micky could take them. "Surely it must bug yer that Scriven rooted yower Mrs before yow did?"

"My wife is dead Hickman!" Tanner gritted his teeth and his black eyes grew larger and more intense. Micky Cole was not impressed with the comment about his mother either, but he said nothing.

"Ar know that Cedric... Surely you owe it to that lad over there to give him his chance to punish the man who abandoned his mother?"

Tanner raised his eyebrows and looked at Cole.

"I owe that lad nothing Hickman...Why would I owe him anything?" Tanner began to feel uncomfortable, he knew exactly what Hickman was referring to. Hickman looked at his drink and then gave Tanner a knowing look.

"I think you will want Mucklow and Scriven punished just as much as we do Cedric." Hickman lent back in his chair and continued to enjoy his cigarette.

Tanner was beginning to feel intrigued. "Oh yeah? Why is that then?" Hickman lent in closer and whispered.

"Ar know what happened to yower ode mon Brian."

Cedric Tanner froze and looked at Hickman. *If the man was lying and trying to use his father as leverage then he would have his guts for garters, but he would at least hear what he had to say.* "Go on."

"Mucklow and Scriven killed him." Hickman whispered his revelation then took another sip of his beer. Tanner remained silent for a whole minute before he finally spoke.

"Well that is very convenient isn't it Dick... Why should I believe you?"

"Ar remember that night back in January 54... We had just given Jimmy Danks a lampin' in The Fountain over in Tipton and he told Harry Scriven that yower ode mon had paid him to hurt our wenches."

Hickman took another drag of his cigarette before carrying on. "Just yower ode mon's style that wore it? Danksy said that yower father had paid him to gew after Billy Mucklow's wife and kids. Apparently, yer ode mon wanted to move in on The Mucklow's turf after ode mon Willie Mucklow retired." Hickman paused again and studied Tanner's face. Cedric Tanner had been heavily involved in his father's business in 1954 and he knew that what Hickman was saying was true. "Naturally, Billy wore too happy with that so him and Scriven picked yower ode mon up and tortured him to death… Buried him in the middle of fuck knows where." Hickman shrugged. He spoke the truth and Tanner knew it. He had come to assume that his father must have been killed, but a small part of him had never given up hope that maybe his father was still alive and had possibly ran away to some foreign country. Cedric Tanner and his father were wicked, twisted, evil men, but they had shared a bond like any other father and son and even though it had worked in Cedric's favour financially, the disappearance of his father had thoroughly affected him and he missed him greatly. This new information was of great interest to him.

"If what you are saying is true then these men will die." Tanner's manner had changed and he was now taking Dickie Hickman much more seriously.

"Just tell me where we can find them and me and the kid will do the job." Hickman had grown in confidence.

"You will do the hit for me? On my order?" Tanner liked to be in control. He smiled perversely at the prospect of having control of Michael Cole again.

"Free of charge." Hickman smiled and reached out his hand for Tanner to shake.

Tanner shook the man's hand and then looked away in thought. "I will find out where they are and get back to you…"

"You know where to find me."

Tanner suddenly paused and nodded towards Micky Cole. "Whatever you do, do not let him anywhere near me. He would slit my throat given half a chance." Hickman did not doubt that what Tanner was saying was true, but he chose to say nothing. They were getting closer to locating their targets and Dickie Hickman felt optimistic.

Chapter 21

An old gas fire on its lowest setting was all that heated the icy cold living room of the big old semi-detached house in High Haden Crescent. The furniture and décor had been completely unchanged since the lady of the house had passed away two years previously and through neglect the once grand house had now fallen into a sorry state of disrepair. Cobwebs hung in every nook and cranny of the once luxurious middle-class home and the stench of damp and urine clung to the cold, moist, nicotine-stained walls.

In an old leather armchair sat the deceased woman's husband with a bottle of Bells whisky, a slice of stale bread and a lump of hard cheese. Eli Davis was vastly approaching his 80th year upon this earth and in his old age his twisted and bitter tendencies had magnified considerably. Night after night he would sit alone in his urine-stained chair and find his way through at least one bottle of blended Scotch, reliving the glory days of his youth. Sometimes in his drunkard state he would hallucinate and look over at the settee where his wife had once sat and in the eerie shadows of the room, he would see her there watching him. They would have lengthy conversations and sometimes he would see others sitting opposite him. His brother Stan who had been killed during the Great War, people who he had caused immeasurable sufferings to during his career as a high-ranking gangster, though more often than not he would see his own father. The man who had beaten him so viciously throughout his childhood, the man who's life had been cut reassuringly short when a youthful Willie Mucklow had slashed his throat to protect his friend. *Davis' father had taught him his greatest lessons in life. How to take an extreme beating and how to have absolutely no expectations of those around him.* His father had taught him that he could not and would not feel pain and this in turn had made him totally fearless. A trait that had served him well during The First World War and throughout his career. *He hated his father, but he felt gratitude.*

Eli Davis had led a full though not necessarily happy life, but now in his old age, the only activity he had to look forwards to was a weekly drink with his stepbrother Willie Mucklow on a Tuesday dinnertime at The Bell and Bear Inn on 'Gosty' Hill between Blackheath and Halesowen. It was the highlight of his week and since his wife died it was the only true companionship he would experience in his old age. He was bitter, he was miserable and he was lonely, but he did not have self-pity. His upbringing and experiences during The Great War would not allow him to feel self-pity.

Davis drained the last of the Bells, lay back in his chair and contemplated whether or not he should get up and use the toilet or simply relieve himself on the spot. It was 7 o clock on a Saturday evening and he had hoped to catch Match of the day later that night to catch up on the results of West Bromwich Albion. The 'Baggies' had been relegated to the second division that year and even though he was not an obsessive football supporter, it was always nice to have an understanding of the results for when he caught up with Willie on a Tuesday. He suddenly remembered that he had another bottle of Scotch in the kitchen and as the night was still young he decided against the idea of urinating in his chair and made his way slowly towards the downstairs lavatory. Eli Davis was a huge bear of a man and in his old age this had contributed towards problems with arthritis throughout his joints, particularly in his knees. As he shuffled painfully across the hallway a loud and sudden knock at the door almost startled him, but nothing could startle Eli Davis.

"Who the fuck is that?" He thought aloud, suddenly relieved that he had not *embarrassed himself by 'pissing in the chair.'* He opened the door to the cold and miserable December night and straight into the wicked and purposeful eyes of Cedric Tanner, Davey Price and an extremely large associate of theirs.

"Hello Eli." Tanner spoke with no respect as the three men pushed past the old man and through to the living room. Davis sneered and shut the door. If he was capable, he would have felt afraid. But he did not.

"What's the matter Cedric? Ran out of little boys pants ter sniff?" Davis' breath stank of Scotch and even though he was old and frail, his eyes and manner were every bit as intimidating as they always had been.

Tanner grunted in mock amusement. "How am yer ode mon?"

"What the fuck has that got ter do with yow?" Davis pushed his face closer to Tanners. He towered above the younger man and he did not know the meaning of fear.

"Eli, Eli, Eli… We can do this the easy way or we can do this the hard way." Tanner genuinely hoped that Davis would talk. He had better things to do with his Saturday nights than to torture old age pensioners. "Where in Spain are Harry Scriven and Billy Mucklow?"

Davis smiled. He knew exactly where they were. He had even visited them with his wife, Willie Mucklow and Mucklow's wife in the late 1960s. It amused him that he knew something that they did not and a strange excitement shot through him as he realised that tonight would be the night that would end his misery. *Tonight he would be finally reacquainted with his wife and his long lost brothers Stanley and Tobiaz. He could take pain better than anyone, he had been trained well and the thought of having to endure one last beating brought about a perverse and bittersweet excitement. It would be a fitting end to his tenure.* Davis' smile turned into an eerie and intimidating laughter.

"Gew fuck yerself Tanner."

Cedric Tanner closed his eyes and shook his head in disappointment before stepping aside so that Davey Price could get closer. Price was a big man himself and was in his late 20s. He grinned, tensed his right arm and then punched Davis hard across the face with a straight right hand. To his surprise the old man did not go down and Davis' laughter became louder and more mocking in its tone. His face was clearly damaged but Davis did not care, it was amusing, it was a challenge, it was a blessed deliverance. Price became frustrated, pulled back his fist and hit him again even harder. Davis stumbled and then fell backwards onto the floor, blood pouring from his face and his aged bones severely broken, but still he laughed. Tanner placed a hand on Price's shoulder to calm him, the last thing he needed was for his right hand man to go in too heavy handed and give the old man a heart attack before he had chance to give them the information they required. Bizarrely enough, as he lay on the floor, gurgling laughter through blood, Eli Davis was thinking exactly the same thing. He wanted to prove himself one last time, he wanted to defy his father, he wanted to experience the extreme pain in the triumphant knowledge that he would not be beaten.

"Come on ode mon." Tanner tried to adopt a less intimidating tone. "It doesn't have to be like this… Just tell us where they are!"

Davis spat blood onto the floor where he lay. "Gew fuck yerself Tanner." Tanner nodded in frustration and Pricey moved in again. This time he did not hold back and he rained down a series of hard kicks and stamps throughout the old man's body, breaking and splintering bones as he went. Davis did not even cry out with the pain. *They were doing a good job on him,* but he beamed with pride as he lay back and did what he did best. As he drifted in and out of consciousness, he saw the face of his dead wife and he imagined that he could hear her haunted voice calling to him. Tanner suddenly raised his right hand and Davey Price stood off.

"I know what yow want Eli." Tanner briefly went into the kitchen and returned with the second bottle of Scotch. "Bet yow want a drink Eli?" Davis tried to laugh. *Did Tanner really think that he gave that much of a shit about the drink?* Tanner asked again several times before becoming frustrated, pouring the entire contents of the bottle onto the floor and then smashing it into Davis' face. He relaxed, composed himself and looked around the room. If they carried on like this then Davis would not be able to tell them anything. He looked down at the elderly man on the floor and feared that he may already have gone too far. "Do yer want me to cut yer fuckin' fingers off Eli? And yer fuckin' toes?" Tanner could feel himself getting agitated again, but Davis just lay there, his eyes closed but he was smiling, trying to nod his approval of Tanner's gruesome suggestion! *The old man really was as tough as his legend had portrayed.* There was simply nothing that could be done to the man that would make him talk and Cedric Tanner almost felt a quiet respect. He stroked his chin thoughtfully and suddenly noticed an old photograph that took pride of place on an old decrepit mantelpiece. The photograph depicted Davis and the Mucklow brothers, Willie, Stan and Tobiaz in their much younger years and dressed in their army uniforms. Tanner looked closely at the picture and a smug grin appeared upon his face. "You know Eli, if you do not tell us what we need to know, then you know where we will be going next don't you?" Davis' eyes suddenly flickered open and the battered old man tried to raise his head. "Next on our list is ode Willie and his wife. I hear he ay bin too well as of late?" Tanner smiled wickedly. He had made a breakthrough and he knew it. Davis' breathing suddenly became even more laboured, he knew that he was beat. "Of course, if you tell us what we need to know then we don't have to go there… Ode Willie Mucklow was like a brother to you Eli." Tanner's tone softened slightly. "You were his top man all them years… Do it one last time Eli, save Willie one last time." Davis closed his eyes and thought of his brother. He remembered their first meeting, how Willie and Stan had got him that pair of shoes, how they had saved him from his own father and how they had taken him in and treated him as one of the family. He owed them everything. He thought about Tobiaz and Stan, he had not been able to protect them during The Great War, but he would save his brother Willie one last time. *Besides, Tanner would need an army to take down Bill and Harry! Let the fat bastard try!* Davis smiled again, he had proven to himself that he could still take a beating. He was utterly fearless.

"Ok Tanner." Blood covered the pensioner's face but Eli Davis managed to speak. "If ar tell yow where they am, ar want yower word that you will leave Willie and his Mrs out of this."

Cedric Tanner was surprised that Davis was able to manage the sentence. "Ok Eli… As long as what you tell me is correct, you have my word."

Davis wondered about the reliability of Cedric Tanner's word, but it was all he had. He rolled back his head and uttered his defeat. "Torremolinos… On the Costa Del Sol." Tanner wasn't surprised. The area was a sort of haven for British gangsters. Davis paused for few seconds and then spoke again. "If yowm a gewin hunting for Billy Mucklow Tanner, then yow better start prayin' yow filthy, sick, kiddy fiddling piece a shit." Davis' eyes were now wide open and he spoke the words with venom, his blood covered face looking demonic as his eyes bulged with defiance.

"You leave Billy Mucklow to me!" Tanner spat his reply before cracking a swift hard kick into Davis' face which left him all but dead on the floor. The other two men took their turn to kick him on the way out and were laughing as they did so. Davis did not care. His time was up.

It did not take long for Eli Davis to pass over. As he died he suddenly found himself back in The Heath Tavern on Cradley Heath high street with his three brothers. They were all young men again and dressed in their khaki green Army uniforms, about to catch the train that would lead them off to war. *Oh how wonderful it was to see them all again as young men, ready to fight and ready to die for their country. These men had taken him in, they were his true brothers and he felt happiest in their company…* As they passed through the door to the pub that one last time Davis suddenly found himself as a small boy again, sat on the banks of the river Stour with Willie Mucklow. His brand-new shoes were clasped tightly in his hands and he beamed with pride in the heat of the Black Country sun.

Chapter 22

The Summerhouse pub stood on Gospel End Road on the outskirts of Sedgley. It was a large building that lay back from the main road which led from Sedgley towards the village of Wombourne. It was 8 o'clock on the evening of Friday 21st of December and a festive party atmosphere spread throughout the region, but as Micky Cole's Vauxhall Cresta PA pulled onto the large car park that led to the Summerhouse, festive celebrations were far from his mind.

Micky Cole had spent much of his childhood in Sedgley and the Summerhouse was particularly significant as it was Davey Price's pub. He did not actually own it, but in the same way that Dickie Hickman and previously the Mucklow family had based themselves at the Haden Cross, Price and the Summerhouse had come to a similar arrangement. He was a high-ranking member of Cedric Tanner's organization and it was only fitting that he had his own 'office' where he could surround himself with fellow criminals who were loyal to him. Cole felt sick to think that he had once been part of the same organization and he remembered vividly how Price had constantly humiliated him in front of their fellow gangsters. He took a hip flask from his pocket and swallowed a substantial amount of cheap brandy before pulling up the collars of his leather jacket and exiting the car into the cold night air.

As he approached the pub he could hear loud music throbbing through the floor and as he drew nearer he recognised the tune of I wish it could be Christmas everyday by another relatively local band Wizard. It had been a big hit for Roy Wood's band in December that year and just like Merry Xmas Everyone by Slade, Cole was beginning to tire of hearing it. He passed through the front door unnoticed and kept his head down as he took a seat at a dark corner of the bar where he could blend into the shadows. He ordered a pint of lager and lit a cigarette as he watched the spectacle unfold. At a large table on the far side of the room sat Davey Price and his cronies. They were immaculately dressed in expensive three-piece suits, smoking fine cigars whilst drinking ordinary pints of beer. They acted like they owned the place and regarded themselves as if they were Mafia 'big shots' sat in a swanky New York club, the reality was that they were overdressed thugs in a back street Black Country 'Boozer.' They were extremely inebriated and Davey Price suddenly rose to his feet and danced around the table drunkenly before coarsely breaking wind to the amusement of the men that surrounded him. They were loud, rude and aggressive but nobody in their right mind would dare challenge them. Cole sat back in his chair and enjoyed his cigarette as he waited for his opportunity to speak to Price.

"Fuckin' hell!" Price eventually approached the bar for a round of drinks and was particularly surprised to see Micky Cole sat casually smoking. "What yow doing in here fag boy?" Price's friends remained at the table and were out of earshot, but he could still not resist the opportunity to humiliate Cole, even though there was no audience for him to impress.

"I wanted to ask you some questions." Cole's eyes were calm and deadly serious, but Price saw no threat from the smaller man. Davey Price was over 6 foot 3 inches tall with wide shoulders, a thick face, short blonde hair and piercing blue eyes that looked intensely aggressive but notably unintelligent.

"What yow want fag boy?" Price found the whole situation amusing but he remembered that his employer Cedric Tanner was in the middle of some important business with Dick Hickman so he decided to at least listen to whatever Cole had to say.

"When we were kids, back in the early days when ar was less than 10 and yow were working for Cedric?" Cole found it hard to contemplate such painful memories and took a long gulp of his beer. "Did you know?"

"Know what?" Price stopped laughing and spat his reply in annoyance. *He should be drinking with his pals, not wasting his time with this pathetic piece of shit.*

"What Cedric did to me?" Cole's eyes widened and when Price replied it took every bit of his self-control and willpower not to slit the man's throat on the spot.

"Of course I did yer dirty little fucker." Pricey erupted in laughter and nodded to the barmaid as she placed a tray of ale on the bar. "We all had a good loff abaaht it."

"So you knew, but chose to do nothing?" Cole found it hard to look him in the eyes. "Instead you took my girl and humiliated me for years?" Price was really testing Cole's patience now, he bit into his lower lip and the metallic taste of his own blood filled his mouth.

"Fuck off fag boy, before ar throw yer ahht… Get aaht of mar fuckin' pub!" Price raised his voice and several locals turned to see what he would do. Davey Price was not a man to be messed with and they held their breaths as they waited to see what would unfold. Cole smiled and stood up to face his aggressor. Price towered over him by a good few inches but the slightly younger man felt no fear. His question had been answered and there was nothing else to say. He stared deeply into Price's eyes and held his gaze for a good few seconds before Tanner's second in command looked away. They would meet again… Soon.

The next morning Micky Cole's Cresta was parked in Cotwall End Road Sedgley. Inside Cole sat and watched Davey Price's house intently. This was the day that he had been dreading, but he knew that it had to happen. He took another generous gulp from his hip flask of brandy and continued to stare at the house. Every Saturday morning it was a ritual for Cedric Tanner to eat a full English breakfast at a back street Wolverhampton café with all of his top boys. Cole knew that Davey Price would soon be on his way and then he could take his first murderous steps of revenge as his thoughts turned to Lucy Price.

At 8:30AM Price emerged from the house in a black Crombie overcoat with a matching black suit. His facial expression and demeanour gave away that he had been drinking heavily the night before and Micky Cole watched on as he got into his red Rover P6, reversed off the drive and drove off for his meeting with Tanner. The time had come. Cole could put it off no longer and as he searched the Vauxhall's glove compartment, he eventually pulled out a short piece of rope. He pulled it taut in his hands and closed his eyes in shame at the prospect of what it was to be used for. *Did Lucy Price really have to die? Was it right to murder a woman?* Cole took another drink of brandy, thought of the day Lucy had humiliated and laughed at him as a teenager and then got out of the car. *It was just, it was deserved, it was part of what he needed to do in order to punish those who had done him wrong.*

From the outside, the house looked well to do and middle class. It was neatly presented and Cole could not help but wonder what would happen to the property once its occupants had been disposed of. It was the sort of house that he would one day like to see himself living in with Cathy Richardson. He suddenly paused and thought of Cathy. *What would she think if she could see what he was about to do?* He thought of his mother. *Was it really right that Lucy Price should pay for the sins of her husband and Cedric Tanner with her life?* He thought for a moment and then again remembered the cruel memories of that teenage day when Lucy had humiliated him by the side of the cut. His eyes narrowed and he felt the coarse material of the rope inside of his pocket.

The front door was still ajar and Cole pushed it open slightly and ventured silently into the hallway. The house was quiet and dark and he assumed that Lucy must have still been in bed so he moved further inside. Suddenly, he heard movement to the left of him in the living room so he slowly pushed open the door and went in. A young toddler of little more than 1 year of age sat in the middle of the room, a blue dummy hanging from its mouth and a filthy bulging nappy clung around its waist causing a red raw discomfort to the infant. Cole could not help but smile at the child but then froze and gazed at the blood stains that were splattered across the off-white woodchip walls of the otherwise well-appointed living room. The child smiled back at Cole and began to chuckle. He had heard somewhere that babies were a good judge of humans and their intent and he wondered why this child had warmed to him when his sick and evil intent was to murder its mother? Cole smiled again and backed nervously out of the room. *What was he doing here? This could not be right?* He went back into the hallway and continued straight on into the small kitchen that stood at the rear of the house. There, directly in front of him was the attractively curvaceous figure of Lucy Price who had her back to him whilst preparing breakfast for herself and the infant. She heard the door swing open and suddenly turned around in fear and panic. Cole froze instantly. Lucy's face was covered in bruises and the once pretty young mother had been beaten black and blue. Cole now understood where the blood stains that covered the walls had come from. She glanced straight into his eyes and recognised him straight away. Suddenly she had no fear, no worry. Her eyes were relieved and Cole was surprised.

"Michael!" She shrieked. "Why? What are you doing here?"

Cole felt awkward and smiled nervously. "Well its Christmas, I thought I would pop in and say hello." Cole lied, but the sight of the woman he once loved, the look of reassurance upon her eyes and the vicious bruising that covered her face caused him to feel instantly guilty for the evil intent on which he had come. "What happened to you? You look like you've been hit by a train!"

Lucy looked at the floor and tears filled her eyes. "Its Davey… He has other women…" Cole felt confused. His natural reaction was to try and console the woman, but he was supposed to be there to kill her! "He beats me like an animal and now he is telling me that our young son must spend time with Cedric Tanner? I know what Tanner is like, I heard the rumours." Cole felt sick with distaste and he clenched his teeth in rage. *He was probably of a similar age himself when Cedric started abusing him and now Tanner was trying to reach out to the young child he had just encountered through the boys own father!* Cole's blood began to boil and he instantly realised that his decision to punish Lucy was utterly wrong. He took a step closer to the young mother and embraced her bruised and battered frame into his arms.

"You must leave Lucy. For the sake of yower kid yer must leave." Lucy Price looked up at him with helpless eyes. She had nothing. All she had in this world were the possessions Price had bestowed upon her in rare moments of guilt for the hideous violence with which he had treated her.

"How? Tanner is King and Davey is his loyal Prince… There is no escape." Cole reached deep into his pocket, past the murderous rope and clenched his wallet. He pulled it out and produced two crisp 20 pound notes. The latest payment he had received from Dickie Hickman and the money with which he had intended to buy Cathy Richardson's Christmas presents.

"Here…" He held out the notes to Lucy and immediately felt reassured in his own humanity. "Ar know it ay much, but get a taxi, leave here, gew to yer parents. Never return." Cole was deadly serious and Lucy could not believe how she readily trusted the words of a man she had not seen in years over the words of her own husband and the father of her child. She gratefully accepted the money and smiled. She looked into Cole's haunted eyes, leant forwards and kissed him on the cheek. She knew there and then that she had made a mistake in choosing Davey Price over Micky Cole, but she had been young and foolish and now she had to do whatever was best for the welfare of her child.

Lucy Price swiftly gathered a selection of her most prized possessions, a few essentials for her baby and waited for the taxi to arrive. Micky Cole supported her throughout and when the taxi appeared she once again thanked him with a kiss and left the house with tears in her eyes. When she left she locked the front door so as the taxi drove off, Cole made his way around to the back of the house where he searched for an entry point. He surveyed the rear of the house and came to the conclusion that his only form of entry would be to discretely smash one of the rear windows and crawl in. He went back to the Vauxhall Cresta and pulled out a black leather sports bag which contained all of the necessary equipment he would need. He returned to the rear garden, checked around for potential witnesses and then smashed a small window that led into the kitchen. His original plan had been to enter the house whilst Lucy was in there, strangle her to death before waiting for her husband to return home, but Cole felt pleased and relieved that he had decided against that. Besides, he had been unaware of the child and murdering a mother was really not his style. It was something he had been dreading for months and he felt as if a load had been taken from off his mind.

    Once inside the house, Cole ensured that his gloves were tightly fitted and then made his way through to the living room. The last thing he needed was to leave any incriminating fingerprints. *He could not go to prison yet, he had other business to take care of.* He positioned himself in the darkest corner of the room and sat and waited. As he sat he took swigs of brandy and thought about the many times Price had humiliated him. That was not his worst crime however. For the years of bullying and humiliation Cole would have quite happily let Pricey off with a beating, but the fact that Price had stood by and allowed him to suffer at the hands of Cedric Tanner as a child was quite unforgiveable. What made things even worse for Price was the fact that he was also planning to make his own infant son available to Tanner in order to gain further favour with his master! Cole felt sick with rage and then joyous in the momentum of the knowledge that the time would soon be here for him to take his revenge.

    He waited for several hours and watched an elaborate carriage clock that stood on the mantel piece and chimed on the hour. At about half past one in the afternoon Cole heard the distinct sound of a car pulling onto the drive and a shimmer of anticipation shot through his veins. He tensed himself and waited for the sound of the key in the lock and when it turned he held his breath.

"Where is that fuckin' bitch now!" Price cursed loudly to himself on realisation that his wife was not home. "She better had cleaned this fuckin' house." Cole could hear Davey Price getting more and more irate as he moved through the house and realised that his wife Lucy had done no housework. He ventured into the kitchen and more loud expletives erupted from his coarse mouth as he realised that somebody had smashed the window and broken in. "Who fuckin' dares to break into my house?" He roared before wondering if the potential burglar was still inside. A wicked smile appeared on his lips and he hoped that the intruder was still inside. *He would punish them, he would tear them limb from limb! Who was stupid enough and had the audacity to break into Davey Price's house?* He bolted into the living room and paused when he saw Micky Cole sat calmly and menacingly in a corner of the room. "You!" Price's eyes bulged and distorted at the sight of Cole in his living room. "What the fuck are you doing here fag boy?"

"Let's just say I got tired from fucking your mother." Cole spoke with a cocky confidence and as Price flew at him in absolute rage he quickly side stepped and caught Price with an almighty right handed punch that was complete with a heavy set of brass knuckles. The big man went down straight away and in that instant Cole unleashed over 15 years of pure venomous hate as he proceeded to kick, punch and stamp until Price became unconscious. He then turned back towards the leather bag, pushed back his sweat covered dark hair and pulled out a pair of hand cuffs. He applied them to Price's unconscious wrists and felt surprised at how quickly the first part of his plan had fallen into place. He had expected Price to put up more of a fight than that, but he had caught him off his guard and hungover.

The next few hours were somewhat uneventful. Cole sat and waited for the sun to go down. He stared at Price's unconscious body, talking to it, reliving unhappy childhood memories. Tears streamed from his eyes and blood streaked from the side of his face where he had clawed at his own cheeks. *"Look at you now… Look at you, you piece of fuckin' meat… Filthy dirty meat, filth, bastard, utter utter bastard."*

Once it was finally dark Cole took a long drink of brandy and wiped the tears from his face. At one point Price had woken up but Cole quickly silenced him again by hitting him over the head with the butt of a small revolver he had obtained through Dickie Hickman. Now he wanted the man awake so he fetched a glass of the water from the kitchen and threw it over Price's face. At first he did not wake up so Cole had to repeat the action a couple of times until his eyes flickered.

"What the fuck?" Price began to regain consciousness and tried to move, but his hands were securely cuffed behind his back. He looked up straight into the cold hate filled eyes of his captor. "What's gewin on Mick?" Cole smiled. He could not remember a time when Price had addressed him as Mick. He had always been referred to as 'Fag boy.'

"I'm sorry about this Davey." Cole lied. "Dickie Hickman wants a meeting, he asked me to bring yer in… Ar'm afraid this was necessary." Cole lied again.

"Fuckin' Dick Hickman calling me in? Who the fuck does he think he is?" Price was shocked at the sheer audacity of the move. *He was Davey Price!*

"That is why this violence was necessary." Cole pulled out the gun and pointed it at Price. The big man on the floor closed his eyes and tried to pull away.

"No Mick, please no! If this is abaaht ode mon Eli, it was Cedric's idea, I just followed orders. Honest."

"Ar dow give a fuck abaaht the ode mon Davey. If you do as ar say ar promise I will not shoot you." Cole stood up and gestured for Price to do the same, but he struggled on account of the cuffs. He eventually rose to his feet and stood and waited.

"I thought Cedric had told Hickman where to find Mucklow and Scriven?" Price was still clutching at straws as to why he was being taken.

"He did yes… This ay abaaht that Davey. This is abaaht the future. Tanner is finished and Dick Hickman has a very lucrative proposition for you." Cole paused to let the word lucrative settle into Price's mind. "Yow ever heard of a fella called Bobby Murray?" Cole was improvising and making up lies as he went along but it appeared to be working as Price seemed genuinely interested.

"I heard the name yeah. Some kind of drug boss up north?" Price's ears pricked up at the suggestion of a lucrative proposition.

"That's right Davey. He is in partnership with Dick Hickman now." Cole was somewhat impressed with his own lies. "They are gunna move Tanner out… It's up to you what happens next. You can die here and now, or you can keep your old job, but working for Hickman. You know how Tanner's distribution network is set up, you can keep it all, only with new associates. Hickman said that whatever Tanner paid yer he would up it by 10 percent. Yow have the contacts, yow have the organisation… It's good business Davey." Cole almost found himself drifting into a pseudo-American accent, Godfather style, *this man was so gullible!*

"Where's the meeting?" Price seemed enthusiastic though he was still slightly confused from the beating he had received.

"Give me yer car kays. Ar'll teck yer there." Cole pushed his right hand out for the keys but suddenly remembered that Price's hands were cuffed.

"They'm in mar pocket Mick." Cole uncomfortably placed his hand into Price's right pocket and pulled out the keys to the Rover P6. He held the gun in his other hand and nodded towards the front door. Price slowly shuffled out into the night air and made no attempt to escape. He was genuinely intrigued by Cole's lies and he waited patiently as Cole unlocked the passenger door. "Cor yow drop the cuffs now aer kid? Ar'm interested in what Dick has ter say. Bay no need for em."

"Ar'm sorry Davey. Dick's a little paranoid. He would prefer it if yow kept em on."

The car journey from the house in Sedgley to Baggeridge woods was a short one but Micky Cole noted that the Rover P6 was a particularly nice car to drive. Just as nice as Hickman's Jaguar MK10 420G.

"So, what's in it fer yow Mick?" Price was full of questions and Cole continued to notice that he was no longer being referred to as 'Fag boy.'

"Ar'm Hickman's number two now Davey, but that woe effect you. Me and yow will be sort of equals. Ar know yer woe like that Davey but it's better than being dead ay it… And you will be richer." Price shrugged and looked out of the window as the night frost began to set in and the landscape sparkled and shone in the light of a half moon. He did feel a loyalty towards Cedric Tanner. He had worked for him since he was a boy, but business was business and it was better than being dead.

Cole drove the Rover as deeply into the woods as he could before switching off the smooth 3.5 litre V8 and turning to face Davey Price. "Ok, get aaht." The gun was still in his right hand.

"We meeting aaht here?" Price was surprised but he did not question the location too much. He knew how these old gangsters loved the 'cloak and dagger' of secluded locations. He got out of the car and waited for Cole to come around to the passenger side. The night was dark but the moon provided adequate lighting as the pair walked deeper into the woods. Through the gaps in the bare winter branches the two men could clearly see the stars in the night sky and it was obvious that a cold winter's night was ahead of them.

As they drew deeper into the trees a small clearing appeared and Price squinted his eyes to look at a deep hole that had been dug in the hard ground. The gun suddenly pressed firmly into the back of his head and as he got closer he noticed that a wooden coffin like box had been placed at the bottom of the hole and that it must have been at least 8 feet deep. Still, he did not question anything. Dickie Hickman was old school and he knew how these old school villains worked. It was all for effect and he was not falling for their scare mongering. He reached the edge of the hole and looked into the dark forbidding tomb.

"Where's Hickman?" Upon sight of a wooden lid that had been placed at the side of the hole, Price began to worry slightly.

"Dow worry Pricey… Ar bay gunna shoot yer. Ar promised… Fag boy." Cole began to laugh, his laughter was eerie and disturbing and Price began to panic. Before he could utter a word, Cole hit him over the head again with the butt of his gun before shoving him forwards into the makeshift grave. Price was unable to move but he was still conscious and as he lay face down he began to plead.

"But I'm not dead! I'm not dead!"

As Micky Cole coolly dropped the heavy wooden lid onto the top of the wooden box, the muffled, anguished and utterly horrific cries of Davey Price became less and less. Cole then picked up a nearby spade and proceeded to slowly shovel dirt into the tomb in which Davey Price would spend his final Christmas and the rest of his anguished, tortured and agonizingly slow death.

Chapter 23

Cedric Tanner sat alone and listened to a recording of Lamento di Federico from the Italian opera L'arlesiana. L'arlesiana was composed by Francesco Cilea in the latter part of the 19th century and debuted at The Teatro Liricio in Milan on 27th November 1897. It was one of Tanner's personal favourites and on this night he was sat relaxing in his living room with a glass of single malt Scotch and a large Cuban cigar. Tanner's family background was originally working class, but the financial success of his brutal father had rubbed off on Cedric and through his continued successes as his own boss he had acquired a real taste for the finer things in life. He had developed a way of talking that hid his Black Country heritage, though in times of violence he often reverted to his native tongue.

As he sat he thought of his father Brian Tanner who had vanished in early 1954. *If Hickman was telling the truth about Mucklow and Scriven, and he had no reason to doubt that he was, then surely he should be avenging his father himself in person?* Tanner tapped the side of his glass and closed his eyes. He missed his father's guidance and in times of crisis or when he needed counsel he would often close his eyes and think about what his father would do faced with a similar situation. *I'm Cedric Tanner, far too important to go off playing 'Wild West' on the Costa Del Sol! Let Hickman take care of it. That way his father would be avenged and it would be Dick Hickman running the risk of spending the rest of his days in a Spanish jail. If Hickman fucked up then he would have no option but to go out there himself and take Davey Price with him, but for now he would give Hickman the benefit of the doubt.* He glanced around at the fine and expensive paintings that hung in his living room and basked in the smug self-appreciation of his own success.

Cedric Tanner lived alone in a large 7 bedroom detached house at a remote location near the South Staffordshire village of Kinver. It stood a few miles south west of the Black Country and Tanner had moved out for the 'clean country air' a few years previously when his wife Lily had been diagnosed with cancer. Due to the nature of his business, Tanner was particularly security conscious and two large iron gates stood at the entrance to his substantial property and a tall thick hedge spanned the perimeter. He also had a selection of weapons that were hidden in random places around the securely locked house including an impressive gun collection. As he sat, enjoying the opera, his fine cigar and his smooth single malt scotch, he did not for one minute suspect that a particularly dangerous intruder was prowling outside in the cold darkness of the Saturday night. He had enjoyed a good breakfast that morning with his boys and Christmas day was swiftly approaching when he would entertain his mother and his sister and her family at his lavish home. Life was good, or so he thought.

Micky Cole parked the Cresta on a remote country lane that ran alongside the perimeter of Tanner's property and got out of the car. He shut the door and looked at the hedge. It was good for him that Tanner lived so far away from any other dwellings as it would enable him to access the property without arousing any unwanted attention. He turned back towards his Vauxhall and moved around to the back of the brash 1950s styled car and opened the boot. Inside was a small petrol chain saw which Cole pulled out and started up. He knew that Tanner often enjoyed loud classical music on an evening and there were no neighbours to disturb so he pulled the cord and felt the vibrations run up his arm as the lethal device sprang into action. He got down onto his knees and carefully applied the saw to a small section of the hedge. After a few minutes of cutting, a small gap appeared in the hedge and Cole used his lighter to try and gauge his work. *The opening was fine, it would be sufficient for him to crawl through.* He turned back towards the car, placed the saw back inside the boot and then retrieved the leather sports bag from the rear seat. He quickly double checked the contents of the bag and locked the car before getting down onto the floor and crawling through the gap he had just created in the hedge. Once on the other side he quickly surveyed the area and was relieved to find that it was still very much the same as when he had visited his dying mother there a couple of years ago. He picked up a large rock that he found in the garden and approached the living room window where he pulled back his right arm and flung the rock at full pelt.

Cedric Tanner suddenly flew forwards in his chair, he dropped his cigar and spat whisky across the floor. *What the fuck was that?* A rock from his garden lay upon the floor and the shattered glass of his living room window surrounded it. Tanner did not hang around to see who had flung it. He quickly scooted around to the door and dived out as quickly as he could. *If this was a gangland hit then he would not make himself an easy target.* He bounded across the large elaborate hallway and into a small study where he flung himself towards a tall wooden cabinet. He quickly pulled it open and without delay grabbed a 12-bore shotgun and a handful of shells before heading back towards the living room. He waited behind the cover of the hallway door and slowly poked his head around to survey the scene.

"Who the fuck is there? Yow gor a fuckin' death wish or sumet?" Tanner waited for almost a minute but there was no reply. "Come on… Show yourself! What you want?" There was still no reply and with each passing second Tanner became more and more anxious. He thought for a minute and then made his way slowly to the kitchen where a back door led to the outside. He lent in close to the wall and decided on a plan. He would creep around to the front of the house and into the trees where he could come up behind the intruder. He held onto the gun tightly, went out of the door and began to creep, looking closely around him as he went. *Probably just fuckin' kids! Ar'll fuckin' teach em.* Tanner reached the front of the house and concealed himself behind a large tree so that he was looking upon the broken window of his living room from behind the point at which the intruder had thrown the stone. He was in his mid-50s and his eyesight was not quite what it once was, but as he strained and focused he was quite sure that he could not see anybody there. He rested for a moment and then cast his eyes around the rest of the garden. Nothing seemed out of the ordinary and he listened hard for footsteps but all he could hear was the sound of his own laboured breathing as he watched the vapour from his breath disappear into the cold atmosphere. He waited for almost 5 minutes and then decided that he should go back inside and call Davey Price. *Whoever had thrown the rock was probably well away by now anyway.* He snuck out from undercover and held his breath, half expecting to hear a bullet ricochet through the night and slam into his head. No such bullet materialised and he felt a sense of relief. As he began to slowly walk back towards the house he suddenly heard a loud knocking sound coming from the bottom of the garden. He flipped his overweight body around as fast as he could and pointed his shotgun in the vague direction of where he heard the noise.

"Come out yer bastards! Ar know yum there." There was still no reply and Tanner deducted that the sound had come from his wooden shed that stood at the bottom of the garden. Since his childhood, Cedric Tanner had found an unlikely hobby in woodwork and one of his favourite methods of relaxation was to go down to his shed and build things with wood. He had no particular talent for the activity, but he enjoyed it and that was all that seemed to matter.

"So, thieving bastards stealing from my shed am yer?" Tanner suddenly became convinced that kids had thrown the rock into his living room window and were now attempting to steal expensive tools from his shed. *He would not allow this!* As he got closer to the shed his groin began to swell as he *wondered if the thief was a young boy, all alone? Oh the fun he would have with him!* He grinned a wicked and lascivious grin and clutched the shotgun as if it were a phallic prize as he neared the door to the shed.

Tanner stopped by the door and forcefully flung it open before slowly pushing his head into the darkness to see who was there…

"Drop the gun Cedric." Tanner recognised the voice straight away as he felt the icy cold steel of a revolver press against the side of his head. He did not doubt for one second that this man was capable of pulling the trigger so he did exactly as he was told straight away. As the shotgun fell to the floor, Micky Cole kicked it away and flicked on the light switch, all of the time keeping his gun fixed firmly on Tanner's head.

"I should have known it would be you…What do you want Michael? I told your pal Hickman all he needs to know." Tanner was nervous, but he did not show it. Cole shut the door and gestured with the gun for Tanner to take a seat at a small table that stood on one side of the workshop. Tanner sat down obediently and shrugged. "Spit it out boy. What's this all about?" Cole sat down opposite his stepfather and kept the gun trained on the gang boss.

"Ar wanna know why Cedric."

"Why what?"

"Why you did those things to me as a child, why you killed my grandad Norman?" Tears began to flow from Cole's eyes and Tanner knew there and then that his time upon this earth was soon to be at an end. *He had no remorse, he did not care, he did what he wanted to whomever he wanted, it was his birth right!*

"Cus I could." Tanner shrugged and quickly brushed away the one question Micky Cole had spent his entire life waiting to ask. "Don't go blaming me for the way your life has turned out Michael. Your real father was a murderous, vicious criminal too, as was his uncle and as was his cousin. My father was exactly the same and that is why we are the men we are today… It's in our blood."

"That may be true… But those men were old school villains, they hurt those who deserved it and they certainly didn't touch kids, unlike you Cedric."

Tanner began to laugh. "Maybe you should go out to Spain and have a beer with the old man Michael?" Tanner laughed with the same acceptance of his own death that his father had had when he had died at the hands of Harry Scriven and Billy Mucklow 19 years previously.

"But you loved my mother… Why would you do such things to the child of a woman you loved?" Cole still wanted answers.

Tanner stopped laughing and suddenly became more serious at the mention of his dead wife. "I always knew that I would never be your mother's number one… I would always be second best to a child that wasn't even my own. For that you needed to be punished." Tanner spat his answer and then began to laugh again. *It both amused and infuriated him that his successful and oh so important life was about to be taken away by this bastard runt. He accepted death as his father had and deep down he should have known that it would be Michael Cole who would end it.* "Plus… I just like kids." Tanner grinned lasciviously again and Cole could not control his rage any longer. He placed his gun down hard on the table, grabbed Tanner by his hair and smashed his face into the table top with all of his might. His nose shattered immediately and blood splattered across the room. Tanner spotted that Cole no longer held then gun and a glimmer of hope flashed through his mind as he tried to make a grab for it, but before he could Cole smashed his head off the table again several times until he was barely conscious and lying on the floor.

"Do you know how long I have waited for this moment Cedric?" Cole stood over him with a crazed and psychotic look in his eyes. "Did you know that I used to call you the ghost Cedric? Did you realise that a little four-year-old boy used to piss and shit himself each night in fear of you?" Cole kicked Tanner viciously in the stomach twice and then restrained himself. "Ar bet yer thought that I had forgotten abaaht Grandad Norman day yer?" Cole took a long gulp of his brandy before stamping on Tanner's face just a couple of times so that he was still vaguely conscious. He placed the hip flask down on the table and then slowly and deliberately pulled off Tanner's shoes, his trousers and his underwear. "Get up… Get up!" He screamed at the older man like a man possessed and Tanner eventually found the strength to pull himself up. Cole grabbed him by his grey hair again and yanked him towards a large work bench that stood on the other side of the shed workshop. Tanner was half naked, shivering and barely conscious and as he slumped over the work bench he suddenly realised with horror what Micky Cole was doing. Attached to the bench was a state-of-the-art metal clamp vice and before he could protest or move, Cole had shoved his shrivelled manhood between the static and sliding jaws of the vice and without warning tightened the handle. The pain was horrendous and Tanner instantly vomited the contents of his stomach onto the worktop as his testicles were crushed between the metal jaws of the cruel device. Cole tightened the handle further and then unwound the screw before throwing it across the room so that Tanner could not reach it. As Tanner screamed incomprehensible gibberish, Cole picked up his leather sports bag from off the floor and proceeded to douse the wooden structure of the workshop with petrol from a small canister in the bag. He put the gun back into his pocket and then pulled out a large hunter's knife from the bag and placed it on the worktop in front of Tanner. The older man was in such intense pain that he almost passed out and Cole truly hoped that he would retain consciousness.

"If you want to live then you know what you have to do." Cole smiled and looked at the knife before opening the door, stepping outside and lighting a match. First he lit a cigarette and then stood and stared at Tanner's agonized face and enjoyed the vengeful moment before flicking the match onto the petrol doused wood. Cole took a few steps backwards and watched as the small building quickly engulfed in flames. He laughed coldly to himself, sat down on the cold grassy floor and enjoyed his cigarette. He inhaled deeply and then cast his eyes upon the burning structure, waiting, hoping that Tanner would emerge. Cedric Tanner did not disappoint. He emerged, half burnt and staggering with the knife in his right hand and a bloody gaping hole between his legs. The cut had not been clean and jagged pieces of tissue and severed veins hung grotesquely from the space his penis used to be. Micky Cole coolly exhaled smoke into the air before pulling the gun from out of his pocket and shooting Tanner twice, once in each knee cap. The bullets would not kill him but they would render him unable to move. He then grabbed his stepfather by the scruff of his neck and flung him back into the fire before sitting back down to enjoy the show as he watched the man who had terrorised his childhood burn to death before his very eyes. It was all very therapeutic and as he watched Tanner burn to the bone he saw the man's eyes explode as flames ripped through his skull turning his skin into a charred mess. Tanner's blood boiled and erupted from the charred blackness of his body and then proceeded to spill out across the garden and sink into the cold mud. The smell was sickly sweet and utterly revolting and Micky Cole savoured every second.

Chapter 24

The first section of the M6 motorway was the Preston By-pass in Lancashire which was opened by Prime Minister Harold Macmillan on the 5th of December 1958. It would later be expanded to become one of the busiest motorways in Europe connecting central England with the North West and beyond. On Sunday the 23rd of December 1973 Micky Cole found himself travelling north on the M6 for what was one of the most difficult car journeys of his life.

With Cedric Tanner's charred remains lying as yet undiscovered and Davey Price languishing underground in his makeshift tomb, Cole was now turning his attention towards the final section of his vengeful plans. Dick Hickman had booked the plane tickets for Malaga airport in Southern Spain and they had arranged to meet a contact in Marbella to pick up guns upon their arrival. The end was in sight and Cole eagerly wanted to resolve this part of his life and move on to a 'happily ever after' scenario with Cathy Richardson. He had not originally planned for that, he had expected nothing but jail or suicide but Cathy had really changed his existence and he longed to achieve a point in his life where he could be truly happy. The rain beat down heavily on the roof of the car and descended the windscreen like long salty tears, the rotten weather accentuated the sombre mood inside the vehicle and both Cole and Cathy were feeling miserable.

"I really don't understand this Mick." Cathy sat in the passenger seat of the Vauxhall Cresta and had sobbed throughout the journey. Cole said as little as possible and focused his gaze on the road in front of him. "Ar thought yow loved me?" Cathy sighed deeply.

"I do Cathy, ar really do... I never thought I would ever love anyone, but I do... That is why I'm tecking yer up to yer Dads for Christmas... With work how it is at the moment and the moves me and

Hickman are gunna meck it's just safer if yow gew away for a bit." Cole found it hard to hide his own emotions and a voice inside of him longed to turn the car around, let Harry Scriven be and enable himself to enjoy a cosy Christmas at home with Cathy making plans for their future. *Tanner and Price were gone, couldn't he just rest at that?* But then another voice gnawed at his mind and reminded him of how *Harry Scriven had broken his mother's heart, abandoned her with a child and left him to grow up being abused by Tanner. Scriven had to pay!* He didn't know how long he would be in Spain for and he didn't want to leave Cathy alone at home in case of any reprisal from Tanner's crew.

"But we woe be together at Christmas? I have only just started getting to know my Dad after all these years and now I'm supposed to spend Christmas with him up north?" Cathy could not get her head around what was happening. She knew that her boyfriend was a gangster, but she certainly did not know any of the 'ins and outs' of his business. She did not want to know. He had always been good to her, he was good looking and he had a distant vulnerability that made him mysterious and alluring.

"Bobby Murray is looking forward to seeing you. He only lives by Stoke on Trent, it ay that far bab. When things are sorted I will be back to pick you up… Enjoy the time getting to know your ode mon and I will see yer in the new year." Cole hoped he would see Cathy again, but he was not convinced. The risks of death or spending the rest of his life in a Spanish or British prison were ever present and he truly hoped that he would be able to return home, get on with the rest of his life and see his beloved Cathy again.

Later that night Cole found himself back at the flat in Old Hill packing his suitcase for Spain. The flat was cold and lonely without Cathy and he couldn't stop thinking about her face as he drove away from Bobby Murray's impressive, detached house. He had kept his eyes upon her in the rear-view mirror until she was out of sight and he had to quickly divert his focus to the road ahead of him. He had never expected to feel like this about anyone and it scared him, *but hopefully it was his future.*

As he packed his bags he thought he heard footsteps on the landing outside of the flat and this was confirmed with a sudden knock at the door. *Who could this be?* He thought to himself. *Could it be Tanner's associates looking for him? The Police?* He placed a bread knife in the back of his jeans and approached the front door. Whoever it was, he was ready for them.

"Hello Michael, can I come in?" Micky Cole opened the front door and was surprised to find Hickman's lady friend Suzy Miller. She was wearing a fur coat, a pair of white knee-high stiletto boots, the tightest white leather trousers he had ever seen and thick make-up with striking scarlet lipstick. *She was probably just old enough to be his mother, but wow did she look good.* Cole waved her in and made sure that the door was shut firmly behind her. *What on earth could she possibly want?* As she took off her fur coat Cole could not help but notice her more than generous cleavage that heaved at the top of her low-cut black top. She walked into the living room and looked straight through into the bedroom where she could see the suitcase on the bed.

"Gewin somewhere nice am yer Michael?" Cole smiled nervously, he wasn't sure what to say and had always felt pleasantly nervous around Suzy Miller since the first time he ever set eyes upon her outside the Haden Cross.

"Just away for Christmas Suzy."

"Ar know what's gewin on Mick... That's why ar'm here." Her eyes were intense and hypnotic and her red hair shone seductively in the light of the flat. She took a step closer and Cole found the intoxicating mix of her cheap perfume and tobacco smoke strangely attractive. She produced a cigarette from her small leather handbag and waited for Cole to light it for her before blowing smoke into his face. *Like father like son.* She thought to herself as she remembered many similar encounters with Harry Scriven. She was a master of seduction. "I think you should reconsider." Her eyes were deadly serious and Cole almost felt intimidated.

"Reconsider what?"

"Gewin after Harry and Bill." The look on Cole's face gave it away completely but Suzy Miller was already fully aware of his and Hickman's plans. *Hickman thought that she was just a dumb slut who was only good for one thing, but she had spent 20 years around loud-mouthed wannabe gangsters who had used her and passed her off as some brainless tart, an easy fuck… The only man who had ever treated her with any respect and who she had ever really loved was now being threatened and she had to do everything that she could to try and protect him.* "Harry Scriven is a good man Michael. I know."

"Oh yeah?" Cole had heard from Dick Hickman that Suzy Miller had once been involved with Scriven though he did not know how much of it to believe.

"We were in love…" Cole tried to hide the smirk. Suzy looked good but he knew of her reputation. "You might think that that is funny Michael, but I haven't always been some overdressed, middle aged slag! Your father saved my life." Suzy took a drag of her cigarette and exhaled provocatively. "20 years I was a barmaid in Tipton where ar'm originally from… This sick bastard called Jimmy Danks held me at knife point." Suzy looked at the floor and Cole was surprised to see her make up start to run as tears formed in her brown eyes. "He was gunna kill me, ar'm sure of it, but your father, Harry Scriven turned up and saved mar life."

"I heard that he was screwing both yow and yer mother?" Cole couldn't resist the dig but instantly regretted it when Suzy raised her head and he saw how upset she was.

"It wore like that Michael. I really got to know Harry… He was nothing like his cousin Billy, he was sensitive and lived by a strict moral code."

"Is that what he told yer to get yer into bed?" Cole turned away and picked up his own cigarettes from off the mantel piece.

"No… It was me who pursued him actually. He was a good man in a bad man's world and I fell madly in love with him… I just know that if he'd have known that he had a son he would have been a good father, I'm sure of it. How can yer punish a man for a crime he dow even know he committed? Give him a chance Michael."

"Like he gave mar mother a chance?" Cole raised his voice in anger. *He would not stand by and have Harry Scriven made out to be some kind of hero!* "Mar mother gave him everything, she betrayed her family to be with him, she was devoted to him and he broke her heart… He broke her fuckin' heart and I ended up being some twisted gangster's plaything whilst he was living the high life on The Costa Del fuckin' Sol!" Suzy Miller took a deep breath and lowered her top slightly so that Cole could see more of her breasts. She knew that he fancied her and she would do whatever it took to protect the man she loved. "Besides, why dow yer have a word with yower current fella? Why yer talking to me? Why not talk to Dick?"

"Because Hickman's too fuckin' stupid to listen to anyone. Besides, they will spot him coming a mile off. You dow know Billy Mucklow do yer Michael? Hickman dow stand a chance against them pair, he'll end up dead ar'm sure of it. My heart is with Harry but as he is married to some Spanish tart and we will never be together I will meck do with Hickman. Ar dow want anything to happen to either of them." Cole grunted, *she had clearly been devoted to many men over the years.* A serious look came across her eyes and she touched Cole's cheek. "You are different Michael. You're not some loud, ten a penny wannabe tough guy, you are one of them, a Mucklow. You're not all mouth and flash, you're a nice guy but I can see it in your eyes Michael, yowm' just like yer father… If anybody can take them down then it's you, but please reconsider." Suzy took a step even closer and pushed her cleavage into his chest. "Ar'm prepared to do whatever it takes to convince you Michael." She held her cigarette in her left hand and took his hand in her right. She raised his finger to her luscious red lips and put it into her mouth provocatively, gently biting the tip and then moving her mouth backwards and forwards in a seductive motion.

"You have a funny way of showing your love and devotion for Scriven and Hickman." Cole grunted his reply but more than anything else in the world at that moment in time he wanted to grab Suzy Miller, drag her through to the bedroom and *fuck her brains out*. He took a deep breath and showed restraint. *He would not fall for the honey trap.*

"I'm not like you, or Dick, or Harry… I can't use my fists, I can't bully and I can't intimidate. I must use whatever means I can… I'm very good at it Michael." Cole did not doubt her talents in the bedroom but then he was not about to fall for it. *Harry Scriven had to die and there was no way around it.*

"I think you better leave Suzy." Cole looked towards the door and tried to feign disinterest. He had wanted her since he first laid eyes upon her but he would not give in. She raised her strong firm thigh, which was clad in tight leather, to his crotch and held him there between her legs before pulling his right hand down into her firm leathered buttocks which he admired through the reflection in the window. "I think you need to go now Suzy." Cole spoke through gritted teeth as he grew dangerously close to surrender. She took one last drag of her cigarette before extinguishing it on the windowsill.

"See you around Michael. Just think about what I said." She kissed his cheek and the overt sexual confidence she had displayed a minute ago had all but gone. As she realised the implications of her failure another tear appeared in her eye. "I see that you are a man of strict morals Michael. I think that you would like your father." She looked straight into Micky Cole's deep blue eyes and could see that all hope was not entirely lost.

Chapter 25

Eddie Fennel waited patiently in the plush lobby of a grand Spanish hotel complex. Having spent the vast majority of his life in the Cradley Heath area of the Black Country, the Costa Del Sol appeared somewhat exotic. It was not overly hot in Spain during January, but with an average temperature of 13 degrees and highs of 16 it was certainly a lot warmer than the climate he was used to. Fennel had been grateful for the opportunity to bring his family to Spain for Christmas, but it was now early January and was time to get down to business.

As he waited, he smoked a rather exotic Cuban cigar, they were considerably cheaper here than in England and he would make the most of it whilst he could. Edward Padraig Fennel was a well-built man in his early 50s, his features were masculine and his face was full and without hair. He wore a black Burton suit, a light blue shirt with a tasteful dark blue skinny tie complete with a gold-plated tie pin. Fennel had always dressed well and today he had made a particular effort on account of his being 'sent for' by his distant relatives and former professional associates Billy Mucklow and Harry Scriven. Fennel's grandmother had been a Mucklow, she had been the sister of Willie and Eliza's father who had died young in a mining accident. She had married Jon Fennel, the son of a convict who had been deported to Australia in the early 19th century and the couple had had 5 children. One of these was Joseph who was Eddie Fennel's father. The Mucklow family in its criminal form had always liked the loyalty aspect of holding family members within its ranks and after returning from the Second World War having served under Billy Mucklow, Eddie Fennel had been recruited into the family's gang organisation. Fennel had not seen his distant cousins for many years though they had stayed in touch via letter and later through telephone conversations. Despite being resident in Spain, Billy Mucklow still had a strong interest in and a sense of responsibility towards what was going on back home. He still had close family members there and Eddie Fennel was the perfect 'bridge' between himself and the Black Country underworld he had once been king of.

As he enjoyed his cigar and watched the sun set on the Mediterranean Sea from out of a hotel window, Eddie Fennel could not help but feel a little nervous. Mucklow and Scriven were family and he had never really feared them in the past despite their fierce reputations, but he had received the call to come over to Spain for Christmas very late and here he was just over one week later. He knew exactly why he had been sent for, but what worried him was the fact that he did not have any firm answers to the questions he would be asked. He had heard rumours and he could give answers based on 'hear say' accounts, but he had no hard facts.

"Senor Mucklow and Senor Scriven will see you now sir, please come this way." A pleasant young Spanish girl appeared in the doorway to a large office and Fennel obediently followed, paying careful attention to her long-tanned legs which were displayed beneath her smart skirt. The office was grand and spacious. Nautical paintings hung upon the whitewashed walls and a majestic leather settee lay beneath a large window which was next to a set of double doors that led out onto a spacious sun terrace which overlooked the Bay of Torremolinos. Bill Mucklow and Harry Scriven were sat on the settee and Fennel noted how they looked hardly any different to when he had last seen them almost 20 years previously. They both carried a little extra weight; they were deeply tanned from the hours spent in the Andalusian sun and their faces displayed a few extra lines but on the whole they looked like the same chain smoking borderline alcoholic thugs they always had been.

"Eddie." Mucklow rose up first and shook Fennel's hand warmly. "How long has it bin aer kid?"

"Almost 19 years Bill. It's good ter see yer mate, how yer bin?"

"Too fuckin' long mate." Mucklow embraced Fennel and patted him on the back, he seemed genuinely pleased to see him and Fennel felt a little relieved. "Ar'm bostin' kid… How am yow?"

"Good thanks Bill." Fennel nodded and smiled.

"Yow remember aer kid Scriv dow yer?" Mucklow gestured towards Scriven who remained seated and the two men acknowledged each other with a well-meaning nod. Mucklow clicked his fingers and the pretty Spanish girl returned. "Rita, get us some drinks please… Eddie, what will yer have? Whiskey?" Fennel nodded and Mucklow spoke again. "Meck sure it's Irish bab, aer kid here is half Paddy." Fennel smiled. He liked all sorts of whiskey and the fact that his mother was originally from Dublin bore no influence on his taste in alcoholic beverages. "Eddie, sit daahn please." Mucklow pointed to a leather armchair that stood opposite and Fennel could not help but notice that despite spending the last 19 years in prison and in Spain, Mucklow's strong Black Country dialect remained intact. Scriven had always been the quiet one, he was content to sit back and leave most of the talking to the family bosses: Billy and previously Willie Mucklow. "Did you have a good Christmas Eddie?" Fennel nodded but he wished that Mucklow would drop the pleasantries and get down to business. Bill Mucklow had always been a straight-talking man and Fennel saw no reason why he should be any different now.

The drinks arrived and Mucklow thanked the girl. "Right… Ar suppose yow'm wondering why we wanted to see you Eddie." Mucklow's face changed slightly and became more serious.

"I think ar know what this is abaaht Bill." Fennel sipped his drink and was surprised to see ice floating in his whiskey. *It was sacrilege but Mucklow and Scriven had been in the Spanish sun for a good few years.* "Is it about ode Eli Davis?" Mucklow nodded.

"Yes… My ode mon phoned me just over a week agew and said he had been beaten ter death in his own home." Mucklow studied Fennel's face for a reaction. He did not for one second suspect his relative but still he looked for signs of the man's knowledge or lack of it.

"Apparently the cozzers told me dad that it was kids… Fuckin' kids, can you believe it Eddie? A bloke like Eli turned over by kids?" Mucklow looked over at his first cousin Harry scriven whom he knew did not give a fuck about Eli Davis, but Eli was family and it was *important that he got to the bottom of this before he returned to England for the funeral the following week.* Harry Scriven however, would not be attending.

"Ar dow think it was kids Bill, but all I have is whispers, gossip." Fennel was not lying.

"Tell me about these, whispers." Mucklow took a long drink of his whiskey, his intimidating glare had not softened in the sun.

"I heard it may have been sumet to do with Cedric Tanner." At the mention of Tanner's name Mucklow and Scriven looked at each other with a little concern. *Why had Tanner gone after their long-retired family member? Had Cedric found out about their involvement in his father's death?*

"I fuckin' hate that kiddy fiddling piece of shit." Mucklow slammed his glass down hard on a small glass coffee table that stood in front of the settee. "Where did you hear this?"

"Some of my lads heard whispers, Tanner's goons had been in the area asking after Eli and the next thing we know is Eli's dead."

"You should never have let that prick get as big as he has Eddie." Mucklow was still annoyed and he suddenly turned his anger towards Fennel.

"What the fuck was ar supposed to do Bill? Gew to war with Cedric Tanner?" Fennel was not intimidated and nor was he afraid to stand up to the great Billy Mucklow. "We always said that we wouldn't get into drugs and that is exactly what Tanner did. It was inevitable that he would become stronger. He also got well in with ode Isiah Boswell and the Brummie boys before Bossie died. Boswell wouldn't come anywhere near us after what happened and then there was the fact that Harry fucked off with Bosswell's youngest son's Spanish Mrs! We couldn't even get knocked off motors from Longbridge anymore." Fennel glanced at Scriven but Scriven was not annoyed, what Fennel was saying was true. Mucklow wiped sweat from his brow and looked at the floor.

"Ar'm sorry Eddie... If Tanner's got a beef with us then I need to get to the bottom of it, my ode mon is still in England and I don't want him threatened." Fennel was unaware of the circumstances surrounding Cedric Tanner's father's disappearance and as a result of which he did not fully understand Mucklow and Scriven's concerns. "What about Hickman?" Mucklow knew that his former protégé was the only other living person besides himself and Scriven who knew the facts of Brian Tanner's disappearance and he also knew that Hickman would be smarting from his time spent in prison.

"Dick's Dick aye he? We aye had much ter do with him since he got ahht Bill... He's in the drugs game now. He hangs abaaht with Barry O'Leary and some kid from over Sedgley way."

"What kid?" Mucklow pulled a half corona cigar from a box on the coffee table and lit it.

"Ar dow know much abaaht him Bill. He's a tough bastard and he's got a reputation. Apparently he used to work for Tanner, I even heard he was related to Tanner? He works for Dick now." At the mention of Tanner's association with Hickman's new recruit Mucklows eyes widened. *His fears were confirmed, Hickman had spilt the beans to Cedric Tanner about his father's death and now Tanner was looking for revenge. This was why Eli had died and now his own father was in danger?*

"Ok Eddie. Thanks for your help. Gew back to the villa and we will see yer later aer kid." Beads of sweat ran down Mucklow's hairless head as he feared for the welfare of his parents in England. Fennel had never seen Mucklow sweat before but he chose to say nothing.

"Ok boys. See yer later." Fennel stood up and smiled. His two relatives smiled back and Fennel closed the door as he left the room. Mucklow waited until he was quite sure he had gone and then stood up.

"Shit Harry, we gorra get back to England... Ar'm gunna cut Tanner's fingers off and meck him fuckin' eat em!"

"Why Bill?" Scriven had similar concerns but the idea of returning to the Black Country for a shoot-out with Cedric Tanner did not appeal.

"Because Tanner knows, he knows what happened to his ode mon and now he wants revenge. Eli was just the start of it... Our parents are still over there Harry... How dare that fuck threaten mar family!" Billy Mucklow had never been one to panic, but Cedric Tanner was a particularly nasty piece of work who did not respect family or civilians. To Cedric Tanner anyone was fair game.

"How do you know Tanner knows?" Scriven was not interested in vengeance for Eli Davis. He was still bitter about Eli's involvement in his breakup with Lily Cole.

"You heard Eddie, one of Tanner's relatives is working with Hickman now. Hickman knows about what happened to Brian Tanner and he is livid with me for giving evidence against him in court." Mucklow suddenly looked sad.

"Yeah, but you had no choice Bill. Yow had Billy Hill and The Kray twins onto yer, you had no choice but to put yourself away for that robbery. It's too bad that Dick had to go down too but what could you do?" Scriven shrugged and tried to reassure his cousin. Mucklow shook his head in shame and sadness.

"Dick day know about the Krays or Billy Hill... He woe see it like that Harry. He probably thinks that ar'm a grass." Mucklow looked at the floor ashamedly. Hickman had been like a brother to him, just like Scriven. It broke his heart that things had happened the way that they had and now his actions were coming back to haunt him. Before Scriven could reply with more words of reassurance, the office door suddenly flew open and Eddie Fennel burst back into the room.

"Ar'm sorry to disturb you Bill but look!" Fennel threw down a British tabloid newspaper onto the table. "It's from a couple of days agew Bill. The papers am late getting over here." The headline read: 'Midland crime kingpin found brutally murdered at home.' The article then went on to reveal how the remains of Cedric Tanner had been found in his garden and how he had been shot in the kneecaps and then burnt alive in a brutal gangland slaying. Mucklow and Scriven immediately turned and looked at each other in total confusion. *What was going on?*

Chapter 26

Micky Cole awoke in an inexpensive roach infested Spanish motel. On the bedside table stood an empty bottle of Jack Daniels and a green glass ashtray that was full to the brim with used cigarette butts. To the left of him and still asleep lay a cheap Spanish prostitute who had entertained him that previous night. He reached onto the bedside table and pulled out a cigarette. He lit it and lay back on the bed to watch a pair of cockroaches climb the grimy yellow walls. He looked at the shape of a woman next to him who was concealed by the grubby bed sheets. He could not recall anything about her and wondered what her face would look like in the cold light of day. *It didn't really matter.* He thought as he blew smoke into the air and wondered how much longer they would have to wait around to get guns and find Scriven. *Had Tanner been lying when he told Hickman Scriven was in Torremolinos? Or maybe whoever had told Tanner lied? Either way, neither of them could be asked again!* He took another drag of his cigarette and watched the tip burn away as he thought of Cathy back home in England. *Was he just wasting his time? Would they ever find Scriven and Mucklow? They were supposed to own a large hotel and casino complex locally but as yet they could not find any trace.*

    Cole got out of bed and slipped into his dirty clothes from the previous day. He hadn't expected to be in Spain for this long and he had long used up his supply of clean clothing. He grabbed his jacket, slipped on his aviator sunglasses and ducked out of the main door and onto an outdoor landing. The sun was out and piercing though it was not particularly warm, though neither was it cold. As he began to walk towards the iron staircase that led down to the ground, he felt his wallet in his pocket and decided that it was probably time to purchase an airline ticket and return home. *This was useless, somebody had obviously got their facts wrong, either deliberately or by mistake. This was just like looking for two needles in a haystack.* As he reached the bottom of the staircase he heard the familiar rumble of a straight 6 engine and then a racing green Jaguar mk2 emerged from around the corner and pulled up outside the motel. Micky Cole didn't pay much attention until the driver's door flung open and out got Dickie Hickman.

"Hey Mick, get in. We're on!" Cole walked quickly around to the passenger door.

"Yow faahnd em?" Hickman nodded and waited until they were both securely in the car and out of earshot before he began to speak.

"Look in the glove box." Cole opened the glove box and saw two pistols with ammunition and a crumpled-up piece of paper with an address written on it.

"Where did you get this car from?" Cole was surprised at Hickman's success. They had been discretely asking around for days but had had no look in tracing their targets.

"I borrowed it." Hickman smirked. "I got the plates changed so that should buy us a bit of time."

"It's a bit ode ay it?" The car was from the very early 60s and had seen better days.

"All the villains used these mate. The big straight 6 can outrun the cozzers. It's a great getaway car and we might need it."

The Jaguar mk2 was built between 1959 and 1968 in Coventry and quickly gained a reputation as the car of choice for criminals. Its 3.8 litre straight 6 engine generated 220 bhp and could accelerate from 0-60mph in just 8.5 seconds. It had proven highly successful as a getaway car and one had previously been used highly effectively in August 1963 when Bruce Reynolds and his gang pulled off a theft of £2.6 million during The Great Train Robbery.

"So where are they? Scriven and Mucklow." Micky Cole was anxious for answers. Just a few short minutes ago he had decided he was going to return home to England and now all of a sudden everything was back on again.

"They've gor a big fancy hotel on the sea front. Apparently they have been operating very low key since they come ahht here… They keep themselves to themselves." Hickman drove quickly and without care and Cole thought it was reckless. *A pull from the local law enforcement was the last thing they needed whilst travelling in a stolen car and carrying illegal guns!* "Apparently Mucklow had some problems in England with the Kray twins. You know, Ronnie and Reggie from London?"

"Ar never knew em personally Dick, but they went inside a few years back day they?" *How could he not have heard of Britain's most famous gangsters?* Throughout the 1960s the Kray twins had mixed with celebrities and had become famous in their roles as West End club owners and prominent gangland figures. They were eventually arrested on the 8th May 1968 and were convicted in 1969 for the murders of fellow London criminals George Cornell and Jack 'The hat' McVitie. Both twins were sentenced to a non-parole period of 30 years in prison, the longest sentences ever passed at The Old Bailey in London for murder.

"Yeah, but they were still abaaht in the 60s when Scriven built the hotel… Ar never met the twins either but I heard they ay all that aer kid."

"They ay all that? Ar thought they were like the fuckin' kings of London or sumet?" Cole was surprised at Hickman's words. "Easy fer yow to say Dick whilst they'm banged up."

"When are was doing mar porridge in the mid-60s, ar was banged up with Charlie Richardson from South London. He med the Krays look like Morecambe an fuckin' Wise mate! Yow must have heard of him and his brother Eddie?"

"He ever bin to Wolverhampton?" Cole laughed. He wasn't up on the gang scene and he didn't really see what it had to do with the job in hand. *Dick was a fantasist, a wannabe, in it for the glory. All Cole wanted was to get his revenge and live out the rest of his life with his woman.*

"Dow be fuckin' saft Mick. Charlie and his brother were twice as hard as the Krays mate. Ar dow know what Billy Mucklow was worried abaaht. He shit his pants over Jack Spot too in the 50s. Ar was surprised at Mucklow."

"Ar guess it depends on how many there are of them and how many there are of yow. Yow can be the toughest bastard in the world but if yow'm outnumbered yum fucked Dick." Cole spoke sense, but Hickman didn't listen.

The Richardson gang had been the Krays main rivals and were fronted by brothers Charlie and Eddie Richardson. They were based in South London and had gained a brutal reputation in the 1960s as a Torture gang. Like the Krays they were also involved in legitimate business activities, they owned a highly successful scrap metal business but it was their alleged use of sadistic torture techniques that brought them notoriety and contributed to Charlie's arrest in 1966 on the day of the World Cup final. Their feuds with the Kray twins had been legendary and it had been suggested by some that the Richardsons were in fact the tougher of the two rival firms. The Krays always craved notoriety and reputation whilst the Richardsons preferred to operate with more discretion. In reality, Harry Scriven and Billy Mucklow had had very little involvement with either gang, but in 1955 when the Krays associate Billy Hill had been fingered by the flying squad for Mucklow's infamous Oxford jewel robbery, it had been Ron and Reg who had 'persuaded' Bill Mucklow to own up to his crime and get Billy Hill off the hook. In return, Mucklow was able to keep the proceeds of the robbery through Harry Scriven who escaped to Spain with the money and the guaranteed safety of Mucklow's family whilst he was inside. Since arriving in Spain, both Mucklow and Scriven had continued to keep a low profile. A lot of gangsters had lost money from the Oxford heist and it was safer to be that way.

"So what happens now then?" Cole lay back and relaxed in the comfortable seat of the Jaguar. "Where we gewin?"

"Ar wanna meck a few quid aaht of this Mick… Apparently Scriven and Mucklow have got a really swanky hotel." Hickman gritted his teeth in anger. "All the time ar was in prison, them pair med millions. With the money I went ter jail for"

"So what we dewin?" Cole wasn't really interested in making money. *He wanted vengeance and vengeance alone, but a few quid would come in handy for the future.* A twisted grimace came over Hickman's face and he smiled smugly.

"Scriven and Mucklow will be at the hotel right now, so we'm a gewin to Harry Scriven's place… I heard his Mrs is mighty fine!"

Chapter 27

Antonia Scriven rarely got out of bed before 11 o'clock. She had no reason to. She had begun her life as a peasant girl living in the Andalusian mountain village of El Acebuchal. It was here that during the Spanish Civil War her father and brothers were taken away from their home and executed by government forces loyal to the dictator Franco. A few years later the village was cleared out by the government and Antonia was forced to move to the coastal town of Nerja with her poor mother. Her biggest asset was her mesmerizingly good looks and she quickly attracted the attention of British 'rich kid' Paddy Boswell whilst working the streets of Nerja as a prostitute. Boswell, son of the legendary and now deceased Birmingham gang boss Isiah Boswell, gave Antonia her first taste of the good life when they became engaged in 1953. However, Boswell treated her badly and when the older man Harry Scriven turned up in the late 1950s, newly rich and smitten, she saw an escape to even greater wealth and she quickly married the Black Country gangster. Now she was 41 years old and living in total luxury. She was slightly plumper now than when she married Harry Scriven, but she still looked good, like a ripe piece of fruit that had matured to perfection. She had long raven coloured hair, hypnotic brown eyes and an olive-skinned complexion that was typically Mediterranean.

As Antonia Scriven lay in her massive bed she wore no more than a tiny pink nightie that was so short that the lower part of her buttocks could be seen when she stood up straight. She casually smoked a cigarette and thumbed a popular Spanish magazine whilst listening to an LP that span on a record player in the bedroom. The current song playing was Gimme Shelter which was the opening track to the Rolling Stones 1969 album Let it bleed. It was not her husband Harry's kind of music so she would often enjoy listening to it when he was out at the hotel and on this day she had it so loud that she did not hear the sound of the Jaguar mk2 pulling up outside on the driveway.

"Nice fuckin' place ay it?" Hickman parked the Jag next to Antonia Scriven's Mercedes 280SL sports car. "Nice an remote aer kid." Micky Cole had still not been enlightened on the plan and he simply nodded in agreement as he got out of the car and followed Hickman to the front door. *The villa was amazing, it had stunning views of the Mediterranean, a massive swimming pool and it must have consisted of at least 8 bedrooms.* "All the time ar was in fuckin' side, Harry fuckin' Scriven has been in this palace!" Hickman bit his lip in anger and raised his voice.

"Hang on Dick, a big place like this has probably got servants, bodyguards… We cor just walk in there. Besides Scriven ay here is he?" Cole put his hand on Hickman's shoulder and spoke in a hushed tone.

"It ay Scriven we'm after." Hickman saw the sense in Cole's advice, lowered his voice and pulled out his gun. "We'm gunna teck his Mrs, leave a ransom note, then when he comes with the cash we will blow him and Mucklow away." Cole did not like Hickman's idea of involving the woman. He remembered his incident with Lucy Price but then took comfort in the knowledge that Scriven's Spanish wife had deprived his own mother of happiness. *It could have been his mother living out here in Spain and his entire childhood would have been very different? Maybe she would have even still been alive? Besides, it would be a good earner.*

"Ar bet its locked Dick." Cole nodded towards the front door.

"Let's find out aer kid." Hickman crept towards the front door and slowly pulled the handle. To the men's surprise the door slowly opened and they slowly moved forwards into a grand entrance hall with elaborate marble floor tiles. The sound of The Rolling Stones echoed through the corridors of the grand villa and Hickman winked at Cole. "Scriv definetly ay in. He dow listen ter shit like this." Micky Cole said nothing, he quite liked the Rolling Stones. Luckily, for Hickman and Cole, there were no servants or staff in the villa at this time of day, but they were unaware of this as they crept silently towards the staircase.

"It's coming from up there." Hickman nodded upwards towards the bedrooms at the top of the stairs and Cole pulled out his gun.

"We ay gunna hurt her am we Dick?"

"Dow get saft on me Mick… Yow'm as bad as yower ode mon!"

"What yer mean?" Both men spoke in whispers as they mounted the stairs. It was hardly the time or place for a discussion.

"Me and Harry did a job out in Himley back in the day… There was this tasty posh slag there but yower ode mon wouldn't let me touch her." Hickman smiled at the memory and placed his foot slowly on the next step to test for a creek. It was silent and he signalled for them to continue. Cole followed but his mind was working overtime. *Maybe Suzy Miller was right? Maybe his blood father was not such a bad guy? His so-called friend Hickman had no qualms about hurting and threatening women, was he on the wrong side?* Before he could think anymore, they reached the top of the stairs and the music was louder. Hickman put a finger to his lips before swiftly kicking the door open and emerging into the large bedroom where Antonia lay on the bed in her revealing and vulnerable attire. She went to scream but Hickman pointed to his gun and placed a finger over his mouth.

"What is going on?" Her voice was soft and feminine and her Spanish accent added to her shear sexual magnetism. "What are you doing in my home?" Hickman was instantly aroused and he stared at her, open mouthed and in amazement.

"Yow'm abaaht ter find aaht love… Ar'm gewin first!" Hickman unzipped his flies and moved towards the terrified woman. "Woe be the furst time ar'v had Harry Scriven's sloppy seconds, but ar'm gunna have the last laugh!" Upon realisation of what was about to happen Micky Cole felt horrified. A million thoughts went through his mind. *What should he do? Shoot Hickman and leave? Maybe he could talk some sense into him?*

"No, not here. The servants could walk in! It will disrupt our plans." Cole was careful not to incriminate anyone by mentioning Hickman's name and Antonia looked at him with wide scared eyes.

Micky Cole could not help but admire her scantily clad form. She was an absolute work of art but using and hurting women was not his style. Hickman laughed perversely and zipped himself back up.

"Guess yow'm gunna have ter wait love." He pointed the gun and nodded for her to get off the bed. "Walk slowly slag."

"Can I please just get a coat?" Tears began to run from Antonia's pretty Spanish eyes and before Hickman could reply Micky Cole threw her a long trench coat that was hanging on a hook in the room. She slowly put it on and Hickman turned and gave Cole a disappointed look.

"Dunno why you need a coat bitch... Ar'm gunna have yow over and over. Ar'm gunna fuckin' hurt you." Hickman blew her a kiss and raised his eyebrows. He was going to enjoy his revenge.

A few hours later a long black 1972 Mercedes-Benz 300 SEL pulled up onto the driveway next to Antonia's sports car and out got Harry Scriven. He wore an elegant black suit and a pair of black wayfarer sunglasses. He locked his car and looked over to the front door. *What's that?* A piece of paper had been nailed to the front door and Scriven hastily hurried over to read a note that had been written on it.

> Mr Scriven, we have your wife. Bring yourself, Bill Mucklow
> and £200,000 in British sterling to Torre de Maro tomorrow
> at noon. If we see any Police or any person other than you
> and Mucklow then your wife dies.

Scriven sighed deeply and shook his head in annoyance. He had constantly been reminding his wife to be more security conscious and now this had happened. *How dare they take my wife!* He clenched his fist and punched the door in anger before immediately regretting it on account of the sudden pain that throbbed in his hand. *Who the fuck was behind this? It was obviously someone who knew both himself and Billy Mucklow.* He went into the villa and straight towards the phone when he suddenly realised the person who must have been behind the abduction of his wife. *It was obvious!* He picked up the phone with urgency and frantically dialled a number.

"Hello?" Scriven was pleased to hear the reassuring sound of his cousin Bill's voice.

"It's me Harry. Sumet bad as happened. Ar think Dick is over here in Spain. He's got mar wench and he wants me and yow to see him with £200,000 or he's gunna kill her." Scriven did not doubt Dick Hickman's capability to hurt a woman.

"What the fuck?" Mucklow replied with surprise. "Yow sure it's Dick?"

"Who else could it be Bill? The twins am in jail and Tanner is dead!"

"Ok mate… Ar'll be right over. We will teck em an empty case, Dick will think the cash is in there. We can teck some shooters and have a chat with him… We need to set the record straight, maybe we can talk him round and he can come and work for us? Like ode times?" Harry Scriven could not believe what he was hearing.

"Bill, he'got mar fuckin' Mrs and yow wanna give him a fuckin' job?"

"Yer know how it is though Harry, ar kinda feel responsible after what happened."

"Fuck you Bill." Scriven screamed down the phone through gritted teeth but he resisted the urge to hang up, he needed Bill to be there with him the next day.

"Look Harry just calm down, if this is Dick he's one of us. Let me talk to him. Just wait there ar'm coming right over aer kid."

Chapter 28

The Torre de Maro was one of several 16th century watch towers that were constructed in prominent locations on cliff tops across the Mediterranean coast of the Costa Del Sol. They were originally built as lookouts to provide warning of historical raids from North Africa. The tower overlooked the beautiful beach of Maro which lay to the east of the resort of Nerja and behind it could be seen the picturesque Sierra de Tejeda mountain range. Dick Hickman had chosen the location as a meeting place as during the short time he had spent in Spain he had noticed the place and noted how the spot was derelict and relatively remote. The perfect spot for him to collect the money and massacre those who had done him wrong.

Hickman, Cole and Antonia had driven from Scriven's luxury villa to the remote Torre and parked up for the night. It was here that Dick Hickman planned to have his wicked way with Harry Scriven's wife and begin his sordid crusade of revenge.

Antonia Scriven stood cold, terrified and exhausted against the abandoned and vandalised Torre de Maro. She had been held against her will all night in the green Jaguar that Dick Hickman had stolen in Marbella and had spent most of the night sobbing as Cole and Hickman shared a bottle of cheap whisky. She was in constant fear of being raped or worse and Hickman made regular references to his dishonest intentions towards her. She had spent the night sat on the back seat of the car, rigid with fear, her mind running away with itself, imagining all of the potential things that could happen to her. *Would she be raped? Would she be beaten? Would she be killed? How?* Micky Cole desperately did not want anything untoward to happen to Scriven's wife, even if she had taken the place of his own mother with his natural father. He had made sure that Hickman drank plenty of alcohol and had done his best to distract the older man throughout the night. Antonia may not have known it but Micky Cole had been her guardian angel that night, staying awake the entire time to watch over her and make sure that Hickman did not get his wicked way. The next morning had finally come and the trio had exited the car for some fresh air. Micky Cole had had the awful job of escorting Antonia as she relieved herself in the bushes and as he watched over her as respectfully as he could he had almost let her run free, but he knew that the consequence of this would be her alerting the Police which would evoke the failure of their quest. Now the three of them stood against the tower and smoked cigarettes.

Micky Cole looked out over the small bay of Maro and admired the view. He had never been to Spain before and he liked what he had seen. *If things worked out then maybe he would bring Cathy here for a holiday sometime.* He sucked the last dregs from his cigarette, cast it over the cliff edge and watched as it made its long descent into the frothy, foamy Mediterranean below them. Micky Cole had never seen such huge waves and he watched as they crashed against the rugged rocks and rose into the air. He had always thought of Spain as a warm country but in early January the temperature was barely into double figures.

"It's time aer kid." Hickman suddenly interrupted the roar of the waves as he threw down his cigarette and eyed Antonia with a lustful want. "Scriven and Mucklow will be here in a bit so ar'm havin' this wench now. Yow wanna gew?" He looked at Cole and nodded towards the shaking woman.

"Senors no, I beg of you please." Antonia tried to protest but Hickman found her fear humorous and a sexual turn on. Cole breathed in deeply, it was time for him to intervene.

"No Dick… This will ruin all of our plans."

"Fuck off kid. Fine yow dow wanna turn, but ar'm havin' mar gew!" Hickman grabbed Antonia's arm and forcefully pulled her towards him.

"Ar said fuckin' no Dick!" Cole raised his voice and pulled his gun from his pocket. "Do you wanna end up dead rich or dead down there?" Cole's eyes were deadly serious and Hickman could feel himself filling with rage.

"Bloody hell Mick, ar thought yow were mar mate?" Hickman's eyes flickered like fire. "Dow threaten me kid." Before Cole could reply, the sound of an engine filtered through the dry Spanish air and they turned to see Harry Scriven's black Mercedes saloon pull up on a dirt track alongside the Jaguar. Micky Cole felt relieved, they could finally accomplish their mission.

"Look Dick, let's just do the business and get the fuck out of here." Hickman looked at Antonia with disappointment. She shivered in her thin coat and *her face looked innocent, pretty and ready for abuse, but alas, he had more important matters to attend to.*

Harry Scriven was still livid at Billy Mucklow for his wish to make peace with Dickie Hickman and bring him back into their business, but he did not show it. He needed his cousin more than ever so he felt it best to keep his frustration quiet for now. The front doors of the Mercedes flung open and the two ageing gangsters got out. Scriven concealed his trusty old Webley revolver inside his jacket pocket and Mucklow tried his best to discreetly carry a Second World War assault rifle. They had arrived early to survey the area but the presence of the green Jag caused them to suspect that the hostage takers were already there.

"Right Harry, yow gew that way towards the tower, ar'll gew this way." Billy Mucklow had served in the British army during World War 2 as a Captain and had proven himself to be a highly successful soldier. Scriven did not disagree with his suggestion and as usual, did as he was told.

Scriven followed Mucklow's instruction and pulled out the Webley revolver. *No way was he going to make up with Hickman after this. There had been too much 'water under the bridge' between the two of them and*

Hickman had had this coming for years. Harry Scriven decided there and then that as soon as he set eyes upon *that bastard Hickman, he would blow the mouthy little mother fucker away!* He crept towards the tower, his eyes peeled in all directions, but it was eerily quiet. All he could hear was the roar of the ocean crashing against the rocks hundreds of feet below and the sound of the various loud insects that lived in the Spanish vegetation. He reached the front of the tower, the strong scent of urine and decay hit his nostrils but there was still no sign of Hickman or his wife. *Where the fuck am yer Dick? Ar'm a fuckin' comin' for yer aer kid.* He narrowed his eyes and his brain filled with macho bravado. In reality, he could not help but feel a little afraid. His way of dealing with fear had always been to 'front it out' and mask fear with violence. He did not want Hickman to know that he was there, but he felt exposed, sure that Hickman was there watching him, mocking him. In his left hand was the empty bag and his palms were clammy and sweaty as he clutched its leather handle. He continued to move forwards and passed by the side of the tower until he came to the edge of the cliff top. He stood there for a few seconds and cast his eyes down at the foamy water below. He had never been particularly fond of heights and he suddenly felt an overwhelming premonition that he would soon be floating face down in the deadly waters below.

"Drop the gun Harry." Scriven suddenly felt the cold steel of a pistol pressed against the back of his head and he recognised the voice straight away. He dropped his revolver to the ground and raised his hands in the air. "Dickie, Dick head Dickman… It's been a long time aer kid. Run ahht of women ter batter yer cocky mother fuckin' bastard?" Scriven laughed and turned around slowly, his hands still in the air. Hickman was stood a short distance away by the tower and was holding his gun to Antonia's head. The man pointing his gun at him he had never seen before, but Scriven thought how he felt instantly familiar. There was something in his eyes that he recognised straight away and he could not put his finger on why the young man felt so intensely significant. The two men stood face to face, staring at each other, one of them confused, the other fully understanding the personal significance of the man before him.

"Where's the money Harry?" Hickman had a nervous, impatient tone to his voice.

"Release the bird and ar'll give yer the money." Scriven held up the leather bag.

"Where's Bill?" Hickman was anxious to see his beloved Billy Mucklow one last time and his voice quivered slightly as he mentioned his hero's name.

"He's by the car. He's coming." Scriven lied.

"Do you know who this man is Harry?" Hickman suddenly became more confident as he pointed towards Micky Cole. Scriven said nothing, he felt as if he knew the man, but he could not think of a name.

"This is Lily Cole's lad Harry." The mention of Scriven's true love's name cut through him and suddenly he knew, he understood fully. "He's your son Harry… You're a fuckin' father!" Hickman erupted into sarcastic laughter and Scriven felt an overwhelming mixture of emotions flood through his mind. *He had always wanted to settle down and have children with Lily Cole but his dreams had been denied by that bastard Davis in 1948.* Tears immediately erupted from his blue eyes and he looked upon the man who held the gun to his head with more love than he had felt for anyone in his entire life. He smiled with an inner joy and an unseen empathy passed between the two relatives.

"Why did you leave my mother Scriven?" Michael Cole finally spoke.

"I had no choice… I loved your mother deeply, but things were taken out of my control." Harry Scriven meant every word, but it still broke his heart that he had followed the instructions of his uncles Willie and Eli all of those years ago. Deep down he had always known that he had made the wrong choice in choosing his family and a life of crime over the woman he truly loved.

"If you love someone you do not fuckin' abandon them Harry!" Cole screamed the words into his father's face with 25 years of anger and pain as tears filled his own eyes.

"I have no excuse... I fucked up. I've regretted that more than anything for the last 25 years. That is the god's honest truth and I swear upon it," Scriven looked at his boy with a mixture of pride and regret.

"Because of yower fuck up Scriven, I had to grow up being abused by that sick bastard Cedric Tanner." Cole was raving, hysterical and he so desperately wanted to pull the trigger, he wanted to punish Scriven for everything, but he could not do it. He had killed men before and it had been easy, but he simply could not do it. At the mention of his child's cruel upbringing at the hands of Cedric Tanner, Harry Scriven shook his head with sorrow and had never felt such utter guilt.

"Micky, shoot this son of a bitch." Hickman barked the command with glee. Cole put his finger to the trigger and closed his eyes... *This was it, the moment he had been waiting for, his chance to punish the man who had caused it all!* He took a deep breath and dropped the gun to the floor. *He had been told so many positive things about his real father by Suzy Miller, Bobby Murray, even Dick Hickman. The last few days with Hickman had really shone light onto his true character. Hickman was a wicked twisted man with no sense of morals, why should he kill at the instruction of such a man? All of his life he had been a puppet for the evil doings of Cedric Tanner, why should he now be the same for Dickie Hickman?*

Hickman watched the gun fall to the ground and instantly punched Antonia to the ground with his boxers left hook. He rushed forwards with his pistol and held it to Micky Cole's head.

"Fuck it Scriven, dow get sentimental over this vicious little bastard. He came here to kill yer!" Hickman spat his words, his face was possessed with anger and a murderous rage was within him. He had been waiting all night to 'have' the woman and the frustration and tension of his need added to his demonic fury. "Ar'm gunna kill your son and your wife and yow'm gunna watch them fuckin' die!" Cole instantly felt a fool. He had thrown his gun away and now his supposed friend was about to take everything he ever had and everything he ever would have. He would never see Cathy again and just when he felt he was finally finding happiness within his cruel tortured life it was all about to end prematurely. *He should have listened to Suzy Miller.*

"Do not kill my son... Kill me in his place." Scriven felt an immense terror at the thought of his newly found offspring being murdered. It was all new to him, but he would do whatever was necessary to protect his child. Hickman laughed cruelly.

"What? You would sacrifice yourself for some chap yow only met 5 minutes agew?"

"I missed out on his life and he suffered because of it... I should have been there for him and his mother... This is my chance to redeem myself as a father." Scriven looked at the floor with sadness and emotion. He meant every word. *He would sacrifice himself for the life of his and Lily Cole's child there and then. His life had suddenly taken on a new precious responsibility.*

"But ar'm gunna kill you all anyway!" Hickman erupted into another fit of laughter. Revenge was sweet.

"Wait." Scriven edged even closer to the cliff and held out his Mercedes keys over the drop. "The money is in the back of the Merc."

"I thought it was in the bag?" Hickman looked confused and Scriven shook his head and tossed the leather bag in his direction. Hickman kept the gun sighted fully on Scriven whilst he opened the bag and checked the contents. It was empty. "You cheeky bastard."

"If yow shoot ar'll drop the keys daahn there Dick." Scriven nodded to the Mediterranean that still raged below them. "Give my wife and the kid the keys to the Jag and let them escape... Then do whatever you want with me and teck the Merc and the cash."

"Why should I believe you?" Hickman was cynical.

"What have you got to lose?"

Hickman stared at his gun in thought.

"Where's Bill? He is supposed to die too."

"That is between you and Bill Dick... Let these two go and you will be rich and have the first part of your revenge."

Hickman smiled and turned to face Cole and Antonia.

"Right yow pair, fuck off." He flung the Jag keys towards Cole and he caught them. Harry Scriven looked on and was not surprised to see his wife of so many years turn and flee without giving him as much as a second glance. He had been fooling himself all along to think that she had really loved him. *There, as his life drew nearer to its conclusion, Harry Scriven felt regret that he had given his life to this Spanish girl when really it should have been Lily Cole all along... He would never see her or his son ever again...*

As Antonia fled, Micky Cole stood routed to the spot. He was glad he had met his real father, he had helped to reinstate his faith in humanity and helped him to understand that not everyone who had done wrong by him was bad, that people could change and that people could make genuine mistakes. Those that were evil were punished through acts of vengeance, those that were genuine and sought redemption were forgiven. Michael Cole felt melancholic and respectful of the sacrifice his father was making. He looked at Scriven and managed a half smile and Scriven returned the gesture.

"What's yer name son?" Scriven did not even know his child's name.

"Er, Michael." Cole hesitated and then revealed his name. Scriven nodded and smiled again. He took one last look at his son before closing his eyes.

"Michael." He said the name lovingly to himself and flung the keys down onto the gravely floor. "Michael." He repeated the name again, expecting nothing but death.

The shot rang out and echoed throughout the cliffs and caves of the rugged Spanish coastline as the dying man fell from the cliff top of Torre de Maro. He plummeted rapidly towards the ever-wicked sea which eagerly welcomed its human prey. A gaping bullet hole stood within his forehead and the blood ran incessantly as the victim died on impact.

As he died, Dickie Hickman found himself as a young man in the 1950s at the Haden Cross on Halesowen Road between Old Hill and Halesowen. There he was, smiling in the back room with his hero, his master and mentor Bill Mucklow. The two of them truly did have the world on a string, they ruled the streets and Hickman was ever loyal to his beloved idol, the same man who had pulled the trigger that sent him to his death…

Epilogue

Harry Scriven returned to the Black Country soon after. He had come to understand the true depth of his shallow relationship with his Spanish wife and all that was of importance to him now was in England. Of course, Bill Mucklow remained in Spain, but Scriven sold him his share of their business and the close cousins agreed to stay in regular touch. Back home, Scriven still had his ageing parents and the opportunity to build a relationship with his newfound son, but what appealed to him more than anything was the chance for him to finally do what he should have done many, many years ago. A chance to rekindle and salvage some kind of relationship with his beloved Lily Cole…

Upon his return and on discovery of Lily's death just a few years previously, a part of Scriven died too… As he sat alone inside the dilapidated, run down and decaying living room of what once was his family home in Talbot Street, he thought of that last day he had spent with Lily as they wondered around Haden Hill park together in the bronze of the late autumn sun. He could think of nothing else. It was cold and dark inside the room and the electricity had long since been cut off, but in the silence of the darkness Scriven suddenly felt an intense anger and a deep sorrow. He thought of his son's horrific childhood that had occurred *as he himself had been living the life of a gangster 'king' on the Spanish coast*. Then, he thought of Lily dying alone with *that evil child molester Cedric Tanner*… He bit into his lower lip and tears filled his eyes, there was no vengeance to be had, nobody left to hurt, nobody to torture, nobody to maim or kill. The only person left to blame was himself…

As the last embers of a small candle in the room flickered, he thought he saw Lily Cole's face in the glow and then it burnt out and ceased to be… Harry Scriven truly was alone…

Printed in Great Britain
by Amazon